SEALED WITH DEATH

JAMES SILVESTER

Print ISBN 978-1-913942-65-6

ALSO BY JAMES SILVESTER

<u>Lucie Musilova Series</u>

Blood, White and Blue

<u>Prague Thrillers</u>

Escape to Perdition

The Prague Ultimatum

For @The3Million

1
———

It was a squalid place for a murder. The forest, cold, damp and its air permeated with an almost supernatural sense of unease, stood across from the remnants of what had once been contemptuously dubbed 'the Calais jungle'; ostensibly a migrant camp for refugees but in reality a box into which civilised society could funnel the desperate while patting itself on the back for its compassion. The camp had long since closed, but the stench of fear and despair it had birthed remained, clinging to and perfuming the trees. Lucie Musilova watched and waited, hoping against hope that she would be spared the task of killing. The camp's legacy was one of cruel abandonment, with pockets of the dispossessed and the neglected, many of them children with nowhere else to go, now calling these very trees home. It was these children she had come to protect.

Unmoving and with her long hair tied back, her trusted black overcoat enveloping her, she was invisible to all but the nocturnal animal life which scurried cautiously away from her position alongside a proudly ancient oak. She had waited long hours for her quarry, and though her body was motionless, her mind had begun to ponder, as it so often did, on the morality of her mission. The mark deserved to die, there was no question of that in her mind, but her years as a military Chaplain were hard to shed, and her struggle to reconcile her faith with her chosen profession brought a constant anxiety, perhaps even more so this time. She was alone in the Field without her mentor, Kasper Algers; to the public merely an outspoken Independent MP, but in reality, an operative of 'The Overlappers', the reclusive branch of the security services to which Lucie also belonged.

She had tackled marks without him of course, and she had taken lives long before her association with the Department, but in even these early days of their partnership, she had learned to rely on him, and he on her. But with him engaged in the Parliamentary business necessary to maintain his cover, and with their superior, the aberrant 'Mr Lake', eager to own the information the mark possessed, Lucie had been entrusted with carrying out the hit alone. She was several hours into her forest vigil before she appreciated how naked she felt without him.

Alone with her thoughts, she pondered how darker hues of the sex industry had brought her here, yet people back home in the UK were getting used to the daily acceptance of its arguably lighter shades. The government's trialling of legalised brothels, while increasing its tax receipts, had in truth had a negligible impact on the problems of human trafficking, forced prostitution and sexual abuse it had been trumpeted to end. In her darker moments Lucie wondered if they had even worsened them. Certainly these 'establishments' had done nothing to counter the objectification of women that so infected society, with groups of young men openly making plans in the country's workplaces for boozed up weekends 'paying their dick tax'; a phrase that had both very quickly and very regretfully entered the vernacular.

The brainchild of Adam Butcher, an aggressively ambitious

darling of the Hard Brexit extremists, the venues had provoked massive controversy that Lucie firmly believed was planned to distract the public even momentarily from the disaster of Brexit. Algers had agreed and pointed to Butcher's own love of his reputation as a 'scourge of feminism'; a badge Algers believed he wore simply to cover his misogyny with a more acceptable label.

In theory the new venues were staffed only by those women and men who wanted to be there; clean from any habitual drug use, happy to ply their trade in a safe environment and content to be classed alongside other self-employed professionals in any other regulated industry. That still left those outside the 'system', those living hand to mouth, those desperate for their next fix and those whose poverty was so extreme that the risk of performing more dangerous activities in unsafe environments, was more attractive than the notion of losing a cut to line the government's pockets. And wherever the service was offered, it was taken advantage of, usually by the hypocritical, the violent and those with more unconventional tastes.

A car approached, and its headlights drew closer before veering slightly away as the driver twisted his vehicle into a halt, the crunch of rubber on stone and bracken announcing his arrival. The click of the handbrake on the modest and unspectacular car confirmed the driver's intent to remain, as did the sudden quiet of the engine. Lucie remained still and stiff, waiting with churning stomach and aching knee for what she feared would come next. She did not have to wait long.

From the trees bathed in the headlights' glow, shuffled a tiny, awkward figure. No more than three feet high and dressed in filthy jeans and a t-shirt inadequate against the cold weather, the figure hesitated for a moment and made to turn back towards the relative safety of the all-enveloping branches. The car door opened, the creaking metal halting the youngster in its tiny stride. As it turned back towards the car, Lucie caught a first proper look at the face of the betrayed innocent caught in the beams: thick, black hair, matted and knotted with dirt, over a little girl's wide-eyed features, the light brown of her skin stained by the woods she lived in and the remnants of the scraps she ate.

A heady cocktail of anger and revulsion bubbled up inside Lucie, as she watched the tiny one turn back towards the car, before being obscured from view as she disappeared on the far side and drew closer to the driver, waiting in his seat.

Lucie's rage would not allow her to wait any longer. She slipped noiselessly from her position in the trees, traversing the rough ground. Reaching the passenger side of the vehicle, and crouching down, she slipped her hand beneath her coat and closed it around the unsettlingly comforting handle of the gun she carried. Pulling it from its position, Lucie eased her head up to peer through the passenger window and check the position of her quarry.

On the backseat of the vehicle sat a paper takeaway bag, spilling its contents partly on the seat beside it. Salty fries lay around an open box of deep fried portions of what was claimed to be chicken; a small plastic toy, wrapped in a branded cellophane bag had been jammed in alongside the meal, and a small paper cup with plastic top and a straw, stood pathetically in the holder between the front and back seats. Partially covered by the snacks, lay what looked like a Smith & Wesson .45.

The driver was a man, heavy-set and with his back to Lucie. He had twisted around to sit with his legs out of the still open driver-side door, his broad shoulders stretching the material of his suit jacket as he struggled to turn his frame into whichever position he was trying to adopt. Berlioz was romanticising voluminously to the night through the car radio; normally a beautiful sound to Lucie, but only serving to add a macabre accompaniment to the actions unfolding before her, though the crescendo allowed her to click open the passenger door unnoticed. She climbed as softly and deftly into the passenger seat as the music would permit her, inching as close to her perverted target as possible, and felt her fury build as she peered over his shoulder to see the youngster, terrified and shivering, staring at the ground while the man began to reach inside his pants.

She wasn't to kill him. Lake had been insistent on that. Instead, she was to break him and bring whatever information he held back to the Overlappers for analysis. After that, once they were sure they had everything, he was to be dragged through the press as a public warning to others in the ring, that they would be next. Lucie understood the mission; understood it and resented it. Yes, this bastard deserved humiliation, but didn't he also deserve death?

He was struggling with the tightness of his trousers against his waist, and as he twisted further, Lucie swallowed back sufficient of her rage to retain self-control, hooking her left arm under his chin and dragging him backwards onto the seat where she pressed down onto his chest. The Target's right hand and wrist were still stuck inside his pants, and he clawed uselessly with his left, in vain search of the gun on the back seat.

"What's the matter?" Lucie hissed as she pressed the barrel of her own gun, a subtler Browning Hi Power, to his temple. "Having trouble finding your weapon?"

Stepping backwards from the car, she dragged her quarry with her, his legs flailing uselessly until she dumped him on his backside in the mud, where she ordered him onto his knees.

"Attends là, chéri," she quickly said in as soft a voice as she could manage to the petrified child, still crouched by the driver's door, hoping both that the little one spoke French and that Lucie's attempt at the language was good enough to be understood. She turned back to the figure now knelt in the filth and levelled her gun at him.

"Pray," ordered Lucie, coldly.

"What?"

"Pray," she repeated. "You don't want to meet your Maker with this shit on your conscience, you've two minutes to get what you need to off your chest."

He stared back, wide-eyed and pale, his head shaking slightly, his fear obvious and emphatic. The temptation to pull the trigger was strong, and before it got the better of her, she wanted to be sure she did it right. She'd been tasked with getting information, and it was up to her how she got it; right now, a death row confession seemed as good a way as any. The righteous anger within her was unwilling to release its grip on her cognisance, but also blunted her senses to danger, so much so that as she turned back to check on the young victim, she failed to register the Target's hand move slowly to his ankle...

Had Lucie not turned back when she did, the bullet which tore through her side would have embedded itself in her abdomen. Instead she dropped to the floor, clasping her hand to the fire raging in her wound and struggling to fill her lungs, her body refusing to cooperate as it processed the shot.

Her quarry giggled as he crawled through the slime towards her, pressing the now burning gun metal against the flesh of her cheek and licking his lips at her pain.

"I found my weapon just fine, thanks," he gurgled into her ear, his breath on her skin. "And now the three of us are going to play with it for a while, understand?"

As Lucie's distraction had been her undoing, so too was the Target's overconfidence his. As he made to pick up the stricken spy, Lucie swung her left fist, charged with the sum of her pain, squarely into his groin; he emitted a loud scream as he fell back to the floor. Lucie had so little strength left, and her eyes were beginning to haze over, but she forced herself upright, ignoring the burning in her side, as to do otherwise would surely mean the death of herself and the little one she was trying to save.

The man was still clutching his gun, and Lucie grabbed his arm, twisting it upwards and back towards his head; his own strength having left him with his scream.

"Wait, wait!" he begged as the barrel touched his temple and Lucie's eyes narrowed. "I didn't touch her, I swear I didn't touch her!"

"Good," Lucie breathlessly responded, "and now you never will." The echo of the shot rolled away through the trees; as it died away so too did Lucie's adrenaline, and the effects of the wound began to slow her. The knowledge that there was still the child to consider was enough to convince her she couldn't yet simply lie down and die. Her hand clasped to her side, Lucie smiled as best she could at the little one, who stared in frozen terror at what she had just witnessed.

"C'est bien," Lucie said, holding out her hand to the infant and hoping against hope the blood on it did not frighten her further. "Je suis là pour vous aider."

The first suggestion of a nervous smile began to appear on the youngster's face, and she nodded as Lucie gestured for her to climb into the car. The engine was mercifully still running. Lucie slid painfully behind the steering wheel, and set off towards the port, leaving the Target in the mud; not to be found she hoped until the vermin infesting the place had had their fill of him. The drive was short, and the young girl was quiet throughout it, save only to confirm she had no siblings or friends left behind in the trees. The blood continued to leak from her and Lucie could feel she was on the verge of losing consciousness as the pair climbed from the car and headed towards the Eurostar.

Lucie knew she wouldn't last long, and she had to be sure

the child was looked after. Focussing all of her energy into keeping herself awake, she scanned the milling and scurrying passengers until her eyes settled on a young couple standing beside one of the white pillars beneath the upper walkways, sipping coffee and bickering in English. Holding the girl's hand, Lucie staggered to the couple and gently pushed the little one towards them.

"This girl is homeless..." she began, the young man interrupting instantly.

"No, I'm sorry, we've no change right now..."

"Listen to me, dickhead!" Lucie shouted back, the couple looking at her in shock, both at her language and her pale and bloodstained appearance.

"I've just stopped some pervert from having his way with her, and now she needs to get somewhere safe. Take her to the authorities and keep her safe."

"Wait just a min..."

"Here," Lucie snapped, ignoring their protestations and pulling a large wad of Euros from the pocket of her overcoat. "Take half for your trouble and the rest is for her. Don't let me find out you've let her down."

With that, Lucie turned away, dismissing their blank and open-mouthed faces and blowing a kiss to the youngster, who had now taken the hand of the young woman and was smiling up at her. She pushed through the crowd, her sight failing and her wound throbbing, staggering into one person and then another as she fought her way to God knows where.

One figure refused to give way. Straining her blurring eyes at the intransigent body, she saw that it was dressed in the shades of grey and yellow trim of the Eurostar staff and she shook her head wordlessly at the young man, willing him to move aside.

"Madame," the boy began, his brow creased in concern, "Vous allez bien?"

The pain reached a crescendo and she felt her stomach convulse as her legs finally gave up the pretence of stability and her eyes surrendered to the mist.

"I'm sorry," she said in her mind as her sight finally faded, "I'm so, so sorry."

2

———

She awoke to the same sensation of harrowing dread that had accompanied her transition to consciousness the previous morning, her senses crying out in fearful protest at the onset of reality and ending of their temporary respite in the dream world. Ines was far from used to these sensations. As a child, in Grand Est, she had never been one to be afraid of the dark, or to suffer a nervous disposition. Indeed, her natural inquisitiveness was matched only by her stubbornness in pursuing it, and it had been those qualities which had led her to travel the word before finally bowing to the expectations of her parents and settling down for a career, choosing London as the city in which she would make her professional name. She quickly secured employment on one of the many graduate schemes the City had to offer, and she had excelled, making many friends and few enemies along the way. Even after her mugging, not long after the Brexit vote, by men who took exception to her speaking in French on her mobile phone, her friends had rallied round. They assured her that things would get better and they would not abandon her to the grim and dangerous forces the campaign had unleashed.

But today, she felt none of her usual confidence. She rose reluctantly from the bed, striving to keep the volcanic clash of emotions within her from bursting forth, almost... almost... giving in to a sob as she showered and then brushed her teeth. She caught herself in time, spurred on by the defiance of her own reflection and spat tooothpaste into the sink with every ounce of the contempt she felt for those who'd shown her such disrespect. She dressed with renewed vigour and breakfasted on a single slice of buttered, wholemeal toast, before heading out of the small, sparsely furnished apartment. It was early, she would be alone in the office. Since it happened, she always was.

It was the crack of her nail, finally giving way to the increasing ferocity of her typing that drew her attention, hours later, to the time. The plain and soulless office was empty save for her, and looking outside she saw the darkness was enough to match that of her spirit. She cursed at the break, before inhaling deeply and shutting down her workstation. The repressed sob from the morning had gathered its strength and returned to haunt her again, insisting on being released, but still she swallowed it back, before slipping her jacket on and making her way through the main door and out into the empty street. The sound of engines, horns and swearing in the distance defied the emptiness of the streets Ines walked, with only what looked like the same car passing her at regular intervals, the eyes of the driver as vacant as the streets.

Pausing at the small deli across from her apartment, Ines collected and paid for her usual bag of fresh groceries, and crossed the echoing street, her normally pretty and mischievous features growing more agitated with each step. With what seemed an enormous effort, she pushed her way into the flat, but it was there, as she surveyed the empty shelves and pictureless walls, that the sob returned once more, this time a cry which forced itself from her throat and pushed her to her knees as it did so.

She knelt there with her tears in full flow for what seemed an eternity, until a voice, disembodied and quietly imperious sounded in her ears.

"Such a shame," the voice softly said, "so nearly successful today."

Ines howled in tearful range at the sound of the voice, her hands clenching tighter and her eyes closed tightly as she rocked back and forth on the floor.

"You were so close," the voice whispered again in condescending tenderness, "so very close. Go now, eat, sleep and gather your strength. You have one final day to seal the covenant, one final day to save yourself if you can."

"Fuck your covenant!" Ines screamed through her hysteria. "Fuck you!"

"The covenant will be sealed, my dear," the softly taunting tones replied, louder than ever over her cries. "It will be sealed with your allegiance, or with your death."

Ines' howls ceased as she turned to stare in bitter anger at the source of the voice; a speaker grill beside the light switch next to the door.

"Va te faire foutre," she spat at the object, her eyes becoming distant and glazed. Standing up, she crossed to the window and looked out onto the earthly hell to which she had been condemned, at the street, the shop and the office all within a stone's throw of her cold and soulless apartment.

The walls of the flat were of cheap plywood: so too were the walls of the shop, through whose window the unresponsive cashier still stood, plainly visible through the window, its waxwork face devoid of expression. The painted, chipped and staring features were shared by the 'driver' of the single car Ines had seen these last few days, a hollow chassis welded to a steel pole, which went round and round the plywood town before her eyes. The noises of traffic, of chatter, of TV, bars and bluster that filled every moment of her normal life were all there but leaking from speakers and grills instead of reality. The night sky she had spent so much of her youth gazing into was now reduced to an image, projected onto the dusty, metallic walls of the enormous warehouse her little cardboard city sat in the middle of; the fluid movements of everyday life now cruelly replicated by automated mannequins which stared up at her in dead-eyed condemnation.

"One day," the voice said again as the young woman continued to stare. "One more day."

3

———

Lucie sat cross-legged on the hospital bed, an oversized, baggy t-shirt covering her, oblivious to the arrival of Kasper Algers, the thin and wrinkled man whom to the world was the Independent MP for Camden. In reality he was a fellow agent of the Overlappers – the cloistered branch of the security services responsible for cases where the lines between the remits of MI5 and MI6 were blurred. Her eyes closed, Lucie held her small, silver harmonica to her lips as she played along to the soulful wail of the gospel singer, busily praising The Lord from her phone. On the table alongside the bed was an ancient, leather clad Bible, resplendent with infinitesimally small writing on tissue thin paper. Algers stepped forward to examine the passage, noting that whatever Lucie had been reading came early in the Book of John. The movement broke his young friend from her trance-like state and she sat up with a start, her body coiling as if ready to fight, before relaxing as she recognised her visitor.

"Mahlia Jackson?" Algers asked, his hands held up in apology for the interruption.

"Sister Rosetta Tharpe," Lucie corrected with a smile. "Sorry, I didn't know you were coming."

She shuffled awkwardly to place her harmonica on the table and stop the flow of gospel music from her phone, shushing away Algers' apologies at interrupting a private moment. Awkwardly, she gently eased her right leg from under her, stretching the ache from her bad knee, the one injured during her service in Afghanistan. She pulled herself from the bed and stood up to embrace her friend, delighting in the sincerity of his concerned embrace.

"What the fuck were you thinking?" Algers snapped the question in the manner of a parent, profanely greeting the return of a missing child with a confused mixture of love and chastisement. "You could have been killed!"

"But I wasn't," Lucie replied, somewhat weakly. She knew damn well she had been sloppy, perhaps even stupid in her actions, and she had thought of little else since awaking in Buckland Hospital, Dover.

"You can't be flippant, Lucie," Algers warned, softly, "either in your attitude or the way you approach this work. I should never have let you go alone..."

"Hey! Grown woman here, thank you very much!"

Lucie's indignance was met with another blast of paternal annoyance from the thin, grey haired MP, whose frightening brow creased accusingly at her.

"Then for fuck's sake, act like one!"

Algers wheeled away for a moment, his hand to his mouth as though regretting the outburst. Lucie understood. The pair had grown close in their relatively brief association and it was obvious he felt more than a degree of responsibility towards her, something that had required considerable negotiation on Lucie's part when persuading him to let her take the Calais job alone. It was because of the sincerity of his feelings that Lucie tolerated his sometimes archaic attitudes towards her, and he wore his worry openly on his face.

"I'm alright, Kasper," she softly reassured him. "I lost a lot of blood, but they've pumped me full again. I'm a bit sore but another couple of days and I'll be good to go."

Algers nodded and turned back to her, his wrinkled features cracking back into a smile at last.

"Aye, I know you are. But Lake won't be as easy to convince as me, you know."

Lucie grimaced at the mention of Mr Lake, their enigmatic Head of Department. Algers was right, he would doubtless be furious, and Lucie was far from eager to find out the depth of his anger just yet.

"I know... I suppose I'll just have to take it on the chin when I see him."

"There'll be a lot to take," Algers warned. "He's likely to blame you for the trail going cold on the ring, not to mention one or two uncomfortable headlines he's had to deal with."

Algers pulled a crumpled tabloid from the ancient brown briefcase he carried and held it out to Lucie, who unfolded it and winced. There was the face of her target – a man named Delauney, the hitherto head of an influential NGO – alongside a sensationalised report of his apparent suicide in France, peppered with an array of tributes from colleagues and industry figures – though curiously few, Lucie thought, from across the political spectrum.

"So, what's the problem?" Lucie asked, a little petulantly. "Lake wanted him splashed across the papers; he's got his wish."

"He's also got a dead body he could have done without, and he's had to go in hock to the French to get you transferred back to Dover, incognito, and have your own name kept out of the press. At this precise moment, he's not a happy bunny."

"He wants to fire me?" Lucie quizzed.

"We've all made fuck ups in our time, even him. I could tell you one or two tales about my early days that'd make your hair curl, but I got through it and nowadays he trusts me to do the job. You're in for a hell of a bollocking, that's for sure, but I don't think you'll be out the door this time anyway."

Lucie shrugged.

"A pity," she finally sighed, Algers raising a mighty eyebrow in surprise.

"I thought you'd made your peace with all this?"

"So did I," she nodded, "but now I'm not too sure. Before, I killed in the course of duty, Kasper, when there was no other choice. I learned to justify killing in self-defence to myself and to God... but this time I wanted to kill him. Lake hadn't ordered me to take a life – in fact he'd ordered me not to – but I didn't care. I saw what he was going to do that poor little girl, what he'd maybe done to dozens of others, and I just wanted him dead."

"You've felt that kind of anger before though, right? You've told me as much anyway."

Yes, I have," Lucie readily agreed. "But before I was always able to snap out of it. This time, it feels like I've actually committed murder."

Lucie's eyes dropped to the floor and for a moment there was no response to her introspection from Algers, until she felt his bony hand beneath her chin, gently raising her head up to meet his stare.

"Maybe in the circumstances it was the right thing to do," he said. "If you hadn't, chances are you wouldn't have been able to save that wee girl, who by the way won't have to sleep in forests at the mercy of any kiddie fiddler ring, anymore."

"Really?" Lucie's heart lifted at Kasper's mention of the youngster. "Where is she?"

"She's safe," Kasper answered, smiling. "The authorities took her in and she's warm and well fed, at least."

"But for how long?"

"Well, apparently the young couple you got mixed up in everything took quite a shine to her and when they found out about her background, they got interested in caring for her. If they decide to go ahead, Lake has apparently said he'll cut through the red tape and help facilitate something."

"That's wonderful," she grinned.

"Yeah, so just bear in mind when you're busy self-flagellating, that maybe you did take a life in anger, but you've saved one too."

"I'm not sure there's a tally system for it," Lucie laughed, appreciating both the news and her friend's efforts to ascribe the success to her.

"Well, there should be. Anyway, I should be getting back up to London; we're voting later on the Prime Minister's latest attempt to defy reality and introduce a Brexit plan that's already been rejected by the EU. I might as well enjoy using the motorway before it turns into a car park in a couple of months."

Lucie would have laughed were it not so serious.

"Is it just me, or does every day feel like a new chapter in a Kafka novel?"

"It's not just you," he reassured her, "but unfortunately hardly anyone else who sees it has their hands anywhere near the levers of power. Anyway, I have to be off, lots on..."

"A case?" she quizzed.

"Nothing to worry about," Algers answered, "just need to keep my eye on something."

"I can help, I can..."

Lucie stopped short, as her injury once more reminded her who was presently in charge, and she breathed deeply, a wry smile breaking onto her face.

"It'll wait until your fit and well," Algers reassured her as he headed towards the door of the private room. "Take another few days to conserve your strength; the mood Lake's been in lately you're going to need it."

"You didn't bring any grapes!" Lucie shouted after him in faux irritation.

"Didn't want to have to explain the expenses," came the answer from down the corridor, as his footsteps began to recede, "Lake's pissed off with you enough already."

Lucie pulled herself back onto the bed and picked up the newspaper Algers had left, quickly flicking past the offending headline, and wondering idly what new mission her friend was working on, as her eyes drifted across the print. In a small column, sat a biting attack on an MP for tabling a parliamentary question about something called '*The Red Mako*', a new defence project claimed by the Hard Right to be the salvation of the aerospace industry and proof that Britain could flourish after Brexit. No details were offered on the project itself, only angry condemnation of the one who dared to question it, and Lucie grimaced at the object of the abuse: none other than her friend and mentor, Kasper Algers himself.

4

———

"Well then, if it isn't the Return of the Saint. I remind you that the Calais job was intended to be conducted in secrecy."

Several days had passed since Lucie's release from the hospital and her journey back to London, to the flat above the chippy she had been moved to upon being recruited by Lake; she had spent much of that time contemplating how he would respond to the situation. Though she was not exactly scared of Lake, there was something undeniably intimidating about his manner, and Lucie knew that he could make life very difficult her. He also habitually, she had learned, recruited people over whom he could exercise at least some degree of control; he had done so with her when he saved her from certain imprisonment with his offer of employment. And while he had assured her that particular threat no longer hung over her, she knew very well he was a dangerous man to cross, which made his lack of contact in that time all the more unsettling.

When the text had finally come to meet with him, it had directed Lucy not to his office, but to the British Library. Lucie mused on her way there that she had never actually seen Lake's office, or even knew precisely where it was, and she reasoned that this was another method employed to retain control of his underlings.

Dressed in her usual attire of flared jeans, paisley shirt and black overcoat. Lucie stepped through the entrance and towards the domed grandeur of the reading room, scanning the imperious magnificence for Lake. She spotted him, sitting alone at one of the many desks which all pointed towards the centre. She swallowed and moved to sit at the desk alongside him.

"I know."

Lake began the meeting without either eye contact or pleasantry, instinct alone apparently telling him that it was Lucie who was sitting alongside him at the green bench he occupied in the cycloidal magnificence of the British Library. His eyes instead moved without interruption across the thin pages of an ancient tome, his words soft and measured in the otherwise echoey chamber.

"Do you?"

"Yes."

"So why instead do I find the front page of every newspaper in the land adorned with headlines of the Target's murder, a hitherto fruitful trail gone cold and myself owing favours to my counterpart in the DGSE for covering up your involvement and getting you back into the country undetected? And that's before we go into the mechanics of creating a cover for why an MP's Parliamentary assistant found herself in a Dover hospital being treated for a gunshot wound."

Lake's every syllable was invested with an obvious effort to contain a boiling and righteous anger and though Lucie bristled with resentment, she knew that he was right.

"A kiddie fiddler is dead; that's something, isn't it?"

"Oh, he very much is," Lake nodded, "along with our leads on the rest of the ring. These people don't operate alone, I made that very clear to you. And while it's safe to say that the Calais orphans should be safe from these particular predators for a while, I doubt they'll remain so forever. Had we been able to expose the whole trail then not only could we have brought them all down, the resultant publicity might well have provoked our various governments to do something about it. As it is, the children will remain in the forests to be picked off by whichever perverted opportunist is next on the list. I do hope you're proud of yourself. Your actions may very well have condemned those children to death or worse. And what's more, there's a good chance that whoever was behind the kiddie trail was also connected to the Parliament Square bomb, a trail that has likewise now gone cold."

Lake's eyes continued to move across the ancient words inked onto the pages before him, as though his absorption of their detail was in no way diminished by the chastising of his agent alongside him.

Lucie could feel herself growing paler with each word the spy master spoke, guilt setting in. She hated Lake right now, but she knew there was at least some truth in his censure, and that her usual brand of sarcasm would in no way make up for her error in judgement, and so instead, she offered an apologetic, conciliatory tone.

"So, what do I do to make it right?"

"Nothing."

"What do you mean, nothing?"

"I mean nothing. There is nothing you, or anyone can do to correct your misjudgement. You erred, and people who have caused immense suffering will go unpunished because of it. How you learn to live with that is your own affair, but you must hope at least that no others will suffer or die because of your stupidity, although I would suggest that's an unreasonable prospect."

A blankness took hold of Lucie's eyes, as though each word he spoke detached her a little further from reality, and she stared at him in silence, willing her voice to engage.

"There must..." her voice cracked, and she began her words again. "There must be something I can do."

"Not on this case," came the immediate, blithely delivered response. "Nor on any case in the field for that matter, at least until I can determine whether I made a mistake with you or not and whether your particular talents are so buried behind your own morality to be of any further use to me."

"So, what? I'm on gardening leave or something? I want to help Algers look into *Red Mako*..."

Lake's eyes lifted from his page to glare in Lucie's own, instantly stopping the flow of words from her mouth.

"*Red Mako* is none of your concern," he firmly intoned, "and not to be discussed here. Leave that to Algers, you can do background research on something else for me."

"Background research?" Lucie scowled, "I'm not an office girl..."

"At this very moment, Ms Musilova, you are precisely what I say you are."

Lake's eyes refused to drop from hers, his face a picture of intensity and an uncustomary anger in his voice.

"You have cost me time and money, destroyed an investigation and placed me in the uncomfortable position of being indebted to others, although I can't imagine why I was disposed to go to such lengths to protect you. So whether it's office work I assign you, or cleaning the toilets in Parliament, you will do it, until I can figure out what use you are to me."

"Bastard!" Lucie hissed, drawing immediate frowns and ill-tempered 'hushes' from the scattered patrons around them.

"The right kind of bastard," Lake whispered in response, fixing her with a look of patronising disappointment.

Lucie's wound began to sting, each stabbing pulse matching the throb of rage and self-reproach coursing through her rapidly clouding mind. She wanted to lunge at Lake, grab him by the lapels and scream her resentment into his condescending little face, to have him see – to force him to see – the validity of her actions and the error of his own... But no movement would come, as though the mechanics of her frame were more attuned to dispassionate reality and were fighting back against the more temperamental impulses of her brain. She had fucked up. She knew it. And Lake was correct to admonish her, which made his words all the more difficult to endure. Instead, she inhaled the musty air until her lungs could take no more and wrestled back the tumult raging in her mind.

"What's the case?" When she finally spoke, her words were clipped and rigid, as if anything more expressive would break the delicate seal she had placed on her emotions and drown them both.

"One the Prime Minister would rather we didn't look into," came the response, Lake's gaze returning to the pages before him.

"Then why are...?"

"We are Civil Servants, not MP's," Lake interrupted. "You and I are permanent parts of the Executive; the politicians chop and change. We are ultimately accountable to the Cabinet Secretary, and it's he who has encouraged this to be investigated."

"Favours for the boys?"

"Actually not, at least this time. There have been a number of disappearances of late; disappearances which for one reason or another are not top of the media's or the police's list of priorities."

"Why not?"

Lake didn't immediately answer, instead perusing the aged volume on the desk before him.

"All of those missing are women," he said softly, a hint of what sounded like shame in his voice. "European women."

The familiar pull of resentment that Lucie had felt so often in the past couple of years began to tug at her again, quickly overpowering the contrition that had hitherto encompassed her.

"When you say 'European Women'..." she began, slowly. "Twelve women have disappeared over the last couple of months," Lake continued. "All the same profile, young, professional, well respected in their individual fields. All single with no dependents and no immediate plans to leave the country, at least as far as anyone can tell."

"And they all come from within the EU?"

"All of them. Not from any one country; French, Spanish, German, Slovak, Belgian... all disappeared without trace."

"I haven't read about this in the press," Lucie frowned, assimilating the news.

"You're not likely to," came Lake's response. "The police are under-budgeted and under-resourced as it is; they've been through another round of cuts and let's just say there is a certain element within the Home Office that is very keen to see what remains of their energies focussed on the more *politically expedient* cases."

"No votes in solving crimes against foreigners, I suppose..."

"Nor in even recording some of them. And with no formal investigation there's nothing for the press to report on. Even if there were, the state the media is in today any Force trying to get to the bottom of this would find themselves publicly castigated for prioritising crimes against 'foreigners' over crimes against the 'indigenous' population. We wouldn't be involved at all if not for the fact that one of the disappeared was friendly with the Cabinet Secretary's daughter, who expressed concern enough that he got in touch with me."

The resentment in Lucie's stomach had reached her throat, joining the lump of anger and hurt that she felt there, and she blinked away a tear that threatened to drop.

"Remind me again why I put my foreign arse on the line for this bloody country?"

"At the moment your rear is quite well protected as I don't want you out in the field; you can investigate and that's it. You report your findings to me and we'll take it from there."

Lucie nodded, swallowing back her emotion and confining herself to the facts.

"Where do I start?" she asked in a hushed voice.

"As luck would have it, very close to home. The latest victim was resident in Camden Town; it was a Detective Inspector there who began to put the pieces together and theorised that these were not all isolated cases, before he succumbed to political pressure to suspend the investigation – I'll email you what files we have. As aide to constituency's MP it won't seem too improper for you to ask a few questions."

"What's his name?"

"Ismail," replied Lake. "DI Asif Ismail."

"And what can he tell me that we don't already know?"

"That's for you to find out, but you at least have an unexpected lead."

"Yes?"

"They've found a body. Ines Aubel – the last woman to disappear – turned up dead last week, not far from her home. She was raped before she died."

Lucie looked away, shutting her eyes, while Lake remained silent.

"I'll, er... I'll get onto it," Lucie eventually whispered,

pushing her chair from the desk and standing up, ignoring the various pains in her battered body.

"I'll expect to hear from you shortly," Lake responded. "Oh, and Ms Musilova?"

"What?"

"Try not to balls it up this time, I'm sure you don't want any more innocents on your conscience, and I'm frankly disinclined to rescue you again."

The barb hit home harder than the bullet had done and burned twice as fiercely. She opened her mouth to respond through her rage, but no words would come. Instead, she silently cursed the bastard who had brought her into this world and turned on her heels, striding out into a day as freezing and frosty as the country itself now seemed to be.

5

———

As she strode, her hand toyed anxiously with the content of her overcoat pockets, and she pulled out the twisted plastic strip which housed her medication; the tiny, white pills which helped her keep the worst of her depression in check. Spying a bin as she turned the corner into Judd Street, she threw the tablets into it, stuffed her hands back in her pockets and headed for the pub before her. She didn't deserve the pills, she told herself, and neither did she deserve to throw her sorrows on the Church she had once served as a military Chaplain in the RAF, back in the days before her capture by enemy forces. Since then, while her faith had remained intact, she had forgotten how to articulate it, and so her days of ministry were over. What she deserved right now, at least what she convinced herself she deserved, could be found in the alcohol behind those doors.

It wasn't long before she had surrendered her senses completely to the spirits she poured inside her. The steadily growing collection of glasses had already attracted glances, some mocking, some wary, by the time Lucie pushed herself up from the table and staggered to the Ladies.

Lake was a bastard. There was no doubt of that. His routine

method of recruitment to the Overlappers was to find someone with the required skill set, struggling to stay afloat in a sea of compromising circumstances. When all hope seemed lost, Lake would sail in and throw a lifeline, but only so that he could own them from that point. It was an odd form of employer loyalty, but it seemed nonetheless effective, as all those Lucie had thus far encountered in the Department, Kasper Algers included, lived in perpetual wariness of the man who could transform their lives for ill in an instant should he so choose. While Lucie's efforts in the recent case of Sir Geoffrey Hartnell had earned her a reprieve from the threat of imprisonment, Lake still exercised his power over her with his threats to remove from her the resources to find her mother's murderer – a former intelligence operative named Trystan Dagonet. But Lake was also well-versed in the psychological manipulation of his workforce. So much so in fact, that Lucie almost thought he enjoyed it; but she was damned if she knew what game he was up to now.

The brass handle of the toilet door slammed against the shiny white veneer of the tiles as Lucie's hostile mind relished replaying the words Lake had spoken to her on a perpetual loop of torment. She knew better than to think that every word Lake said was true, but if there was even the slightest chance her mistakes in Calais would lead to more innocents suffering, then...

Her legs were going, she could feel it. Leaning her hands on the sink she looked up at the mirror above, her spinning vision settling on the face that stared back, and she hated it.

"Fucking idiot!" she slurred at herself contemptuously, "Stupid, murdering idiot!"

The mirror offered no answers and merely spewed the insults back at her, mixing them with her intoxication and guilt, and allowing a cocktail of dangerous instability to ferment. Lucie could hear that part of herself begging her to step back from the brink, but she shook her head free of its warm and comforting words, fixating instead on the creature in the mirror, which stared maliciously back at her, at once taunting and chastising her for her failure. She screamed at it to shut up, to look away and leave her in peace, but still it stared with such intensity that she could bear it no more. Drawing back from the sink, Lucie flung herself forward, her forehead meeting the image with such ferocity, it shattered into a hundred pieces as she slid down, exhausted and weeping, blood spattering her skin.

The sound of the door swinging open, and the cries of the aggrieved bar staff, forced her to stagger up and push her way out of the pub. Though she may not have cared about personal consequences, she was aware of her responsibility to Kasper, who for all his faults had been her friend. An MP's assistant may not be very newsworthy in themselves but turning up drunk and vandalising a pub toilet would inevitably bring both of them an unwelcome degree of attention if she hung around. Mercifully, the other patrons were in no mood to challenge her, and she barged her way out of the doors and into the busy, afternoon street, quickly losing herself in the crowd.

She cursed herself as she struggled to stop the spinning in her head and regain proper control of her mind and actions, and cursed again as she tripped on the doorstep of the coffee shop she now sought refuge in. Her behaviour in the pub could easily have got her into trouble and Lake would undoubtedly have taken her off the case if she had, not to mention the embarrassment she might have caused Kasper. Her rage spent, all that was now left was regret and as she sipped the large, black Americano she held between her cold hands, she resolved to make amends.

The alcohol still toying with her system, Lucie raised the mug high, her voice a little too loud for the comfort of those around her, and toasted the object of her new assignment, heartily.

"To Ines Aubel," she vocalised, earning tuts and half glances from the other patrons, that Lucie neither acknowledged nor cared about. She took a sip and clunked the cup down onto the saucer, already stained with Lucie's spillages. "To Ines," she repeated, softly to herself. "I'll find the bastard who killed you, Ines, and by God I'll make them pay…"

After swallowing two of the strongest painkillers she could find in her flat, Lucie spent the first hours of the morning studying the files emailed to her by Lake, and cursing in irritation at their brevity. This 'DI Ismail' her boss had mentioned had put together the bare bones of a report on the matter, connecting the murder of Ines with the previous disappearance of six other women, all from EU Member States, but annoyingly light in other details. If she was to get any further, she needed to speak with him, and thought the best way to do it was to arrange a meeting on behalf of Algers, who as local MP would have a legitimate concern in the case. Algers though was proving difficult to track down. There was no answer from his office and his mobile cut straight to voice mail, leaving Lucie to opt for the direct approach.

Never one for business clothes, Lucie nonetheless dressed as conservatively as seemed appropriate for a supposed Parliamentary assistant, donning brown corduroy trousers and a black polo shirt with just the white trim as a nod to her Sixties preferences, wrapping herself finally in her increasingly tattered overcoat. Her discomfort with navigating the Underground had never completely left her in these past few months of living in London, but without too much uncertainty, she found herself disembarking at Kentish Town station a short while later, before heading up Holmes Road to the building where DI Ismail was supposedly based.

To her surprise, her smile to the desk sergeant, coupled with a quick examination of her Parliamentary pass card and her claim to have arranged a meeting with the Detective Inspector on behalf of the local MP, did not result in her ejection from the premises. Instead, the shaven-headed and somewhat stocky officer cheerily advised her that DI Ismail was currently unavailable, but that she could take a seat and wait in reception if she wished. The wait itself was not too excessive and eased by the coffee the sergeant provided her as she flicked through a day old newspaper left on the plastic chair beside her.

Lucie's eyelids had begun to droop by the time she heard the sergeant's voice pipe up, advising someone that there was a woman from Parliament waiting to see him. Opening her eyes, she jumped up, hoping not to look too groggy as she walked to the desk with her hand outstretched.

"DI Ismail?" she asked, a large smile adorning her face.

The Detective took a moment to respond, a slight frown appearing across his face as he took in the woman before him. He was about forty, tall and reasonably slim and dressed in a simple, grey suit, worn with a colourfully patterned tie loosely knotted beneath it. His face, though handsome, was lined by an obvious exhaustion with which Lucie sympathised. His movements were as cautious as his voice as he raised his hand to take the one she offered.

"Yes," he quietly confirmed. "I'm sorry, you are?"

"Lucie Musilova," she answered in her best 'chirpy professional' tone. "I'm here for our meeting."

"Erm, sorry, what meeting?" Ismail's brow furrowed deeper still in confusion.

Lucie frowned too, wincing apologetically to reinforce the lie. "Ah..." she began. "I'm the Parliamentary aide to Kasper Algers MP. I was told by our office that they'd booked a meeting with you about a case Mr Algers is keen to discuss."

"I don't discuss cases with the public."

"I'd guess not, but this is official business. Mr Algers has been invited by the Mayor to discuss crime concerns in the constituency, and I know that the Home Secretary is taking an interest too..."

"Ok, ok," Ismail interrupted, holding his hand up, his tone suggesting to Lucie that he knew full well she was bluffing but didn't want to debate the issue here and now. "I've got ten minutes, alright? Sarge, can you sign her in please?"

The formalities of registration ended with a friendly smile from the desk sergeant and a walk up a couple of flights of stairs to the Ops room, pounding with the sound of ringing telephones and cursing CID officers. Ducking his head through a side room door to check it was free, Ismail beckoned Lucie in to follow him, leaning against the desk inside and not inviting Lucie to take a seat.

"Let me see your pass," he curtly demanded; Lucie obliging, not entirely surprised by the coldness of his manner. After glancing down briefly as she held it out to him, Ismail nodded and folded his arms tightly.

"Ok, what's this all about?"

"Sorry?"

"There's no 'meeting', there never was."

"I am Kasper Algers aide though, and I am here to talk to you in confidence about a case."

"I told you, I don't talk about cases. Data protection laws, you know."

"I'm afraid I'm here on a higher authority than that."

"Oh yeah?" Ismail laughed. "Whose?"

Lucie swore under her breath. She hadn't wanted to show her cards, at least not so early, and certainly not on a case that the government she supposedly served would not be completely happy about were they aware of it, but without Algers' status to support her story she had little choice. Reaching into her pocket she pulled out the Security Services ID card Lake had issued her with and held it up to the disgruntled Detective.

"Have you seen one of these before?"

Ismail's face hardened as he examined her card, clearly conscious that the situation was falling even further out of his control. He nodded stiffly.

"SIS?

"A branch of it, yes."

"I've worked with MI5 before, which branch are you with?"

"None of your business, I'm afraid. Suffice to say you're obliged to answer my questions, and if you repeat this to anyone, I'm authorised to shoot you in the bollocks." Lucie gave a half-smile as she finished, reasoning that if she was going to pull rank and exaggerate her reason for being there, she may as well try to sweeten the atmosphere with a joke. Fortunately for her, the gamble seemed to pay off as Ismail returned the ID with a half-smile of his own.

"Which case?"

Lucie hesitated for a moment and took a deep breath in. "Ines Aubel."

Ismail gave a harsh, sardonic laugh and shook his head.

"Ines Aubel," he repeated. "You know, I've been a rozzer for twenty years, and I've had a lot of cases I wish I'd never been involved in, but never have I been so sorry a body was found as I was with Ines Aubel, God rest her soul."

The lament surprised Lucie, but she didn't question it,

reasoning that allowing Ismail to unload the obvious stresses he was feeling would see the information he carried flow more freely.

"What was the cause of death?"

"Gunshot wound to the head."

"And she was raped before she was killed?"

"It appears so," Ismail snapped in confirmation. "Her injuries certainly suggest as much although there's no trace of DNA evidence; at least none I'm aware of. I'm sorry, how do you know all this?"

"You filed a report, linking Ines' death to the disappearance of six other women," Lucie said, ignoring his question.

"Indeed I did, and immediately after filing it I was contacted by the Home Secretary's office and told in no uncertain terms to drop it and focus my energies on other cases. When I objected, I was threatened with suspension, so you'll see why it grates just a little to have to make time to dance to your tune – or is that MP you claim to work for pulling the strings? If he is then for what? So he can score points in some debate?"

"Kasper Algers is an Independent," Lucie responded, "he doesn't do Party politics."

"Maybe not, but he still needs to get himself re-elected, doesn't he? If he sticks his nose into a few cases before too long he'll have made quite the name for himself, won't he?"

"Listen!" Lucie loudly demanded. "This isn't about political one-upmanship, ok? Algers may be an MP, but I'm not and I'm just interested in the facts of this case. A woman has been murdered, six more are missing, nobody's come up with a better theory than you, and maybe I might be able to do something about it without getting screwed like you've been. Now if we can get to the bottom of something, and make a bit of noise about it, then maybe the government won't have any choice but to let you re-open the case, yes?"

Ismail's eyes narrowed and Lucie could tell he was feeling the burn of resentment at the impotence of his situation, and it was a feeling with which she fully sympathised. A few moments passed before he finally nodded his acquiescence.

"Right then," Lucie said, her voice returning to normal. "What first made you think the cases were linked?"

"Chance really," Ismail shrugged. "When the body was found, I looked into her background and found there'd been a missing person's report filed on her a few days previously, and I remembered a mate of mine on the MET telling me of a couple of disappearances she'd been working on until she got shifted onto other cases. After that I went looking and found ten other disappearances in similar circumstances: all young women, single, professional and living alone..."

"And all originally from somewhere in Europe," Lucie interrupted, the police officer nodding in response.

"Yep, and not from one country in particular but right across the EU. I thought maybe some nutter from one of these 'yellow vest' groups that have sprung up recently might be involved, but before I could dig any deeper, I was called up and told the case had to be closed."

Lucie squinted as she processed the information. Ismail's thoughts about the yellow vests – the usual Far Right groups, some of whom had taken to donning high visibility jackets in mimicry of the gilets jaunes movement in Paris – were intriguing and the involvement of such people was always a possibility, although they had never previously acted so subtly. More interesting to Lucie right now was the reason for closing the case.

"You said your mate was told to close her investigation, too?"

"So she told me," Ismail responded. "Pretty much the same thing that happened to me; a call from above telling her there was political pressure to divert our resources to more 'pressing matters' as they described them."

"And the case is left open-ended?" Ismail shifted uncomfortably.

"Not exactly," he said. "I wanted to leave mention of my theories in case of future investigation but was categorically told that wasn't acceptable. Instead the bigwigs upstairs picked out what they saw as the most likely option in the circumstances and that was that."

"And what was the 'most likely option' DI Ismail?" Lucie quizzed, her suspicions suddenly aroused by the CID man's uncomfortable body language. Ismail inhaled slowly before answering, a hint of shame in his voice.

"The body was found not far from one of the new trial legal brothels; the one just outside the town centre, you know? It's common knowledge that there are ways to bypass the registration requirements, and there are some pretty desperate people who hang around nearby, looking to undercut what's on offer legally…"

"Ines wasn't a 'desperate' person, Detective Inspector, she was a well-paid employee of a blue chip company in the centre of London; what need would she have to supplement her income like that?"

"Look, I agree, alright?"

Ismail held up his hands, clearly as frustrated as Lucie herself with the situation.

"I agree. There was no evidence of payments other than her salary going into her account, no evidence of drug use, either in her system when we found her, or at her flat. There was nothing whatsoever to indicate a predilection for risky lifestyle choices or anything that could explain why she ended up where she did. I tried to investigate further but thanks to cut after cut to our budget, and now with this fucking Brexit shit about to kick off, my time was demanded elsewhere; what's more it had to be seen to be utilised elsewhere."

"What? More of that 'British services for British People' bullshit the papers are full of?"

"Hey!" Ismail shouted back at her, anger clouding his face in an instant. "Asian guy standing here, hello! You don't get to lecture me about institutional fucking racism after what I've had to put up in my life and doing this fucking job! Believe me, Miss Government Agent, I get more shit each day from the people I'm trying to help than I do from the bloody criminals! Do you know what it's like to be looked at with suspicion by everyone the day after a bomb goes off somewhere? To be stared at with pure hatred by the witnesses you're trying to question, because they think you're more likely to blow yourself up alongside the suspect as arrest them? Even today, I get nasty looks from anyone who has to squeeze up next to me on the Tube. And you think I get off on kowtowing to the fascistic bastards steering us into the sewer?"

Lucie stayed silent for a moment, resisting the urge to snap back with details of her own life and the prejudices she and Europeans had faced since even before the Referendum had been called. Instead, she dialled back her emotions, refusing to again allow them to control her and cloud her actions on a case. Anyway, it was clear the case mattered to the DI. She held up her own hands and spoke again, softening her inflections.

"Ok, I understand, I'm sorry. It's not a competition to see who's taken the most abuse in life. It's obvious you did everything you could."

"Yeah, well it wasn't enough, was it?" Ismail replied, gathering his own emotions and sighing in resignation. "She's officially noted in the records as a suspected prostitute, no-one is out there looking for the killer and six other women are still missing. Meanwhile I'm increasingly finding my job transformed into being part of the judiciary wing of the Conservative Party..."

A small smile formed at the edge of Lucie's mouth at the officer's black humour, which she was pleased to see mirrored on his own face, the tension that had filled the room beginning to ease.

"Well, fortunately I don't answer to the bloody Tories, at least not yet. I'm going to be picking this case up Detective Inspector, and I'll get to the bottom of it, you can count on that."

"Call me Asif," he answered, his smile widening. "And I wish I had your freedom. Is there anything I can do to help?"

"You can start by calling me Lucie," she grinned back, "and by keeping this conversation secret, right? Needless to say, I'm not too keen on the idea of finding my face on the News at Ten."

"Absolutely," Ismail nodded. "I've done enough work with counter terrorism and Interpol to know how these things go down."

"Good. Have you got a pen?"

Ismail patted his pockets and retrieved a ball point pen, handing it to Lucie, who took it and scribbled something down on the back of a receipt recovered from the capacious pocket of her overcoat, handing the scrap to the police officer.

"That's my number," she smiled. "If you think of anything you can reach me on that."

"I will," Ismail promised, his voice now far lighter and devoid of the stresses apparent within it earlier. "I definitely will. Let me sign you out."

For the first time since her brief touching of lips with the late Della Quince, whom Lucie could not now think of without succumbing to a medley of anger and love, she sensed the glorious tingle of new attraction inside her as she walked back down the steps towards the exit, with Ismail beside her. The tension now replaced with a nervous warmth and curiosity that the police officer's face told her was mutual, they bid each other a warm goodbye before Lucie set off back towards the Underground station, focussing once more on the case. The only lead she had was the location of the body, and though she was not entirely enamoured of the prospect of visiting such an establishment, she knew the brothel near the crime scene was the only place to begin. By the time she reached Kentish Town station, she had dialled Algers' number three times without answer and she frowned as she scrolled instead to Lakes' details. Lake had demanded a direct report and while the prospect of speaking to him posed no greater anticipation than visiting the brothel would, it was likewise an unfortunate necessity.

The dial tone rang once before the spy master answered, Lucie advising him blandly that she had met with DI Ismail and would soon be following up a new lead. It was as she finished and made to end the call that Lake stopped her, an urgency in his voice she was unaccustomed to.

"What is it?" she queried.

"Where are you now?"

"In Kentish Town, heading back to Camden Town, why?"

"Meet me in Westminster as soon as possible. There are things we need to discuss."

"Such as?"

"Such as Mr Algers," Lake slowly intoned. "There's been an attack."

7

Lucie spotted Lake outside the imperious magnificence of Number One Parliament Street, wearing both his regular ensemble of casual suit and expression of mild irritation at seemingly everything and everyone around him. Though the anger stirred up by their most recent meeting still frothed within her, Lucie pushed her resentment to the back of her mind and rushed across the road to meet him.

"What's happened?" she demanded. "Where is he?"

"Walk with me," Lake responded, setting off at a nonchalant pace in the direction of St. Stephen's Tower.

After a couple of steps of silence, Lucie could contain her worry no further and repeated her demand to know what happened, Lake eventually responding, though his eyes never once met hers.

"Mr Algers is alive," he confirmed, "though he may not remain so. He is presently at Chelsea and Westminster hospital."

"I have to see him," Lucie interrupted.

"There's little point, he's quite unconscious; his attendants have yet to give an altogether positive view of his chances."

Lucie thought for a brief moment that she could detect the

faintest of cracks in her Superior's voice, though as she turned her head to face him, his features displayed their usual look of annoyed rigidity.

"What happened?" she asked.

"He was on a visit and was confronted by a group of Yellow Vests who crowded him, shouting their usual repertoire of abuse, but rather than ignore them he chose to engage and challenge their remarks. He earned several bottles to the head for his trouble and was beaten further after he collapsed. If the police hadn't arrived when they did, he would have probably been killed at the scene."

Lucie stifled the reaction she could feel brewing in her gut and cursed under her breath. Violence and intimidation towards anyone who dared to call out the illegality and gerrymandering of the Referendum was yet another unpleasant hallmark of the new Brexit Britain, and Kasper, with his outspoken views and refusal to 'get behind' what he and so many saw as damaging at best and fascistic at worst had long been on the list of targets. While politicians of all parties were used to the close attentions of the various Yellow Vest groups roaming Westminster, who would routinely menace MPs in order to score likes on social media, away from the 'bubble' they were altogether more unpredictable.

"Did the police get them?" Lucie probed.

"Regrettably not. Two Police Response vehicles attended the scene, but the Officers' immediate concern was Mr Algers himself."

"But they can identify them, surely? Those thugs never go anywhere without a camera phone, there must be some video evidence the cops can rely on?"

Lake shook his head, his customary frown creasing further. "Nothing I'm afraid that suggests immediate identification. One or two videos have begun doing the rounds on some of the darker corners of the internet, presented as a 'warning to remoaners', but everyone in them, save for Mr Algers, has their face obscured."

"But still, there must be some distinguishing marks, some way of identifying them that the police can look at?"

"If they're given the time to do so," came the fatalistic reply, "which in the current climate, isn't likely. The government don't dare allow a full-scale investigation in case it brings up any awkward questions about Brexit or the validity of the process. I'm afraid the attack on Mr Algers will be put down officially as a simple case of being in the wrong place at the wrong time."

Lucie stopped dead on the pavement, eliciting the insults of the person closest behind her, who stumbled and walked around her. "So that's it then?" She quizzed, giving in to her anger. "We're just going to forget about it?"

Lake took her gently by the arm and encouraged her to keep moving through the ever-increasing crowds, his voice typically low. "Calm yourself, Ms Musilova," he said. "I said that the hands of the police would be tied. You, I and this department are not the police."

Her chest relaxed in relief at his reassurance and she pushed her anger back down, to be dealt with later.

"So where did this happen?"

"WaterWhyte Defence Systems," Lake answered. "The Chairman and CEO of which coincidentally is one Jarvis Whyte MP, the Conservative Member for Heaton South. Mr Algers was looking into some queries about the..."

"The *Red Mako* project," Lucie guessed.

"I remind you, Ms Musilova, that you are not assigned to enquiries into the *Red Mako* project."

"Yeah, well maybe not, but you can at least tell me what it is." Lake sighed in resignation and spying an unoccupied bench, led

Lucie to it and sat down, the pair watching the bustle of London life as he outlined the background to Algers' case.

"The *Red Mako* is the name of a new, high speed military interception boat being developed for the Saudis for use in the Yemen campaign. Six models are being produced for deployment from a strategic platform in the Red Sea – hence the name – designed to patrol the coastline and protect Saudi Arabia from any attacks launched from the water or attempts to break the naval blockade of Yemen."

"What, just trading in guns isn't enough for the government anymore?" Lucie asked in obvious disgust.

"Regrettably not. With business after business making plans to leave the country after Brexit, and the loss of so much of the financial sector for the same reason, the government feels it must attempt to plug the hole somewhere. After being embarrassed by some of the comments made by Airbus and the like, and the very real threat to the defence and aerospace industries, *Red Mako* offered the Hard Brexiters in the Cabinet the perfect opportunity."

"But surely they'll still have the same supply chain problems that the other major companies are facing?"

"Actually, no," Lake replied. "As fate would have it, the tendering process for the sub-contracts, while of course being entirely fair and above board, have resulted in exclusively British companies being selected to supply parts, all under the umbrella of WaterWhyte Defence... strange that."

The cynicism in Lake's voice was obvious and sincere, and Lucie began to grasp the nature of Alger's investigation.

"So, Kasper was looking into the tenders? Fair enough, it just seems a bit low key for a guy of his skill..."

"It wasn't just that," Lake interrupted. "Let's just say that we had one or two concerns that the project isn't as completely defence oriented as the official documents would have us believe."

"You think it's an attack vessel?"

"There are certain indications in that direction, yes; suggestions that the *Red Mako* may actually be a sea-based weapons platform from which to attack Yemeni outposts; but getting to the bottom of things isn't easy. This is the government's pet project, the proverbial middle finger to Remainers and doubters out there, designed to show them that while Brexit Britain may be something of a turd, it can at least be polished."

Lucie smiled at his uncommon vulgarity, but her mind quickly returned to the severity of the situation Lake described.

"Polished by building an attack ship to worsen a humanitarian crisis," she mused.

"If it makes money for them and makes Brexit look even vaguely successful then they consider it worth it. The human cost of anything has never weighed heavily on the minds of that lot."

"But if this is the government's baby, and this Jarvis Whyte bloke is on the government back benches, then how are you able to get away with looking into it?"

"Who says I've told them I have? I follow paper trails every day and I exercise my judgement as to which of those to inform my superiors of; if I'm not completely open about what I'm investigating I can't be told not to. Likewise, I am very careful to protect the identity of my operatives, which is why to the rest of the world, Mr Algers is merely a crusading Member of Parliament, and his real obligations remain hidden."

Lucie squirmed in sudden discomfort, her conversation with Ismail earlier that day now racing to the forefront of her mind.

"Listen, about that," she began. "I was following up on the

missing women case you gave me today, and when my cover was getting me nowhere, well I..."

"You've said who you are and what you do."

It was a statement rather than a question, and Lucie simply nodded in response, not ashamed of her judgement call, but annoyed that there had seemed little other way to get the information she needed.

"Such an admission is not typically to be advised," Lake intoned, in a surprisingly dispassionate voice. "Whom precisely did you tell?"

"Just the DI you set me up with, Ismail. He's a good man and he's worked with SIS before, so he understands what's required.

"Does he now?"

"Yes."

Lake was quiet for a moment as if pondering, before turning to Lucie requesting details of what she had learned, nodding sagaciously as she recounted the specifics of her meeting that day and the victim being officially recorded as a prostitute, murdered by an unknown punter.

"What's your next move?"

"Visiting the brothel she was found near, I suppose," Lucie answered. "See if there are any records of her on the books there or if anyone saw her around. Can you get hold of a fake police ID for me? I'd rather not have to reveal my true motivations again."

"No, indeed," Lake responded, "and I might be able to do rather more than just provide an ID. Wait to hear from me before you go there. In the meantime, there's somebody else you could be talking to."

"Who?"

"Amber Robyn."

Lucie's heart sank, and she guessed her expression joined it in sympathy. Amber Robyn MP was notorious in the Commons and with the public as one of the few hard-line Brexit supporters on the Labour benches and had courted controversy through her willingness to share platforms with characters on the extreme fringes of debate. Her comments on immigration and what she perceived as the 'flood of foreigners pouring in from Europe' had long since made her a figure reviled by both anti-Brexit campaigners and the European nationals she sought to denigrate. "Why her?" Lucie asked, scowling. "I'd get a more stimulating conversation from half the Yellow Vests outside Parliament than I would do going inside to talk to her."

"Don't be so sure," was Lake's answer, clearly amused by Lucie's reluctance. "She was a very public opponent of the trial brothels opening in the first place and she sits on the Home Affairs Select Committee, which has access to all the relevant regulatory documents. In fact, I've always said, if you want to know the whole truth about a project, don't talk to its supporters, talk to its opponents – they'll know the facts behind every dotted i and crossed t. Plus you're able to legitimately quiz her without the need to blow your cover again."

Lake's voice took on an accusatory tone as he spoke the last words, turning his head at last to Lucie and fixing her with a customary look of annoyed disapproval, which Lucie decided it was best to take on the chin.

"And while I'm doing that, what about the *Red Mako*?" Lucie asked, desperate to play some part in the assignment which had put her friend in the hospital.

"I have other operatives, Ms Musilova," Lake answered disdainfully, standing up from the bench and moving to head back down Parliament Street. "Concentrate on the assignment you've been given. Good day."

Lucie watched him walk away, soon losing him in the throngs of oblivious and distracted people crowding the street. She cursed to herself that she hadn't been able to help Kasper and offered a quick prayer for his recovery, before professionalism took over and focussed her mind on what she had been tasked to do. She knew very well that Lake still had significant doubts about her abilities; she could only win back his respect by doing her job. If Lake wanted her to meet with the notorious Amber Robyn, then meet with her she would; and Lucie hoped she would make it a meeting the politician would never forget.

8

"I t's a pleasure to finally meet you, Lucie, please have a seat."

The coldness in her words conveyed Amber Robyn's reputation as an intimidating and even fearsome woman. Having first made a name for herself in the early Eighties as a vocal and passionate opponent of the Thatcher governments, she was no less inclined to ruffle feathers now, relishing her reputation as a Brexit contrarian and relying on the relative safety of her seat to chastise the significant portion of her own constituents who voted to Remain. Though age had faded her once vibrant red curls into a more becalmed grey and white, the ferocity and intelligence behind her blue eyes left none in any doubt that the flames within her were undiminished.

Lucie had fully expected that this would prove to be a frosty and uncomfortable meeting, and so the ice in the MP's greeting surprised her little. Lucie after all was the half-Czech Parliamentary aide to perhaps the fiercest anti-Brexit campaigner in the Commons. While Amber Robyn revelled in her role as the pantomime villainess of the debate's opposite side and had been a vocal campaigner for the end of freedom of movement. Both women knew there was little love lost between them, but Lucie hoped that they could avoid the elephant in the room long enough to at least talk professionally.

Accepting the politician's proffered hand, Lucie entered the small and cramped office, taking a brief moment to assess the woman she would be dealing with before opening the conversation. The beauty of her youth was still evident, and the vibrancy of her character reflected in the bright energy of the clothes she wore.

"Thank you for seeing me at such short notice," Lucie began, "I appreciate how busy you are."

"Not at all," Robyn answered, her face twisting into an expression of exaggerated concern. "How's Kasper?"

"Still unconscious," Lucie replied, a little too curtly. She had never enjoyed the posturing so prevalent within the world of politics and the faux expressions of friendship between bitter opponents who would happily step over each other in the street if cameras weren't present.

"Still, I'm hoping when the police catch the bastards who did it, it'll help perk him up no end."

Lucie sailed as close to the edge as she dared with her words, conscious of the need for the information Robyn held, but equally determined to let her know that she didn't consider those on any side of the argument who had fostered the violent climate that clung to the country above blame when it came to the attack. Robyn though, with a politician's natural ease, deftly deflected the inference and continued in her vein of artificial sympathy.

"Absolutely," she nodded. "It's so sad that the days when we could all disagree on things without resorting to such violence seem to be behind us. I lie awake at night wondering how we can put things right."

"Well maybe a few less headlines and speeches talking about

'traitors' and 'enemies of the people' might be a good place to start."

This time the barb hit home, and the ice blue stare of the MP burrowed into Lucie from across the desk she sat behind.

"Yes, perhaps," she quietly answered, though her tone implied anything but agreement.

Lucie took her cue to change tack and fixed Robyn with a faux smile of her own, leaning across the desk as though taking a trusted friend into her confidence.

"Actually, it's to do with the spread of violence that I wanted to speak with you, Amber."

"Oh?"

"There was a body found recently, in Kasper's constituency; a young woman. She'd been raped and murdered."

"How awful," Amber Robyn answered, the inflection of political sympathy returning in full to her voice. "Have the police been able to help?"

"Unfortunately not," Lucie answered, "they're massively under-resourced and they haven't the capacity to properly look into it."

"But surely a murder…"

"The victim was French."

Silence at once took possession of the room as Lucie made the revelation, leaving the women to stare at each other uncomfortably. 'British services for British People' had long been a slogan of the hard-line Brexiters and was one more controversial platform Robyn had merrily shared with some of politic's more unsavoury figures. Lucie's accusatory tone had been undeniable, and she half-expected to be immediately ejected from the room before she had got to the meat of the matter.

"I see," Robyn eventually spoke, her words not so much

breaking the ice as plunging the temperature of the room still further. "Look, if you've come here to argue politics..."

"I haven't," Lucie interrupted, firmly. "I want to talk about where the body was found."

"And what's that got to do with me?"

"She was found in Camden Town; a stone's throw from one of the new brothels decorating the country."

The silence returned, but this time fuelled by a sudden and obvious peak in Robyn's interest. Without asking, the older woman stood and moved to a side cabinet, from which she pulled a bottle of Scotch and two glasses, quickly pouring two large measures and handing one to Lucie, who wordlessly accepted.

"I think," Robyn began as she sat back down and took a sip from her glass, "that the issue of these brothels is one of the areas where you and I might find some common ground."

Lucie, against her better judgement raised her glass towards her counterpart, who reciprocated the gesture before they both drank, Lucie relishing the burn of the spirit as it travelled through her chest.

"You've campaigned against them for a long time," she began. "Since the day they were mooted, and I've come under all kinds of attack for my efforts."

"It's a controversial subject."

"You surely can't be in favour?"

"No, not in the slightest, but I understand the argument. Sex is the oldest business in the world; if someone wants to sell their body for profit, it's not the government's place to question their morality. But as it goes on anyway, they can save lives by providing a clean and safe and regulated environment to practice it in."

"Ensuring that the objectification of women in society

continues apace while the government counts its tax receipts and closes its eyes to the social repercussions."

"Men are employed there too," Lucie countered, putting forward the justifications the government had utilised upon the launch.

"Perhaps so, but it's women who bear the brunt of this, whether through sarcastic comments in the office tea rooms from young boys wanting to 'pay their dick tax', or the poor unfortunates too destitute for these damn places to employ, who end up selling themselves for even less three streets away. You're an intelligent woman, Lucie, you must be able to see that these things have solved nothing at all and caused twice as many problems as existed before!"

The passion in Robyn's words matched the ferocity of her stare and Lucie allowed herself a brief smile before raising her glass to her lips once more and draining the contents.

"Then perhaps you're right," she smiled. "Perhaps we do have some common ground after all."

The women shared a brief smile and Robyn visibly relaxed, the tension removed from her voice.

"I suppose," she began, "that you want to find out whether your victim was employed in the establishment? I'm afraid I can't help there. The committee does of course keep a full list of those operating on the premises, but data protection regulations are quite explicit..."

"I know, you can't confirm or deny, I understand. Between ourselves I already know she wasn't on the books."

"So, you think she might have been undercutting the market, one of the street girls in the area?"

Lucie sat back, finding herself beginning to relax into the older woman's powerful company despite her inherent opposition to so much of what she stood for, and offering her a fresh smile as Robyn replenished her glass. She didn't immediately answer the politician's question but pressed on with her own probing.

"You've long campaigned to get women and girls off the streets, you're probably the foremost authority in Parliament on the issue of prostitution and trafficking; I've always imagined it was desperation that led to people putting themselves into that position, I suppose I'm looking for whatever I've missed."

Robyn took another healthy sip from her glass and placed it down on the table, inhaling for a moment before addressing Lucie's question.

"Desperation comes in many forms, Lucie," she said. "We're years into a programme of austerity, some people have absolutely nothing and no way to feed themselves other than by selling their bodies. Others might be addicts so lost in a destructive spiral they lack either the will or ability, or both, to climb out of it, and with services decimated and being cut further all the time there's no-one to help them."

"But what would motivate someone with a well-paid, respectable job to get involved in that kind of work?"

"Danger?" Robyn shrugged. "All too often people are tricked or trafficked in believing they have a good job lined up and end up forced into sex work..."

"Not in this case, her job was legit, her passport and documents were all at home. She'd even applied for the damn Residency scheme."

Lucie spat the last words, her contempt for the government's insistence that all EU Nationals apply for permission to stay in their own homes after exit day obvious. Other than a quick flash of her blue eyes, Robyn didn't rise to the comment.

"Maybe a desire for excitement. Did she have a partner?"

"No. And no family either, at least in this country. By all accounts she had a good circle of friends, none of whom were aware of this kind of behaviour. It's been recorded as a score gone wrong, but the report isn't very thorough; this could all be supposition and the location of the body a coincidence."

"What time was she found?"

"Early morning by a dog walker; they reckon she'd been there a couple of hours, so about four I think."

"Well then, however circumstantial it might be, I'm sorry but I think the police opinion is right."

"Why so sure?" Lucie frowned, lifting the re-filled glass to her mouth, her mind furiously racing over the sparse details of the case as far as she knew them. She had never met the victim, nor had any reason to pre-suppose her motivations, but nonetheless the case had reached into Lucie's heart and gripped it tight. She felt as though she knew Ines, and was advocating not just for justice for her murder, but also for her character. To hear Robyn assert so casually her belief that prostitution really was behind all this sent a pang of resentment through her chest. The certainty in Robyn's voice, and her apparent ease with the judgement she had made, only served to intensify that feeling, and Lucie found herself swallowing the whole measure in one gulp, stifling the cough that toyed with her chest.

"It just seems to fit, that's all," came the answer. "The brothel in Camden is on Chalton Street, isn't it?"

"Yes."

"And how far away was the body?"

"Hidden by the trees on the corner of Chalton and Polygon Road."

"Well there we are," Robyn said, shrugging, a strangely inappropriate smile forming on her face which only served to deepen Lucie's frown. "I'm sorry, but everything seems to fit. She was found within a few hundred yards of the legalised venue which is precisely where the street girls operate. Plus, there's the nationality thing to consider..."

"What 'nationality thing'?" quizzed Lucie, irritation returning to her tone.

"You've heard of honour among thieves? Well there's a hierarchy too," Robyn explained, clearly relishing her superior knowledge on the subject and in so doing, diluting whatever goodwill had thus far built up between them. "Believe it or not, there's a rota of sorts to these things. You'll find British girls working the streets in late evening, until about two or three. After that, the foreigners take over."

"The foreigners." Lucie repeated the word with distaste in her mouth; a reaction which did not go unnoticed by the politician, but did little to affect her stride.

"From anywhere and everywhere really," she brazenly continued. "The statistics acknowledge that there's greater risk at that time of night; fewer punters, more extreme tastes, and less money at the end of it too. Working the streets in those hours really is taking your life in your hands, but most of those who find themselves trapped into it don't care about the risk – or at least consider it a worthwhile one to take in return for their next hit."

"Or their next meal," Lucie added, coldly, adding another layer of tension to the room.

"Quite."

The heat of the whiskey warmed Lucie's breath as she sighed in frustration and stood up quickly and threw her overcoat over her shoulders.

"Listen," she began, as Robyn looked up at her with her typical intensity. "I know we don't agree on everything politically, and I know you can't give me the employee details, but you can still help."

"And how can I do that?"

"You're on the committee, you could raise it in session.

Someone of your stature asking questions like that won't go unnoticed; it could even allow the police to re-open the case..."

Lucie's voice was rising as her passion began to get the better of her, coupled with her incredulity that the politician was not jumping at the chance to help. Instead though, the firebrand was simply shaking her head in a further display of exaggerated sympathy.

"Lucie, Lucie," she interrupted in a voice only a shade below patronising. "The police have been slashed to the bone and face more cuts every day. There's talk in Parliament right now about deploying the army to help them with knife crime! There's simply no point in asking them to allocate resources to such an open and shut case."

"No political mileage, you mean."

"Excuse me?"

Lucie checked herself, not wanting to allow Robyn the satisfaction of seeing her lose control, but pressed home her point, fully intending to make clear she would not be letting the matter drop.

"Just like there's no political mileage in looking into the others?"

"What others?"

"Six other women have gone missing, Amber," Lucie quietly relayed. "All of them with similar backgrounds to the murder victim, all of them European Nationals, only there's no trace of them and guess what? The investigations were all stopped before they got started, because of the need to 'prioritse' police activity. You know? British services for British people?"

The women's eyes locked, neither wishing to break away or display anything that could be perceived as doubt in their own positions to the other. Robyn eventually rose from her own chair, leaning forward on the desk and never once dropping her eyes from Lucie's, even to blink.

"I think that this meeting has come to an end. You may think me callous, Lucie," she said, any trace of the temporary warmth between them now vanished, "but in an era of austerity, when the Will of the People is set against the influx of foreigners, sparse services should and must be reserved for the benefit of the indigenous population. Foreigners can always just go home."

Lucie's face twisted in contempt, the politician's display of casual disregard for the lives and contributions of so many more than sufficient to light the flame of angry resentment in her gut. There was little point in arguing. Amber Robyn delighted in her reputation for controversy, and even if she had made her comment in public in full view of the cameras, she could be confident it would earn her praise from the army of internet warriors who hung on her every utterance to justify their own prejudices. This was a woman whose priority was hashtags and likes, not reason and argument, and Lucie stifled the urge to respond in fury at the barb, calming her voice and offering her counterpart a disdainful look of disgust.

"Just like that, eh?" she spat as she turned and headed for the door. "Maybe you could make us all wear little badges; a yellow star perhaps? It'd be easier to decide which ones to deport that way."

Opening the door of the cramped and cold office, Lucie turned to stare a final time into the politician's uncompromising gaze, and shook her head, her anger almost diluted by a sudden sense of pity. The contempt in Lucie's eyes melted instead into sadness at the knowledge that there was nothing she could do or say that could bring the MP out of her intransigence, and she looked away as a lump began to form in her throat.

"Thanks for the drink," she said.

9

Lucie replayed her conversation with Robyn again and again in her mind as she made her way back to Camden Town and the refuge of her flat. It had been as awkward a conversation as she expected, and she questioned for the hundredth time why Lake had insisted she go through with the meeting. One thing was certain, and that was that no political will existed to look any further into the disappearances, and that no matter how circumstantial it was, the evidence suggesting Ines was a closet prostitute was sufficient to close the minds of anyone with any kind of influence over the process.

The bustling of people on the pavements and spilling into the road beside her jogged Lucie from her introspection and she paused to stretch her lungs with a deep and satisfying breath and smiled as she took in her surroundings properly for the first time that day. It was nearly lunchtime and the glory of Camden Market was in full swing; the heart-warming colours and mouth-watering smells reaching out to tease Lucie from the trap door of her mood. All around her, stores, outlets and eateries were crammed together, filled with buzzing crowds. Opening up her senses as wide as her smile, Lucie allowed her nose to choose whichever scent was the most appetising and followed it to a stall where a grey haired and plump woman with rough, coarse hands and a radiant smile merrily filled a large wrap with her wares and handed it over; Lucie passing a crumpled note in return and dismissing the offered change which was instead gratefully dropped into a plastic tub marked 'Staff' beside the till. Sinking her teeth into the copious and bursting flatbread, Lucie cupped her hand beneath her chin to stop any falling contents from staining the grey paisley she wore and sucked a contented breath through her teeth to cool her mouth from the spices and heat which threatened for a moment to overwhelm her, before she swallowed and bit in again.

She had missed this. In the few months since she had been plucked by Lake from certain imprisonment and dumped in her run-down flat in this unfamiliar part of London, Lucie had isolated herself somewhat from anything and everything around her, choosing instead to focus on the jobs she had been assigned and the healing of her own precariously balanced mind. Her concentration had for the most part kept her from falling back into the depression which had tormented her so often since her hellish experiences in Afghanistan, but it had also blinded her to so much of what life was offering around her. In her days as a Chaplain in the RAF, she had tried each day to celebrate the little things, the simple joys which could, if allowed, outweigh so many of the negatives the world so consistently provided. Yet the coping mechanisms she had adopted had not only robbed her of her usefulness as a Minister, but also clamped her eyes shut against the pleasures in which she used to revel. Yes, the state of the country made her sick to her very soul, but she had allowed the emptiness and betrayal to ferment within her, by refusing to look for or even acknowledge the wonder of life around her.

Carrying on past the market Lucie composed a new resolution in her mind. She could never go back to how she was, too much had happened for that. Neither could she ignore the truth of both the world around her, and the world of espionage she had been plunged into the day she accepted Lake's deal. But she did not have to define herself by it anymore. Lucie rounded the corner and glanced up at the brown and white bricked building she found herself beside. Two pillars guarded the blue doorway and a painted board in faded brown, upon which a white cross had been daubed, invited people inside for services and prayer. Lucie allowed herself a short laugh and a quick nod towards the building.

"Ok," she smiled, "I get the message."

Flicking her overcoat tails behind her, Lucie stuffed her hands deep into her jeans' pockets and strode on towards home, her chest and her step lighter than she could remember. She was worried about Kasper, and despite the certainty of Amber Robyn, she still could not reconcile the thought that the murder victim she had begun to care for had died in the way the record insisted. Ordinarily thoughts and worries of this kind would marry together to tease and tempt her into an emotional response which itself would invariably lead to the depression that hung forever in the wings. As she walked, Lucie resolved not to allow herself to follow that pattern this time. Instead, she would be sure to take her medication as prescribed and make adequate time for the prayer and meditation she had ignored for too long, harnessing the focus it provided instead of clouding it with pure emotion. She would contact Lake, advise him of her morning's discomfort with the obstinate Amber Robyn and follow through the investigation until she could be certain of the cause of Ines' death; and while she was at it, find out what the hell had happened to the other missing women. And if by doing so she could persuade Lake to involve her in this *Red Mako* business, then all the better. If – *when* – Kasper awoke, she would be there to greet him with news of not one but two successfully resolved cases to help him on the road to recovery.

Anticipating her friend's inevitably sarcastic reaction spread the smile which had crept onto Lucie's face still further as she reached the decaying chippy, above which sat the crumbling and barely adequate flat she called home. Stepping around the corner towards the wooden front door, Lucie fished into her pocket for her key, her smile still wide upon her face, only to stop dead at the unexpected and tumultuous curse which greeted her appearance from the street.

The smile retreated instantly, replaced by a look of surprise and confusion as her eyes shot to the source of the profanity, only to be greeted by the furious stare of Detective Inspector Asif Ismail, who promptly swore once more.

The Police Officer stood outside Lucie's front door, his eyes wide and projecting a mien of anger so unadulterated, Lucie was unsure at first if he was entirely stable. His forehead glistened with the tell-tale sign of day old sweat, accentuated by unshaven cheeks and chin above a shirt open at the collar; the tie that had adorned it the previous day now stuffed untidily into the pocket of the suit jacket which today appeared crumpled and unkempt. Lucie instinctively poised herself, ready to respond and reciprocate any attack, but taking the figure in, she knew that no assault was forthcoming. Ismail made no move towards her, instead remaining stood by the door and repeating his pointedly accusatory swearing. As his tone became increasingly despairing, Lucie held her hands out, hoping to clam the man long enough to discover both the source of his anxiety, and the reason why he was now outside her door with his mouth full of imprecations.

"Asif?" she began, her voice calm and measured as she stepped slowly towards him. "What's wrong Asif, what are you doing here?"

The question was met with a harsh and cutting laugh.

"What's wrong?" he repeated. "What's bloody wrong? I could fucking kill you, that's what wrong!"

"Why?" Lucie pressed, still calm and stepping closer still, her arms now out to the side in as open a posture as she thought safe. "What have I done to upset you?"

Ismail didn't answer straight away, instead leaning against the faded paint of the door and sliding down until he was awkwardly sat on the ground beneath it, his head dropping into his hands.

"You know damn well what you've done," he finally mumbled through his fingers, "you and that bastard mate of yours."

"What mate?" Lucie frowned, her confusion increasing by the second.

"Lake!" Asif cried, lifting his head up to shout the name as though it were a despised incantation. "Mr fucking Lake!"

Lucie's stomach tumbled at once into a sickening churn and she exhaled in frustration and anger as a thousand thoughts flashed through her mind, punctuated by the memory of her own first encounter with the enigmatic man who never gave away his first name. Lake only made open contact with people outside the Overlappers if he intended to recruit them, and he only recruited those he could enjoy some hold over. As she crouched down to join Ismail on the gravel by her door, watching as he shouted his impotent rage into his hands, Lucie could only wonder what the hell had happened to this man that had allowed Lake to plunge his hooks into him. And with her knowledge of the spy master's modus operandi pushing its way to the front of her mind, she pondered with trepidation whether the Detective Inspector would ever be completely free of him.

10

The bright early afternoon sun had retreated behind grey and heavy late winter clouds, and the Inspector's anger given way to exhaustion by the time Lucie persuaded him to come inside and talk through whatever disaster had befallen him. Her mood had not in any way brightened by the time he finished his outpouring. Between calming breaths and sips of steaming hot tea, Ismail recounted how barely hours after meeting and speaking with Lucie the previous day, he had been unceremoniously hauled into a meeting room to be confronted by a po faced Chief Superintendent, a frowning HR officer and a somewhat flustered looking Fed Rep, to be informed of his immediate suspension pending investigation into allegations of security breaches and leaking confidential information to unauthorised persons. Though no specifics were forthcoming he quickly reasoned that the root of the accusation was his conversation with Lucie, but his protestations that he had been liaising with the security services were dismissed quickly, as were his protestations of the rushed and very much flawed interpretation of the discipline process he was now subject to. After being curtly ordered from the premises, Ismail found himself immediately accosted on the street by a short, blading man with an unreadable face and a folder containing detailed notes of his life. The man introduced himself as 'Mr Lake' and presented Ismail with an immediate proposition: accept secondment to his team, working under the woman he had met that morning and the process he was now subject to would disappear. Refuse and he would find himself very quickly out of a job with an uncomfortable level of press attention following him.

Lucie grimaced as he recounted his story, recognising with grim distaste the similarities with her own induction onto the Service. Only on that occasion Lake had taken advantage of her situation, whereas now he had been the willing engineer of Ismail's misfortune, and had used her as the unwitting tool to facilitate it. "Bastard," she whispered in condemnation of her boss as she looked across to the dishevelled Ismail, who sat crumpled on her sofa, his face as wretched as the story he had told. The DI's ears pricked at the profanity and a cynical sneer tugged at his lip in response.

"Yeah," he softly replied. "Isn't he just..."

Lucie sat down in the chair opposite Ismail, and leaned forward, the concern on her face unguarded and sincere, though he pointedly ignored it.

"You're all a bunch of bastards," he mumbled, shaking his head as his anger began to visibly swell within him once more. "You're as bad as him! Swaggering around like Janey Big Tits, with your SIS pass and your national security bullshit. You came to me for help and what the fuck do I get in return? Shafted by you and your bastard friends!"

His voice reached a crescendo and such was his rage that Lucie thought for a brief moment that he might actually try to attack her, but instead he clamped his hands once more to his face and sunk deeper into the sofa.

There was no point arguing with him, Lucie rationalised, as everything he said was right. It was his willingness to help her investigation that had brought him here, and if she was honest with herself, she had enjoyed being the one with all the cards when she quizzed him in the police station the previous day. But having lived through a similarly discourteous introduction to the Service, Lucie also knew that looking for people to blame and shouting at the moon wouldn't help anyone, and it certainly wouldn't aid the case. With the officer still emotional and raw, Lucie recognised the importance of keeping hold of her own emotions and making sure at least one of them in the room remained calm.

"Asif," she began, inching forward further still as he turned his tired head away. "Hey, Asif, look at me!"

The command in her tone was as clear as her concern and the policeman's face snapped back to her as though she were a superior on the parade ground berating his unpolished boots.

"I'm sorry you've been put through this," she said, "truly, I'm sorrier than you know, but like it or not you are where you are. Now, do you want to clear your name?"

"Of course I bloody do!"

"And do you want to get back to work?"

"After this?" he stuttered, a note of hesitancy in his voice which ultimately gave way to one of determination. "Yes, yes I do."

"Then that means you're stuck with me until we get to the bottom of things and Lake takes his hooks out of you. I know you probably blame me for getting you into this mess, God help me, I would, but right now I'm your best and only chance of putting all this shit behind you and getting on with your life."

"I'm a police officer," came the indignant reply, "I'm not a bloody spy!"

"Do I look like a spy?" Lucie asked, laughing. "Spies aren't what you think they are; the best ones are just normal people doing an unusual job and not gobbing off about it in the pub. You're a DI, you must have been in more than your fair share of scrapes in your career?"

"Just the odd one or two…"

"Then if you handled that, you can handle this. Come on, I need help on this!"

Ismail stood up and headed towards the door, pausing as he reached it and inhaling deeply, stuffing his hands into his pockets and letting his head drop to stare at the floor beneath him. Lucie stayed in her seat, knowing full well that only he could properly process everything and calm himself.

"You really need help?" Ismail finally asked, his voice calmer, the anger it had contained diluted into irritation.

"I do," Lucie answered. "And I'd like it from you."

"I don't suppose I have much choice," he rhetorically spat. "Not much."

Ismail turned back to face her, his handsome, if somewhat stressed features beginning to crease into a half smile.

"Do I at least get an Aston Martin?"

"You have to wait your turn," Lucie smiled back as she stood up and held out her hand. "Janey Big Tits is using it right now."

The name smashed through the tension in the room and Lucie was delighted to hear the hearty laugh that forced its way out of Ismail's mouth and see his grin widen in self-conscious acknowledgement. "Yeah…." He grinned, shaking his head at the bizarre situation that had taken hold of his life. "I didn't think calling you 'Johnny Big Balls' was the most appropriate thing."

"Quite right too," Lucie grinned back, pleased to see the police officer regaining control of his emotions. Her empathy for the man was absolute, and casting her mind back to her own recruitment, she remembered how much she had benefitted from the kindness shown her at that time by a seasoned professional on the team, who had taken the trouble to spend time with her and ease her into her new life with a drink and a considerate word.

A lump of emotion threw itself maliciously into her throat as the irrepressible Della Quince flitted through her mind, bringing with her the explosive cocktail of sensations she had been responsible for fermenting within Lucie. Della had been at once Lucie's dream and nightmare, having proven in the end to have manipulated her with an equal mixture of expertise and precision in her quest for vengeance against a whole country. Lucie, having eschewed personal relationships ever since the abuse she suffered while chained up in an Afghan cave, had felt herself falling for the older woman. To this day half of her yearned to know whether Della's professed reciprocity was genuine, while the other half no longer cared. After her death, Lake had presented her with a note Della had written to her, but in her obstinacy, she had refused to accept it, and though its mysterious contents tormented her heart daily, her soul declined to alter the decision, accepting and stubbornly taking pride in the self-inflicted pain.

Nonetheless, whatever it counted for now, Della's actions had been of immeasurable help in those first days, allowing Lucie to slip into the role rather than crash into it, and as she stood smiling at the bemused and emotional Asif Ismail, the desire to be of similar use ran through her. The tension may be gone, and he may have accepted the reality of his situation, but that didn't make living with it any easier, and the sooner he learned to do that, the sooner they could work properly together.

"Listen," she began, hoping her voice sounded as full of understanding as possible without tipping over into condescension, "did Lake give you any instructions? Anything at all?"

Ismail shook his head, tiredness beginning to show through his smile. "Nothing much. He just told me where you live and said we had some missing women to find; he said you'd take it from there."

"Well then, I guess we should have a chat. Any plans for the day?"

"All of a sudden my diary looks pretty empty."

"Well then," Lucie answered, grabbing her overcoat and keys from the table and stepping past Ismail through the living room door. "It looks like we have time for a drink."

11

———

The idea had proven as successful as Lucie had hoped and more, the one drink quickly turning into several more as the pair began to relax into each other's company. Ismail, she learned, was a more than accomplished officer, having received several commendations for bravery and a scar across his abdomen from a knife attack. Although reluctant to talk about it, he had finally admitted that the knife had been wielded by an elderly member of a golf club in Primrose Hill, who had taken exception to what he perceived as cheating by other members and decided to deal with the matter with a sheath knife he had kept since the war. Although fortunately nobody else was injured, the young PC Ismail had ended up with a slash across his flesh after the old gent tripped up as he walked forward to surrender the weapon. Though she had listened intently to that point, Ismail's sheepish revelation led to a mutual roar of laughter and another round of drinks.

She had liked Ismail when she first met him, and she warmed to him further still during the evening. Though the light in the bar was dim, the setting and the music seemed to accentuate the stress lines she had noted on his face at their first meeting, which strangely added an extra layer of complexity to his handsome, if tired features. He had been full of questions for her, probing cautiously at first before quickly moving through inquisitive gears and pressing for more details of the job, the nature of the work and Lucie's involvement in it. She didn't answer everything in detail – she couldn't – but she endeavoured to provide the same level of reassurance that Della had given her barely months before. She watched his eyes as he absorbed the information as readily as he imbibed the alcohol they drank; his eyes flicking ferociously as she described the nature of their work to him as unglamorously as she could. When she had been sure his queries were finished, she ordered him another beer and probed him on his background, wanting to be sure his homelife leant itself to this type of work, and also satisfy her natural curiosity about a man in whose presence she had begun to feel the earliest twinge of nervous excitement. He was 39, a divorcee and lived not too far from Lucie, in a flat off Highgate Road, where the extortionate rent left few funds for anything else.

"Well don't think that espionage is going to make you any richer," she'd joked, earning a laugh in response.

When the stress of the day's events began to catch up with him and he had started to stifle yawns, Lucie had called it a night, shaking his hand and suggesting he get some sleep before they met the following day. His refreshed and altogether more human appearance the following morning showed that her advice had been wisely taken. As she watched him collect the two large cups from the half empty coffee bar they had entered minutes earlier, Lucie took in his altogether more relaxed features, complemented by the business suit he wore with causal elegance, and caught herself before he could notice her smile. She still had no time for that kind of thing – at least she told herself that she didn't – and certainly not when there was work to be done. Throwing her overcoat over the back of her chair and pushing up the sleeves of her blue paisley shirt, Lucie took one of the cups from Ismail, thanking him as he joined her at the table.

"No problem," he answered, "thank you for picking up the tab last night."

"Least I could do," she grinned, "since it was my lot that led to you getting pissed in the first place. Did you have time to go through your notes?"

"Better than that," Ismail answered, pulling a flash drive from his inside pocket and holding it up to Lucie.

"What's on that?"

"What isn't on it? Let's just say we can be thankful for at least one consequence of Tory cuts."

"Yeah? Which cut?"

"The one to the Met's IT department. In the old days, my suspension would have meant instant loss of intranet and database access and a block on my email account. Unfortunately, the loss of so many of the team means they're not as on top of that as they should be. First thing this morning I logged on to my police laptop and wouldn't you know? I still had access to all the files."

"The rest of the missing women?"

"Everything that was recorded by police up and down the country," Ismail grinned, his pleasure at being of immediate use in his new role both obvious and palpable.

Lucie shared his elation. This was just the break they needed, and her mind began instantly and impatiently race, yearning to simply absorb the information the drive contained, rather than waste time asking questions.

"Fantastic," she exclaimed, leaning forward to look at the small, flat stick as though it were a sparkling jewel of unparalleled beauty.

"What have you learned?"

"There are a couple of things that stand out," Ismail began, handing the drive to Lucie who clutched it tight in her palm for a moment before pushing it securely into her pocket. "The first one you can probably guess."

"The investigations were all pulled before they got going?"

"Spot on," he confirmed. "No surprises there. But something else got my alarm bells ringing, something which puts Ines's murder in a whole new light."

"What's that?"

Ismail paused to take a sip of his scalding Americano and fill his lungs with the coffee shop's warm air.

"Something a DS in Leeds picked up on before the case was pulled from her. She was looking into the disappearance of Isabella Garcia, a Spanish woman who went missing in the city a little while back, and she found something interesting in her social media history."

"How interesting?" Lucie asked, her attention entirely focussed on her new colleague's words.

"Extremely. It seems that Isabella belonged to a Facebook group called 'PeopleToo'. It's an online campaign page for women's rights; people use it to campaign for all sorts of things under that umbrella."

"What did Isabella push for?"

"A few different things," he answered, taking another sip from his coffee. "Equal pay, EU Citizens rights... she was very anti-Brexit as you'd expect, but something else stood out. She was a vociferous campaigner against the government's introduction of trial brothels."

"Really?" Lucie mused, assimilating the information and reaching finally for her own drink.

"And she wasn't alone either," Ismail continued. "Pages like that often generate sub groups and connections between members. In the weeks leading up to her disappearance, Isabella had dialogues with a number of fellow campaigners, including..."

"Including the other missing women," Lucie finished, her mind picking up the thread of the police officer, who nodded in confirmation.

"Precisely," he answered. "All of them, including Ines Aubel and quite a few more besides."

"How many more?"

"There are seventeen women Isabella regularly communicated with, all passionate campaigners. Three of them British and the rest from various EU countries."

Lucie nodded quietly, her brain locked fully into analysis mode and busy formulating hypotheses, as she absently sipped the scalding hot coffee.

"Shit," she whispered as her tongue screamed in protest and she clinked the cup back to the saucer. Her elation at the existence of the information had been tempered by the new questions it posed and what looked like a very real danger to even more women.

"We need to check on the whereabouts of the other women Isabella was in contact with," she said, her forehead furrowing as she spoke, "including the British ones. It might look so far like British women aren't being targeted but we don't know that for sure, and even if they're not they might know something about all this."

"True." Ismail replied. "There is something you can be pretty sure of now though: Ines wasn't out looking for punters the night she died."

Hearing him say the words infused a sensation of justification in Lucie. "No," Lucie readily acknowledged, "she wasn't. Which means either she'd taken her campaigning to a dangerous level and this was a protest gone wrong, or else someone is targeting those specific campaigners; someone who could be back at any time for the rest of them."

"Agreed," nodded the detective. "But if you're thinking of organising protection for any of them you'll be disappointed; the cops just don't have the resources."

"You're not a cop anymore," Lucie answered, immediately regretting the coldness in her voice. "What I mean is, you and I have different resources available to us now."

"I suppose that's true," replied Ismail, a touch defensively, "but what about the political pressure? Police up and down the country have had their investigations curtailed and been threatened with all sorts of crap if they continue. What's stopping the same pressure being put on us?"

"We have a degree of insulation against that, for now at least," Lucie answered, risking another sip of her coffee. "Lake, for all his faults – and believe me I know all about them – is a tenacious bugger. There are still one or two people in high positions who want this looked into and Lake is canny enough to be cagey with exactly what he tells who. We can crack on for now."

She pushed her coffee away from her with a grimace, her burnt tongue letting her know in no uncertain terms that it did not relish the prospect of further sips, at least not right now.

"I don't even want this," she said with a laugh, only for Ismail to pick it up and gratefully drain the still steaming contents himself.

"Do you have an asbestos throat?" she asked, a look of quizzical amusement on her face.

"Nope, just a headache that could floor a rhino," he answered with a grin. "There was a lot of beer flowing last night."

She laughed, "I wish I looked as good as you when I'm

hungover; it's normally tea time before I've stopped drooling onto my pillow."

"Getting up and ready isn't the problem for me," Ismail said, dabbing his lips with a paper serviette. "It's staying up I struggle with. A pot noodle sandwich for brekkie and as much coffee as I can lay my hands on helps a treat though."

"Pot noodle butties, eh?" laughed Lucie as she rose from the chair and wrapped her tattered black coat over her shoulders. "I've always been a cheeseburger with everything kind of girl when it comes to hangover cures."

"Each to their own," the cop smiled, picking up the cups and sliding them onto a bus trolley near the counter before following Lucie to the door and staring in concern at the garment she had just thrown on.

"I thought it was," he said as she opened the glass door. "Thought what was what?"

"That's a bullet hole," he answered, pointing to the frayed and untidy circle hanging over her midriff.

"You're mistaken."

"Don't patronise me, I know what a bullet hole looks like."

"What if it is?" Lucie answered, a challenge in her eyes. "Nothing," he answered, "I just don't like the thought of you having been shot, that's all."

There was the slightest hint of what sounded like affection in the man's voice, but now was not the time and she found his question both inappropriate and clumsy. She had been burned before by revealing too much information about herself and her history too quickly, and she had no inclination to repeat her error now. Instead she fixed him with the firmest of gazes and repeated her assertion that he was mistaken, her eyes leaving him in no doubt that further questioning would not be received politely.

They stepped out into the late winter morning sunshine and

biting cold air, and Ismail stuffed his hands into suit pockets as they walked, Lucie wrapping her trusty coat tight around her.

"We need to get the social media records of everyone in that group Isabella communicated with, look for any correlations in their activity, any indications they were planning any direct protests or any connections we can find."

"That'll be quite a task," Ismail cautioned. "Seventeen people, probably all with multiple accounts across multiple platforms; that kind of research will take a hell of a long time for just the two of us."

"Yeah, you're right," Lucie concurred. "I'll ask Lake to have people look into that side of things for us. In the meantime, we should check out the scene of the crime. At least the potential scene of the crime."

"I take it you mean the 'Adult Leisure & Entertainment Centre'?" Ismail quizzed, a cynical tone to his voice as he gave the official, government approved name of the new establishments.

"The brothel, yeah," Lucie answered. "I want to find out exactly what went on there that night, question the employees, view any CCTV footage..."

"I don't have my police ID anymore."

"Yes you do."

They had reached the famous Chalk Farm Road bridge, Lucie stopping as they passed under it, and Ismail following suit with a curious frown on his face. Reaching into the inside pocket of her voluminous overcoat, Lucie pulled out two small, black wallets, handing one to Ismail and keeping one for herself.

"I asked Lake for these," she explained as Ismail opened his to reveal a shining, metal police badge and corresponding photo card.

"Fake police IDs?" he frowned, clearly somewhat

professionally irritated as well as appreciative of the convenience.

"Nothing fake about these," she replied. "Everything's real apart from the names."

"Spy names?" Ismail laughed heartily, "No way! Let me guess, DC Mike Oxlong and DS Gloria Spoobs?"

"Piss off," she laughed, "this isn't a bloody Bond film; we've got sensible, every day names. I'm Agni Tadialova, and you're Zishan Ellahi, at least as far as this case is concerned."

"I suppose that'll do," Ismail smiled, pocketing his new identity securely. "So, Lake's lot can look into the electronic trails and you and I will do the good cop, bad cop routine at the knocking shop. Sounds like a plan."

Lucie took a deep breath and winced a little as she came clean to the once more confused looking Ismail.

"Actually," she began, "I was thinking of a slightly different approach."

"Like what?"

"Come with me," she said, "I think you might need a bit of hair of the dog."

12

The bright winter sun had long since faded by the time Lucie reached the threshold of the Camden Town Centre for Adult Leisure and Entertainment that evening. Having eschewed her usual paisley and denim, Lucie climbed the steps to the grand, illuminated entrance dressed in unusual finery. A velvet cocktail dress as red as the lipstick she uncharacteristically wore, clung to her frame. Her dependable, if somewhat tired, overcoat having been left at home, Lucie instead carried the kind of small and impractical handbag she had so often laughed at in the past, cursing both it, the stupidity of the high heels she wore, and whomever had decided that they were an appropriate look for a woman. Outwardly cold but inwardly warmed by irritation at her attire, Lucie pulled open the door to be met by a duo of impeccably mannered bouncers.

The woman, the shorter of the two, stepped forward, imposing in black leggings, boots and bomber jacket, while the man hung slightly back, resplendent with shaven head and goatee beard.

"Good evening, madam," she said, her voice politeness itself, though her lined and somewhat 'lived in' face remained unflinchingly stern. "Welcome to the Camden Adult Centre. Are there others in your party this evening?"

"No," Lucie answered, her eyes quickly taking in the pair. There was little question both could handle not only themselves but probably several others besides. The woman, whom the goateed man seemed to defer to, looked a few years older than Lucie, and her jacket prevented a thorough assessment of her physique, but her thigh and calf muscles, around which her leggings tightly clung, were testament to her strength. Her colleague also possessed the aura of the genuine article. Both, Lucie thought, looked more than capable of causing serious physical damage – or worse – to anyone who found themselves on the wrong side of the establishment's rules. Faced with a young woman like Ines, they would barely even break a sweat.

"If I may check your bag please, madam," the female bouncer continued; Lucie handing it over and inwardly sighing in relief that the new wallet was not opened to reveal her fresh new ID. Alongside that lay a passport also made out in the new name, which the bouncer did open and inspect, looking up to compare its picture with Lucie's face, before closing it and handing it back. "Thank you" she said in her monotone delivery. "The reception desk is through the doors; your details will need to be recorded before you enjoy the facilities."

With that, she stood back, gesturing with her arm for Lucie to head through the doors. She complied and pushed through to a spacious and dimly lit room, at the far end of which was a bar, while next to her was a small alcove, housing an individual desk with computer, phone and scanner. Aside from a small desk lamp at the reception, the illumination in the room came from a myriad of blue and red neon lights decorating the walls, the obvious intent being to keep visibility, and perhaps recognition, at a low. Sofas and chairs in burgundy leather punctuated the floor space, while dance music pumped its way through the sound system, making any conversations in the room inaudible to all who didn't strain to hear. The room was largely empty, save for a group of five young, suited men, fresh from some office somewhere, who sat grinning to each other with drinks in their hands and their eyes displaying the undisguisable signs of a well-satisfied coke habit. As she watched them, two young women, clad only in exotic underwear, came through a door beside the bar and headed towards the group, informing them that the 'party room' was prepared and bidding them to follow. Lucie grimaced in distaste as the group stood up, laughing in poorly disguised nervousness and peppering their journey with all manner of boorish comments and unrequested touching.

"She sounds German," she heard one of the group shouting to his friends over the music. "That's another one off the list. I had a black girl and a chink last time I was here..."

Lucie scowled at the crass display as the group disappeared to continue their churlishness behind the closing door.

"Can I help you madam?"

Lucie turned back to the reception alcove, her frown deepening as she realised the young man who had appeared behind it must have likewise heard the racist vulgarities and opted to do nothing about it. Tempted though she was to unload upon him, her plan for the evening depended on her keeping her cool, and so she quickly adjusted her features and stepped closer, reaching into her bag for her fresh new passport.

"Good evening," she said, loudly enough to be heard over the pumping music. "I was told to come through and book in with you."

"No problem at all," came the response in what seemed to Lucie an unnecessarily obsequious tone. "Is madam awaiting company?"

"Madam is not, madam wishes to use your services alone this evening, unless the establishment has a problem with that?"

Lucie already loathed the conversation she was having and was sorely tempted to feel the same way about the man she was having it with. A man obviously older than he was trying to convey, the long hair tied back into a ponytail looked wholly out of place, lending a sinister edge to his unashamedly sleazy expression. Deep lines ran across his brow, which creased further as an unsavoury smile tweaked his red cheeks and his tongue flicked snake-like over his lips.

"No problem at all," he answered, repeating his apparent catchphrase in a broad cockney accent as he pulled a laminated black card from beneath his desk and handed it to her.

"If you would like to purvey this week's offers while I process your details?"

Lucie put her fake passport on the counter and took the card from him, struggling to keep the wince from her face as her eyes moved quickly down it, taking in the exotic names for all manner of sexual acts, with a column of steadily increasing prices listed opposite. The desk clerk's voice piped up again, his jovial inflection a clear indication of his enjoyment at conversing for once with a single woman.

"We do have a two-for-one offer on tonight," he chirped, Lucie looking back to him with steadily narrowing eyes. "And quite a few of them will ask you outright if you plan on leaving a tip but if you ask me it's best to be cagey about that until the end; you'll find they do a better job if they think they might make a few quid extra out of it."

"I'll bear that in mind," Lucie answered, tossing the card back onto the desk and picking her returned passport off it.

"So, what'll it be?" the seedy man quizzed, the formality of his language dropping as his lasciviousness rose. "Man, woman or maybe one of each? There's a few things we're not allowed to put on the price list but once you get in the rooms most of our people are prepared to negotiate. If there's anything special you want and anyone says no, just you come back and see me and we'll find someone prepared to do it. Oh, and there's a twenty-five per cent discount if you're prepared to sign up to the streaming service."

"Streaming service?"

"Some of the suites are fitted with webcams where we can stream you straight onto the web – that's a big revenue stream for the owners, and a lot of punters like the idea of being a pornstar for the night."

"Do they?" Lucie replied in rhetorical deadpan.

The man leaned forward, the creases on his forehead and the red of his cheeks deepening as his unsettling smile widened and he leaned closer towards her.

"So, what do you think?"

She could feel the man's sickening attempt to intimidate and embarrass her and for a moment pitied him. She had survived infinitely worse than this seedy little shit and one look at him was enough to tell her that he would crumble in a second if faced with the same horrors that she had come through in her life. Toying with him, she put her hands on the counter and leaned just as closely in, her face so close to his she could smell the stench of stale alcohol and cigar smoke.

"I think," she said, as his grin grew wider, "that there isn't a discount in the world big enough to convince me to get my kicks in front of a camera while you sit behind your desk, pulling on your pathetic little cock to my moves."

The lecherous grin disappeared, and the man straightened up and stood back as the redness in his cheeks became the purple of embarrassed ego.

"I want someone to dance for me, that's all. No cameras and no crap from anyone."

"What kind of dancer?" came the chastened and sheepish response.

"A woman, I don't care which, just someone with some good moves and who's been here a while; I want someone who knows what they're doing."

"And will you be requiring additional services…?"

"That's between me and her, I presume I can pay her direct?" Lucie forcefully answered, receiving a curt nod in response. "Good, I'll wait over there, shall I?"

Not waiting for an answer, Lucie stepped away from the desk and sat in one of the deep leather seats, breathing deeply to compose herself and trying to take in as much as she could about the place, the people and the attitudes. It wasn't just in places like this that single women found themselves the subject of unwanted advances, but she was surprised at quite how brazen the receptionist's approach had been. Had Ines or any of the other women been here alone, it was easy to think they could have quickly found themselves in trouble, but Lucie wasn't prepared to make that judgement quite yet.

The depth of the seat was making her right knee, which had been badly injured years earlier, ache and throb, and she stood to stretch it. As she did so, the inner door opened, and a young woman began walking seductively towards her, making Lucie's eyes widen in surprise. Dressed in only skimpy, frilled white underwear, the woman was stunningly attractive, with long dark hair worn loose and hanging down her back. A petite nose sat above red lips and a neatly pointed chin, while her eyes, round and blue, gave an air of innocence which defied the way she moved her shapely frame towards Lucie.

"Your room is prepared," the newcomer informed her in a soft accent Lucie immediately identified as Polish. Taken a little aback, Lucie struggled for a moment to swallow her embarrassment and play the role of someone seasoned in the enjoyment of this type of interaction, with firm ideas as to how she wished things to proceed.

"You came quickly," Lucie said after a moment, adding a mischievous edge to her smile that was far from natural to her.

"The first one's always quick, it's the rest that take longer."

"Excuse me?"

"You're my first customer of the evening," the young woman answered. "The room has been prepared a long time; they have to be cleaned up at the end of sessions. Shall we?"

She looked at Lucie with a naughtiness which bore through the outward innocence of her eyes.

"What's your name?" Lucie asked, accepting the professional's proffered hand.

"Ludmita. And yours?"

"Agni."

For a brief moment they locked eyes with the stare of two people who knew the other to be lying, but to whom the deceit was not important. Names, after all, hardly mattered in places like this.

As Lucie followed 'Ludmita' through the door from which she had entered and down the corridor, she damned herself for her plan. This was not a field in which she was comfortable or, she guessed, convincing, and she was sure that while she had pulled the wool over the eyes of the man behind the desk, this 'Ludmita' had already seen through her façade as the dominant punter. While Lucie had been ill at ease with the plan from the beginning, together with Ismail she had decided that trying to get into the premises as a punter would garner more information than simply flashing an ID and playing good cop, bad cop. Now as she followed the shapely woman before her she worried further still that it had been a poor choice.

The corridor was peppered either side with doors or different colours, each under a polished metal sign screwed meticulously into place and displaying a unique name hinting at the pleasures contained within. Walking gratefully past the 'dungeon room' and the shouts that came from within, Lucie stopped as Ludmita opened the dark blue doors to the 'dancing suite' and beckoned her inside.

The quiet beat of muffled background music immediately leapt though the doors to meet her, and Lucie entered to find a dimly lit lounge in the middle of which sat a cream velvet sofa placed before a small, raised stage with a metal pole erected in the centre. On one side of the sofa stood a small, round table upon which sat a full bucket of ice, cradling Lilly Bollinger's finest, a glass alongside it, while opposite was an open mini bar stacked with miniatures and cans of every description. Ludmita gestured for Lucie to sit as she closed the doors, then turned to her, her demeanour changed at once to one of pure business.

"Okay," she began, moving in front of Lucie and placing her hands on her hips. "Ground rules: We can do pretty much whatever you like so long as we agree it in advance; I don't want anything going anywhere I'm not expecting, ok? I'm an open-minded girl but I absolutely won't do scat; if you want something like that tell me now and I'll find you someone else..."

"No," Lucie raised her hand and interrupted, both to maintain her façade of control a little longer and to avoid going any further down the list of acts the working woman found too extreme.

"Good. If you want a drink, help yourself. The price list is next to you and a choice of music."

Lucie picked up the card beside her and scanned it.

"The booze is double the price in this room than at the bar?"

"Anything sold at the bar goes to the owners, in here it goes to me."

"An admirable business plan," Lucie replied in tones matching Ludmita's for firmness even if there was little confidence behind them. Taking a thick wad of banknotes from her bag, she placed them next to the ice bucket, reclined into the sofa and crossed her legs, keeping her eyes on the young woman's as she did so.

"I presume that's enough for an hour? I don't want any booze, whatever music is already on is fine, and I just want a dance."

Ludmita picked up the notes and flicked through them, the amount far exceeding anything on the House's 'price list' and narrowed her eyes as she looked down at Lucie.

"It makes a change to see a woman in here by herself. I usually have to put up with drunken boys who can't get it up, or middle-aged businessmen cheating on their wives. You're unusual."

"You don't know the half of it."

"Just a dance?"

"Just a dance."

"That's a lot of money for just a dance."

"Then don't make it a shit one."

A wicked smile flickered across Ludmita's face for a moment, made all the more alluring by the paper innocence of her eyes.

"I told you I don't do scat."

Lifting a remote control by the side of the stage, Ludmita raised the volume of the music by a few notches and began to bend and stretch herself into readiness before standing still and focussed behind the silver pole, her eyes closed as though entering into a state of meditation. For a moment, Lucie wondered if any capering would ever come, before a long and perfectly formed leg kicked upwards in perfect rhythm with the building crescendo of music in the background. Ludmita, or whoever she really was, fell instantly into her stride, her arms and legs enveloping the pole as though it were a missing limb to be re-claimed and absorbed by her hungering body.

Lucie watched as Ludmita climbed, contorted and writhed

to the music, not moving from her cross-legged position on the sofa, but finding herself curiously unsettled by the nervous energy which continued to grow within her. Before meeting Della, it had been a long time since Lucie had allowed herself to think about love or sex, or even entertain an attraction, and after the betrayal she had retreated from the field once more. In recent days though the desire for love, or more truthfully the desire for companionship, had begun to flicker within her again, and she had found herself growing ever fonder of Ismail and wondering how things might develop once their mission was over. Ludmita inspired no such sensations of warmth or affection, radiating instead only a raw sexuality.

Lucie had no time for labels, and she had never particularly cared what a person carried in their pants, being drawn instead to what they carried in their souls. She had loved and been loved by women and men before choosing to put all of that on hold and follow her calling into military chaplaincy; her past drawing condemnation from some of those she had studied with. Though it was Ludmita's soul that had caught Lucie's eye this evening, as the dancer slid herself out of the slight, white underwear and moved with deliberate intent over to the sofa.

Ludmita placed her hands on Lucie's knees and pushed them firmly apart before straddling her and leaning against the sofa as she continued to dance just close enough for her breasts to brush across Lucie's face.

"Are you sure you only came here for a dance?" Ludmita whispered, her hot breath on Lucie's ear raising goose bumps on the spy's flesh.

"Maybe I had other ideas as well..."

"I'm all ears," said the dancer, laughing softly as she slid from Lucie's lap and knelt on the floor before her and began to move her head up between Lucie's inner thighs, pushing the hem of her dress up as she did so, the hot breath now on her legs and getting higher.

"Maybe we could start with a game?" Lucie said, a hint of her nervousness breaking through into her voice as she pushed herself back into the seat.

"Mmmh," came the voice. "Sounds fine to me, what type of game?"

"How about twenty questions?"

"I like that." The naked woman had begun to kiss Lucie's legs, slowly and deliberately moving up and down, each time moving closer to the top before dropping back to begin again. "What kind of questions?"

"Oh, I don't know," Lucie answered through short breaths. "Maybe for starters I'd like to know if the name Ines Aubel means anything to you."

Ludmita's head stopped pushing and Lucie exhaled in what she thought might have been disappointment rather than relief as the young prostitute sat back and straightened up, her face at once consumed by a scowl.

"Fucking hell," she spat with contempt. "You're one of that lot, aren't you?"

"Which 'lot'?"

"Those fucking campaigners. I knew it couldn't just be good luck I got a woman tonight..."

The angered Ludmita stood, shut off the music and flicked on the lights, the brightness highlighting thin worry lines and heavily made up bags under the woman's eyes, noticeable even as Lucie squinted in the brightness. Picking up a white dressing gown from a hook on the wall, Ludmita quickly covered herself and tightened the strap, raising a finger to Lucie and shouting her indignance at her.

"Let me fucking tell you something," she started, "and you can tell this to all your do-gooding friends too. No-one trafficked me here, no-one is keeping me here against my will and no-one is going to tell me how to fucking live my life, ok? I might be a whore but I'm an honest one, and if I don't have the right to do what the fuck I want with my own body then what do I have?"

Lucie remained in her seat, far more comfortable dealing with the woman's rage than her sexuality.

"I'm not here to judge you," she calmly replied.

"No? That's just what your friend said, right before she came out with a list of everything that could go wrong in this profession, that we're putting ourselves at the mercy of men who might want to fuck us but would never *give* a fuck about us. How we were putting other women at risk who couldn't afford to get set up in a place like this. That sounds pretty fucking judgemental to me."

"I'm sure she was just worried about you all..."

"Ha! Worried about us? I grew up under the fucking Communists, I had nothing, I was in fights every day with people who had absolutely nothing to lose, do you think I can't handle a few pissed up guys with floppy dicks? And anyway, if things ever get out of hand do you think the guys at the door would just let it happen?."

Lucie stood up from the sofa, ignoring the twinge in her knee as she rose, and stepped closer to the fuming young woman.

"Did things get out of hand with Ines?"

"What? Who wants to know?"

"I do."

For the briefest of moments, Lucie thought she may actually get a worthwhile answer, Ludmita's deceiving eyes flickering for just a second with concern and what looked like a desire to tell the truth. Instead, she walked stiffly to the wall and slammed her palm against a bright red button alongside the door.

"That was bloody stupid," Lucie sighed, shaking her head. "I just wanted to talk."

"I'm here to fuck and be fucked," Ludmita spat, with a new and profound contempt in her voice that didn't quite suit her. "If you want to talk, go see a priest."

The suite door thumped open, and in the frame stood the female bouncer and her bearded friend from earlier, accompanied by another black-jacketed figure of equal stature.

"Problem?" The female asked, her fists clenching and unclenching, and her eyes narrowed and fixed upon Lucie.

"She's another one of *that* lot," Ludmita shouted, her passions rising with each syllable. "The fucking do-gooders. This one wants to know about the last one that was here."

"I just want to know what happened to my friend," Lucie protested, her voice calm and her hands raised.

"Who can say?" said the new woman. "The world's a nasty place. It's time you left, madam."

The bouncer strode up and gripped Lucie tightly by the arm with a strength the spy would not have suspected from a woman her size. Although she fancied her chances in a fight with her, this wasn't the time or place and would have blown the whole point of being there. In any case, she had no way of knowing just how many security were there and would pile in if she started throwing her fists around. Instead she simply let herself be guided from the room, casting a glance over to Ludmita as she left and offering her a defiant stare.

"You should have just told me the truth," she said as the door closed behind her, just slowly enough for her to see the certainty drop from Ludmita's face.

"That sounds like a threat," one of the men grunted as he led the march down the corridor. "We don't like threats in this establishment."

"Why? Too much of a pussy to deal with them?

Lucie's voice was confident and strong, and she felt the immensely powerful hand around her arm grow tighter still as she spoke. Far from being simple thugs, most bouncers Lucie had known were professionals, with an excellent level of self-control; such traits were essential in fact to do their job well, and Lucie knew that she would have to press harder than that if she were to get a rise from them, harder still if she wanted to see quite how far they were prepared to go. In any case, if there was any truth in the theory that the venue's security were responsible for Ines death, she knew at the very least they would do nothing on the premises, where every movement was recorded. To get the response she wanted, she had to get them outside.

Marching past the reception desk the seedy assistant looked up from his enjoyment of the activities going on in one of the streamed suites to grin in malicious triumph at her. They reached the main entrance, where Lucie began to drag her feet and claw at the woman's taut grip.

Lucie's other arm was quickly pulled behind her, and she could feel the bouncer's breath on her neck as she struggled, the stench of strong cigarettes and stronger coffee overpowering her as she felt herself pulled closer to the woman's chest.

Shit, she was strong, Lucie thought as she played up to the role of the uncontrollable punter, kicking her legs out and shouting profanities in as many languages as she could muster at her escort. "Bloody hell, we've got another foreigner, Debs," said the second male, grabbing a hold of Lucie's kicking legs so that she was effectively being carried through the door. "I thought they were all supposed to be fucking off home now?"

"Not here, Jim," 'Debs replied, a note of irritation in her voice for the first time. "Wait 'till she's outside."

'Good,' Lucie thought as they carried her through the main doors and down the steps to the path, whereupon her legs were promptly deposited back on the ground, so roughly her bad knee howled in protest. She looked around quickly and noted the camera attached to the front gates and guessed that they wouldn't do anything here either; a guess that proved accurate as she was frog-marched down the gravel path, nerves for the first time beginning to trouble her as she contemplated what must surely now be a physical confrontation.

One of the men held back at the gate, standing, Lucie guessed, so as to block the camera's view of the street outside, while Debs and Jim walked her tightly onto the street and continued down it for a few yards, before coming up alongside an alley and making to turn her into it.

"Where the fuck do you think you're taking me?" Lucie shouted, as loudly as she could without risking the unwanted intervention of any passers-by.

"For a chat," answered Debs coldly, twisting her clasp on Lucie's arms and pushing her forward.

The alley was filthy, unlit and strewn with the stench of dirt, rotting food and waste.

'This is it," Lucie thought to herself, the adrenaline she had supressed until now beginning to freely pump through her body and the instinct to fight becoming almost impossible to ignore. She needed to know what they'd do, and if she fought back as she could, she would never find out. She could only hope that by the time the full extent of their intentions was clear, she had retained sufficient control to prevent them.

The blow, when it came, was hard enough to make Lucie stagger, but not so hard to knock her to the floor. Debs had in an instant released the painful grip and pushed her back, hard, following up with an enormous cuff around her head which made her ear throb and sting.

Lucie spun around, poised and ready to fight off the expected lunge of the ape-like male accompanying them. But the lunge didn't come. Jim simply took a step towards her, his face screwed into a vision of utter contempt that was obvious even without light. "I've had it up to fuckin' 'ere with you and your sort," he said, his finger jabbing into the air in front of Lucie's face. "You ain't fuckin' English, are you? Well you don't get a fuckin' opinion then, alright? Nobody 'ere gives a shite about what you think about the time of day, and if you don't like it, fuck off back where you came from, alright?"

"Is that what you say to the girls in the club?" Lucie spat, her body tense and her voice shaking.

"They're different," the ape snarled. "They're alright, it's the uppity ones like you who fuck me off. Stay the fuck away from here, got it?"

Jim turned away and began stomping back towards the brothel and those foreigners he considered 'alright', Lucie too shocked from not finding herself in a life-threatening scrap to shout anything in response. Debs, for her part stayed a little longer, not quite a smile appearing on her face, but little by the way of aggression, either.

"You heard what the man said," she said after a moment. "Sorry we had to get physical, but we can't have you upsetting the staff. Stay away, alright?"

"What happened to my friend?"

"I haven't got a fucking clue, and that's the truth. Now stay away." Offering what could have been mistaken for a look of sympathy, Debs turned away and followed her colleague out of the filth strewn alley. Lucie didn't follow, but replayed the confrontation in her head and cursing the new puzzle it had presented: if the bouncers weren't responsible for Ines' death, then who was? The receptionist may be a seedy little shit, but try as she might, she just couldn't picture him as a killer.

"That's one plan that didn't come together."

Lucie spun around at the unexpected voice and exhaled in

relief as Ismail stepped from the shadows and walked up to her, a concerned smile on his face.

"Bloody hell," breathed Lucie, laughing the surprise away. "I'd wondered where you'd got to."

"Tailing you as instructed every step of the way," he answered. "And no, it wasn't nice watching you being roughed up and not being able to stop it. I nearly jumped in a couple of times."

"If you had done, I'd have kicked you in the bollocks myself," said Lucie, the pair walking together to the end of the alley and heading back up the main road to where Ismail had parked. "I needed to know how far they'd go; turns out not very far."

"Which doesn't really help us," Ismail finished, plucking out the gun from his pocket and holding it distastefully in his hand. "At least I had no call to use this thing..."

Lucie looked at him in sympathy for a second. Considering the manner of his recruitment into the Overlappers, he had taken the situation remarkably well and had displayed no malice towards her, quite the opposite in fact. The mask had slipped for just a moment earlier that evening when she had handed him her weapon and told him to watch her back and be prepared to shoot if need be. It had been difficult enough for Lucie to adapt to the role when she first been press-ganged into service, and she had had cause to kill before, but in Ismail's case, the request had only served to expose the culture shock he was feeling.

She took the gun from him and carefully placed it in her bag as they reached the car, a silver-grey Peugeot 306 that appeared to Lucie to be almost as world-weary as its owner.

"So, what do you think?" he asked her as he turned the ignition. "I think my arm bloody hurts and my ear will still be throbbing this time next week, but other than that I'd almost swear they had nothing to do with Ines' death."

"That big one isn't too keen on foreigners, though is he? He said some pretty nasty shit back there, I'm not sure I'd have held back from swinging for him."

"Being a racist arsehole doesn't make him a murderer," Lucie countered as they pulled onto the relatively empty road. "Aside from a few insults he didn't lift a finger to me back there; if he'd killed Ines, why would I get away with just a mouthful of shite?"

"Maybe. Did you get anywhere inside?"

"One or two things intrigued me," Lucie answered, squirming a little. "I met a young woman named 'Ludmita', or so she says. Ines had definitely been there, and caused a bit of a scene apparently, but that's as much as I learned before they kicked me out."

"Well tomorrow I'll pay an official visit to this 'Ludmita' and see if anything gives. Maybe..."

Whatever it was he pondered remained unspoken as the Peugeot's rear window shattered into a thousand shards of glass, showering the two spies, who swore and cursed in surprise.

"What the fuck?" screamed Ismail, as he gripped the wheel tighter and pulled the car out of the skid.

"Gunmen, front and back!" Lucie shouted the words, her eyes everywhere before settling on the window in front. A black car was pulled horizontally across the road, a man stood in front of it, gun drawn and pointed towards them.

Other vehicles screeched and swerved past to avoid collision, blocking the other lane with horns blaring and passengers screaming, as the Peugeot drew ever closer to the obstruction and Ismail began to ease off on the accelerator.

"Foot down and drive!" Lucie ordered, pulling her gun from the bag.

"But..."

"DRIVE!"

Ismail swallowed hard and did as he was bade, gritting his

teeth, dropping the car into third and slamming his foot to the peddle.

Firing one shot back through the shattered rear window, Lucie twisted back to the front and braced herself as the battered old car gathered speed, praying that this would pay off.

"One, two, three... DUCK!"

13

———

The aging, fourth hand Peugeot smashed into the rear end of the vehicle, Ismail having turned the wheel just enough to avoid a full-on collision, knocking the attacker's car backwards with an almighty crash, and freeing the road behind it for the pair to screech into.

The black clothed and balaclava wearing gunman, who had thrown himself clear, scrambled back to his feet and fired at the escaping pair, but was soon passed by his colleague in the pursuing vehicle, who sped up in ferocious pursuit.

"Normally when people shoot at me it's because I'm trying to arrest them!" Ismail shouted over the noise of the wind as he tried to keep his speed up while dodging oncoming traffic and hysterical civilians.

"Good to have a bit of variety now and then!" Lucie shouted back. "We need to get off the main road, too many people; head up to Primrose Hill!"

She twisted in her seat and pulled herself onto her knees as another bullet came through the broken car.

"Where the fuck are you off to?"

"Sunroof!"

"You need more fresh air in here?"

"Just keep driving!

Lucie pressed the switch and the roof panel receded, whirring and groaning. Lucie squeezed her head, arms and upper torso through the gap and pointed her gun towards the pursuing vehicle, shrugging off the shot which whizzed inches past her head. Firing as accurately as possible in the speeding car, she took out one of the pursuing black Audi A8's headlights and put a hole through its windscreen to match the one in their own car, before losing her balance and clutching the roof for support as the Peugeot slid dangerously around a corner.

"Careful!" she shouted down to Ismail.

"Oh, sorry! Was I not escaping the nasty gunman safely enough?"

"Don't worry about the gunman," she bellowed, firing again, "you've got a gun woman!"

Despite her sarcasm, Ismail had skilfully pulled the car away from the main roads and led them into Primrose Hill, the Audi still relentlessly in pursuit and getting closer.

"Get back in here!" he shouted to Lucie, who slid back in alongside him.

"I'm nearly out of ammo," she said.

"That's not all we're out of," Ismail replied, pointing to the bright orange petrol pump illuminated on the dashboard.

"Shit..." She looked around, her eyes searching for a solution or a way out, as more bullets flew past them, before fixing on something and allowing a wicked smile to play on her lips. Reaching out, she grabbed the wheel and spun the car into a tight, angled turn onto a narrow and deserted gravel path. Their pursuers overshot the road and Lucie saw them slow down and spin to pick up the chase, before she turned back to the ornate black and gold gates standing imperiously before them.

"Fancy a trip to Regent's Park?" she asked Ismail, who grinned back and slammed his foot down hard.

The impact shattered the car's front chassis, jarring and jerking the two spies inside, but succeeded in bringing the imposing metal gates clanging down to the ground. The car was stuttering and belching, and Ismail pulled it off the path, using the last of its juice to reach a small cluster of trees and spinning it into a final stop.

The Audi had corrected itself and was speeding through the broken gates towards them, and Lucie knew as she kicked open the door and knelt behind it that she would get only one shot. Straining from the brightness of the car's remaining headlight, she levelled her gun and peered inside, aiming for as low in the driver's seat as she could, and fired.

The black car spun to the side, filling the air with the stench of burning rubber, before it thudded into the trunk of an unyielding oak, crumpling its bonnet and blowing airbags into the faces of its occupants.

Lucie and Ismail eased out from their cover and began heading from the stricken vehicle, as a figure began squirming and wriggling from the passenger door.

"Freeze!" Lucie shouted, her command unheeded by the attacker, who instead pulled himself free and swung his arm up wildly, ready to take another shot.

Lucie was too quick for him though, and he dropped the weapon as a bullet from Lucie's gun tore through his bicep, the man letting out a cry of pain. Still he refused to remain still, and instead made a run for the broken and twisted gates. Lucie clicked the trigger again, but the cartridge was empty.

"Check the other one!" she shouted back to Ismail, "and be careful, he might be armed!"

She set off on the heels of the would-be assassin, driven as much by the animal desire to punish his actions as her professional need to understand them. He was proving deceptively fast despite his injury, but Lucie pressed her tired body forward nonetheless, until her knee, already strained and sore from the day's exertions, clicked and wobbled beneath her, pulling her up into a stuttered hop.

"Damn it," she hissed to herself as she limped breathlessly back to Ismail, who leant on the wrecked Audi, staring back at his own half-destroyed car.

"I had my MOT due in the morning," he mused as Lucie drew level with him.

"Well at least that's your diary clear for the day. What about the other one?"

"Dead."

Lucie's spirit dropped, as though a boulder had been placed between her shoulder blades; she closed her eyes for what seemed like an eternity. Lucie leaned into the car and stared into the face of the man she had killed. There was nothing special about his appearance; the pale, unshaven features of a slightly overweight man in his thirties tarnished only by the blood splatter on his cheek caused by the gunshot wound to his chest.

Reaching into the car, she placed her hand on the dead man's forehead and clamped her eyes shut tight.

"Lord," she began, "I'm sorry for having once more offended you..."

Her words disappeared into a whisper, and the suddenly embarrassed Ismail looked down at his feet, and back into the car, anywhere except directly at her, unsure of what steps to take next but unwilling to break her meditation.

"I know him," the police officer suddenly exclaimed.

"What?" snapped an irritated Lucie, trying to keep her mind focussed on her lamentations.

"I know him!"

The words, combined with the rapid approach of wailing

sirens dragged her back into the present, Lucie finishing her confession and pulling herself back to her feet. The sirens had reached the destroyed gateway, two response cars pulling up to the pair, uniformed officers spilling out and screaming for immediate surrender.

"This is a bit of a pickle," Ismail opined. "I'm normally on the other side of the fence."

Lucie though simply offered the first constable the beamiest of beaming smiles and stepped towards him.

"Evening, Officer! Nice night for a drive, eh?"

"Get your hands in the air," ordered the young officer with an uncertainty in his voice that was mirrored in his expression.

"Nah," Lucie said, shaking her head. "Is now a good time for my phone call?"

14

It was late afternoon the following day when Ismail met Lucie as she came out of Westminster Abbey, dressed in the more comfortable attire of jeans and a polo shirt, the increasingly frayed looking overcoat hanging on her shoulders and her hair untidily down.

Their spell in custody the previous evening had been as brief as Lucie had expected it to be, her call to Lake surprisingly well received and resulting in immediate release for the pair of them. Though one or two eyebrows had been raised at the appearance of Ismail in the custody suite, they were soon satiated by cryptic references to the 'special secondment' he was involved in.

"It's hardly a secondment, it's a bloody suspension," he had spat as the pair had walked free from the station in the early hours. But Lucie, tired of games and repentant of her latest killing, was in no mood to respond, the pair retiring to their respective flats an agreeing to liaise in the morning. While Lucie had spent the morning in a tense de-brief with Lake, before heading to the Abbey to sit in morose contrition, Ismail had made good on his offer the night before to track down 'Ludmita' and press her further on what she had let slip the previous evening. He relayed the tale as the pair strolled around the historical beauty of the Abbey gardens.

The 'entertainment centre' had released Ludmita's address on site of Ismail's faked ID. He had found her that morning, tired and angry, at the studio apartment she rented in Elephant & Castle, disposed to give Ismail successive mouthfuls of the foulest language she could muster until she too had lain eyes on the shining badge of the Met. As it had turned out, whatever the secret of 'Ludmita's' true identity, she was so desperate to keep it that she didn't allow the resentment she felt to inhibit her answers. Over an early morning bottle of vodka, she had spilled what she knew about the visit of Ines to the centre in return for Ismail's assurance he would not take her in and set about uncovering who she really was.

His bluff had evidently worked, and by the time he had caught the tube to meet with Lucie, he was satisfied that the young prostitute had told him everything she knew. Ines, Ludmita revealed, had been well-known at the centre, along with several other women who had actively campaigned against the opening of the brothels since they were first mooted by one of the Cabinet's more libertarian Members. At first the protests had been confined to comments and messages to the centre's social media pages; never aggressive, quite the contrary in fact, but relentless. One night, not long after the messages had been blocked, a small group of four women had arrived at the centre asking to be entertained by a selection of girls, Ludmita among them. Almost before the door to the suite had closed, the group had begun what amounted to a sermon, urging the women to abandon this career and not let themselves be used and abused by the people who frequented it.

Security had swiftly arrived, and the women escorted from the premises. One woman however, who spoke in a French accent and introduced herself as 'Ines', appeared again later that same night. It had been in the early hours when Ludmita had finished her shift and was leaving for the night that this woman approached her on the steps outside the centre, begging her to listen and asking her to at least take her number and meet sometime to talk, away from the centre. Though she was sick to death of people screaming their morality at her, there had been something in the woman's eyes that almost compelled her to accept the number and agree to meet, and had the bouncer, Jim, not come outside and intervened at that point, she might well have done so. As it was, she was marched from the grounds in much the same way, Ismail noted, as Lucie herself had been the previous night. That had been the extent of Ludmita's involvement with the mysterious Ines, and for what it was worth, Ismail had finished, he had believed her.

"Doesn't tell us much," Lucie mused, "but at least we know for sure she'd been there. Thanks for taking care of that, mate."

"No problem," he said with a sly smile. "*Mate.*"

Lucie's cheeks flushed for a moment and Ismail switched the conversation back to the matter in hand.

"You still think the brothel guys weren't involved, even after the fun and games last night?"

"If I wasn't sure of it before, I am now."

"What's convinced you?"

"You did," she smiled at him, enjoying the bashful look that briefly appeared on Ismail's own face. "The name you gave me last night after we finished up with your chums in blue."

"Ah," Ismail acknowledged. "The infamous Mr. Healey?"

"The very same. How did you come by him again?"

"It would have been the beginning of last year," Ismail sighed. "Uniform brought him in on a D&D arrest after a demonstration, and then the next week he was nicked again for harassment when he started following certain MPs around and turning up on their doorsteps at night. CID got involved when we had an anonymous tip he was funding his political activities with a bit of, shall we say, freelance gardening."

"Weed in the attic?"

"Yeah, a shit load of it if I recall. It can be hard to tell where the farms are sometimes, but in this fella's case he opted to grow his stash in the middle of the cold snap. When every house on the street has a snow-covered roof except for one, and the upstairs windows all have tinfoil curtains, you get a pretty good idea of what's going on up there. I think he got twelve months in the end, though he'd have been out in six. I never had him cut out for serious shit like this though."

"Well thanks to your memory for faces, Lake was able to dig into things. Turns out that upon his release, the late Jonathan Healey had returned to his political activities, although in a more organised manner than before."

The pair had passed through the gardens and headed for the beer garden of one of the trendier bars in the area, Ismail ordering them a beer apiece as Lucie continued.

"Healey got himself involved in one of these bloody yellow vest groups, wandering around shouting at people and disrupting traffic, but that isn't the most interesting thing."

"Then what is?" Ismail quizzed, handing a crumpled note to the waiter who placed tall, green beer bottles and half-pint glasses on the table between them.

"Who he worked for," Lucie answered as she tipped her ice-cold beverage into her glass. "Your friend and one of his chums were nicked again not long ago. Turns out they both worked for *WaterWhyte Defence*."

Ismail frowned and swallowed the ale in his mouth. "*WaterWhyte*? The place building this *Red Mako* thing you told me about?"

"The very same," Lucie confirmed. "Healey was employed as on-site security for the last few months, coincidentally at the same company and the same project that Kasper was looking into when he was attacked. I wouldn't mind betting that Healey was the one behind it."

"That's supposition, Lucie," Ismail warned, his rational, police mind resisting such leaps. "Healey had no form for firearm offences or attempted murder. He's just been in a bit of a thug with a weed habit and a big mouth."

"Is that all he was though?" Lucie pressed. "He tailed us through London last night, shooting bullets at us, remember?"

"He was the driver," Ismail corrected, "not the shooter."

"Potato, potahto," shrugged Lucie. "He was in the car, he knew what was going down."

Lucie could feel the anger building once more within her and she was grateful that Ismail did not press further. When Kasper was injured she had yearned for revenge, before regaining control of her emotions and accepting that revenge was, according to her long-held beliefs, The Lord's to take. And after learning that she had taken the life, albeit by necessity, of one of those who had likely been involved in her friend's suffering, the momentary pleasure the death had given her was now troubling her greatly. Had she really fallen so far?

Shaking her head free of such musings, she picked up her train of thought and continued.

"So, much as you might hate suppositions, all we have right now is the hope that the people who came after us once we'd visited the brothel, were the same who went after Ines when she'd done the same."

"But you still don't think the brothel itself is involved?"

"No," Lucie confirmed, "sorry, I just don't. I think the answer is at *WaterWhyte*. That's who Healey worked for and that's where I'm heading next, and I told Lake the same this morning; he wasn't best pleased...

She allowed herself a small smile of victory at the look on

Lake's face when he had told her of Healey's connection to *WaterWhyte*, and the need to expand her investigation in that direction. Triumphs over the spy master she had soon discovered were small, rare and to be cherished when they occurred, and she would have been lying if she'd said this one hadn't brought particular pleasure. Regulations be damned, it was for her to get to the bottom of the attack on Kasper, not one of the other 'operatives' Lake frequently boasted of. Fuck them, and fuck him for taking her off the assignment in the first place...

She quickly drained the beer and ordered two more. It was a bright if cold late winter's day and she had no wish to waste it. It wasn't until she tipped the second bottle to her froth-stained glass and sat back to take in the opulent splendour of the nearby Abbey against the blue sky, that the emotions she had been pushing back down into her gut began to grow within her again.

Ismail was looking at her with the concern of not just a friend, but someone who quite clearly would welcome more, and she looked away as she felt the tears threatening to come.

"First time you've killed someone?" Ismail quizzed suddenly, his voice soft and with what sounded like a hint of compassion.

"If only," came Lucie's response. "No, I'm not a stranger to taking lives; it's just that killing them is the easy part, but at the end of it one of you has to stay alive. The only thing worse than being killed is living with having done the killing. You must know what I mean..."

"Do I?" Ismail replied, with just a suggestion of indignance. "I'm a Police Officer, or was until your mate Lake had anything to do with it. My job was to arrest the bad guys, not put a bullet through them."

He immediately regretted his choice of words and offered a perfunctory apology to Lucie, who shrugged away any presumed offence and simply drank deeper from her glass.

"It's a hellish thing to do; to kill someone," the spy mused, staring into the rising bubbles in her glass as though hoping her guilt would rise up and pop away with them. "When the blade goes in, or the gun is fired, they always fight it, like they know death is bearing down on them but their pride or their will or whatever, refuses to accept it, right up until the last second. You can see it in their eyes, that anger, that resentment that this really is it and their refusal to give in until the last possible moment..."

"But Healey wasn't like that?"

Lucie shut her eyes, trying to force away the image of the felled killer that obstinately refused to budge.

"You won't believe this," she almost whispered, "but killing someone is one of the most intimate things you can do with them, closer than friendship, closer than sex. There's a moment, when you connect utterly with them, soul to soul. You know you're taking everything away from them and they know they're losing it to you and despite all the fight and all the anger, for that final second, they accept it... I killed Healey, but I didn't see him die, the connection wasn't there and... and it feels harder because of that, as though I've denied him his moment of peace."

Ismail, though the rest of his face remained the picture of sympathy, couldn't disguise the eyebrow raised in confusion at her words, and he remained quiet for the longest time, before refilling his glass and raising it to his lips.

"Well if you'll forgive me for saying so, those must be some weird-ass friends and some pretty bizarre sex you've been having."

Lucie's expression shifted immediately to one of shock and surprise, before the laughter within her erupted in a crescendo of noise that drew annoyed tuts from other tables but more importantly dragged the relaxing smile she had grown so fond of onto Ismail's face.

"I'm sorry I've not been myself today," Lucie said, sincerely. "It's ok," he reassured her, "I get it. You need to make your peace with...." He gestured upwards towards the sky. "Yep," she nodded, "and it gets harder every time."

"It's meant to be hard," Ismail said, sagely. "To keep your faith in a world like this, I mean. If it was easy everyone would be doing it."

"What about you? Do you follow any faith?"

"Sure," Ismail nodded, "I'm a Muslim, even though you can probably tell by the beer that I'm not the world's best."

"All any of us can do is try."

"Truth is I don't get to the mosque very often these days, what with shift work, and also being a bit of a lazy bugger on my days off. I used to go every Friday with my folks and there are days when I really do miss it."

Lucie thanked the patient waiter for the further beers he placed on the table and shared a brief joke with him about whose turn it was to pay before turning back to the man who had quickly become a friend.

"The last place I went to with my old man before he got ill was church," she said. "He hadn't been in years then out of nowhere he said he wanted to take Communion, so off we trotted. Six weeks later he was dead."

Ismail stayed silent for a moment, not wanting to simply give the obligatory 'I'm sorry' but unable to think of anything else.

"It's ok," Lucie said after he had given in to the inevitable. "May I ask, how...?"

"Cancer," she answered, blinking back a persistent tear. "Testicular. Make sure you check your balls."

Lucie pointed to him with the look of an army recruiting poster as she issued her command, her little attempt to stifle her sadness and lighten things bringing an affectionate smile to Ismail's face.

"I just got thinking about it since last night," Lucie continued. "You know, I spent every waking hour sat at Dad's bedside, not wanting him to be alone when his time came; I was there for days. Then one morning I went to get a coffee from the kitchen and when I came back, he was gone. Right at the very end I let him down... because of me he died alone."

Ismail heaved in an enormous breath and shook his head gently. "He wasn't alone, Lucie," he said. "He had his heart full of you and his mind full of memories."

"Yeah," she mused, a smile finally returning to her face. "And they were great memories ... music, booze and football, that's what he was about. I'll never forget my first trip to Maine Road."

"Bloody hell," Ismail grinned, "a City fan!"

"In the flesh," Lucie grinned back, "and before you ask, yes, I was there when we were shit."

"That's what they all say."

"It's true! I had posters of Uwe Rosler and Paul Walsh all over my bedroom in the mid '90's; I still can't believe we got rid of Walshy..."

Ismail's grin grew wider. "I felt a bit like that when Arsenal sold Anders Limpar, but then we got Dennis Bergkamp a couple of seasons later, so that turned out ok."

"Yeah? We got relegated twice in three seasons," Lucie laughed. "We lived between Manchester and Prague in those days but whenever we were this side me and my dad would trot along to see us get beaten by whoever we were playing that week..."

She took a sip of her beer as she allowed the memory a moment to caress her, Ismail patiently listening, a sincere smile on his face. "There was a social club, a couple of streets away from Maine Road," Lucie picked up, "and we'd meet up there with my dad's mates for a drink before the game. They were a good bunch of lads, they'd always apologise for swearing in front of me, as though I'd never heard the words before. And they always called me 'Tom's girl'. It didn't matter how old I got, it was always 'Tom's girl', and 'sorry for swearing, Tom's girl'. It used to piss me off at the time, but it always makes me smile now... And then after a few drinks we'd walk to the stadium, grab a pie and wait for our mighty blue heroes to emerge and get stuffed."

"Here's to memories," Ismail toasted, raising his glass towards her.

"And to making new ones."

They drained their glasses and stood up to leave, Lucie wishing they could just forget the case for a day and continue relaxing into each other's company, but duty continued to tug at her senses, and she re-organised her thoughts once more, shuffling the matter of Ines, and *WaterWhyte* to the front.

"We need to find a way to get into the company," Lucie pondered aloud as they continued walking, the cold afternoon air beginning to chill their skin. "I want to know more about this *Red Mako* of theirs, and why they'd employ a man who spends his off hours speeding after people with a gun."

"We could question the HR Manager, or someone with access to the employment records. We should be able to find out who hired him and work from there."

"Yep, that's good," Lucie nodded, "but let's see if we can kill two birds with one stone."

"What do you mean?"

She pulled out her smart phone and grinned, the cogs of her mind clicking into gear.

"Time to phone a friend."

15

"Fantastic to see you, Lucie," exclaimed Professor Tanja Bueltmann, standing up from behind the wooden table to embrace her friend. "Beer okay for you?"

Lucie agreed with a grin, delighted both to be in her friend's company, and to find that she had already adorned the pub table with two large, frosted glasses of German lager. Throwing her coat onto the window sill behind them, Lucie sat down and clinked glasses with the Professor, swallowing a deep and satisfying mouthful of the cold beverage.

"Beer is very much okay for me, Tanja," grinned Lucie, "how are you?"

"I'm well," Tanja replied. "You're lucky to catch me though, I'm only in London for the day to work on the campaign; I'm heading home first thing."

The Professor was a woman for whom Lucie had nothing but admiration and respect. An ardent campaigner for the rights of the EU Nationals scapegoated and abandoned in the country's pursuit of a pernicious Hard Brexit, she had never given up her campaign despite the horrendous abuse and almost constant threats against her. Looking at her now, her smile wide and her lipstick as fiery as her hair, Lucie would defy anybody to say that the pressures the Professor faced showed obviously in her features, and the spy mused how her friend daily displayed as much courage and more as anyone she had known.

"Then that's another reason to be glad to see you," Lucie said.

"Nice to have more than one reason. How's Kasper? Any better?"

Lucie shook her head quickly, not wanting to dwell too long on the topic. To Tanja, and to the world, Lucie was simply the Parliamentary aide to the injured MP, safely out of the limelight and anonymous to all outside the Westminster bubble, and thought it pained her to deceive a friend, that was the role she played up to again now.

"No. Bastard yellow vests..."

"I'm sorry."

"Don't be. He'll be alright, I can feel it, but the thought that the swine are still out threatening people every day is sickening, and precious little seems to be being done about it, at least not by this useless Prime Minister."

"I don't know how we come back from this," sighed Tanja, "I really don't. I'm grateful for every single person who has stood up for us, donated, or just said 'no, this is wrong'; I just wish there were a million more beside them..."

Lucie could only offer what she knew was a wholly inadequate smile. She understood her friend's feelings only too well, her own heart having broken a little further by the inescapable lack of vociferous protest at the treatment of Europeans since the referendum.

"Wilful ignorance," the spy lamented, softly. "Too many people just refuse absolutely to accept the evidence of their own eyes; when you show them how people are affected, how so many are suffering, they just deny that it's happening."

"Or claim it's nothing to do with Brexit," The Professor added. "And those that do see it wring their hands and say it's not what they voted for while doing nothing to stop it."

"Even though it was obvious to anyone with a mind to look what the consequences were bound to be."

They clinked their glasses again and Tanja sighed, heavily.

"To tell you the truth, half the time I'm trying to convince myself to stop because of the negative impact all this is having on me, the rest I'm so angry I tell myself there's no way I could ever stop. God only knows what's going to happen."

"Tell me about it," Lucie concurred. "Have you applied yet?"

"Oh, don't even get me started on that bloody 'EU Settlement Scheme'," Tanja replied. "Bad enough that they refused to give us a say despite happily collecting our taxes for years, but then they design this fucking app which won't work on anything and is so full of glitches it isn't fit for purpose. Then they tell us we have to apply for permission to stay in our homes with our own families. Not register to stay mind, apply to stay and become second class citizens. And in the next breath they say they 'want us to stay'."

Lucie could feel the burning anger of her friend and shared it in every sinew of her body. The latest insult saw the government demanding an application to stay, via a flawed and decidedly user-unfriendly app, with prior contribution to the country and society – not to mention familial circumstances – completely ignored.

"Believe me, I know. And every second Kasper is lying unconscious in hospital, Parliament is robbed of one of the few sane voices it has left. Sometimes I wonder if that was the point..."

"You think it was an organised attack?" The Professor frowned.

"I don't know," Lucie said softly, not wanting to say too much. "All I do know is the clock is ticking down to a colossal punch in the face. Everyone knows it's coming, but the ones in charge are too proud to admit it and the opposition are too busy sitting around with their thumbs up their arses, hoping to capitalise on the fallout. Meanwhile the nation ticks closer to the bloodiest of bloody noses and an almighty kick in the ego."

The women drank in melancholic salute to the intricacies of the injustices they pondered, steadily draining their glasses.

"Speaking of Kasper," Lucie said, "I'm checking into a few things on his behalf; actually, that's what I needed to talk to you about."

"Oh?"

"Do you know anyone who works in the defence industry?"

"Defence?" Tanja repeated, her eyes widening. "Not really my scene. I would have thought you'd have the contacts there, working in Parliament?"

"Well that's the problem. Kasper wanted me to do a bit of research into the treatment of EU Nationals in the industry for him and I'm struggling. I've tried the official approaches but the second you start waving a Parliamentary pass in people's faces they tend to clam up. I want to get in at the ground floor and speak freely to the people at the receiving end of shit. In particular I want to get a look at *WaterWhyte Defence*."

"Ah," nodded Tanja. "The famous *Red Mako* project eh? The saviour of Brexit Britain..."

"Exactly. With all the hype around it I wanted to see how people on the ground have been affected, and whether all this 'British services for British people' crap extends to the job market too. And as Jarvis Whyte has his hands all over the company, I don't think he'd take too kindly if one of his

Parliamentary opponents just rolls up and asks to see his project specs and who he's getting in to staff it."

"No, perhaps not," Tanja laughed. "I'm sorry though, I don't think I know anyone in the industry I could put you in touch with, although…"

The Professor took out her mobile and began scrolling through her contact list, trying to recall the name that danced at the edge of her memory. Moments later, her finger pressed down on a name and the wide smile returned to her face.

"Found her!" she smiled. "Great!"

"Monika Barenyi." Tanja revealed. "A friend of mine who works in recruitment."

"A recruitment consultant?" Lucie winced. "They're about the only people convicts are allowed to shout abuse at, aren't they?"

"Monika's not like that," laughed Tanja, "she's excellent and extremely professional. Plus, she specialises in defence and aerospace, and with this *Red Mako* stuff all over the news, she's bound to be involved in recruiting for it. If you like, I'll drop her a text and tell her you want to get in touch?"

"Tanja, you're an absolute star!"

"Do you want me to say what it's for?"

"Er, no, not straight off thanks, people can get a bit worried if they think an MP's office is chasing them. If you can just say I'd love to get in touch with her for a chat, that'd be great."

"No problem," the Professor replied, quickly rattling off a text. "I'm sure she'll be happy to help. The last time I spoke with her she told me about how the level of abuse she was getting was on the increase since the Brexit vote."

"Really? What kind of abuse?"

"Nothing physical, at least not yet, but a lot of verbal crap. When she turns candidates down or gives bad interview feedback, she's getting all the old 'you're not even from here, who are you tell me X, Y and Z' bullshit. You know the kind of stuff."

"Yeah, the kind of shit spouted by the 'why's a foreigner telling me what to do' brigade."

"Monika's tough, but nobody should have to put up with that crap."

"I don't know anybody who can face up to it better than you, Tanja," Lucie said, holding her glass out to her in a toast, the academic blushing a little at the unsolicited praise.

"Thanks," she acknowledged. "I just wish I could do more; I would have given up long ago were it not for people like you, Julia, Axel and Maike... you all keep me going."

Lucie could feel the smile on her face grow every bit as strongly as the admiration she had for her friend, and even if she embarrassed her, she couldn't let the moment escape without making her feelings plain. Tanja had suffered verbal abuse, physical threats and even been stalked in the street, but still she came back, day after day, never giving up the fight for citizens as the country lost its mind. There were those who heaped praise on Lucie, but she knew that the real champion sat before her now with flushing cheeks.

"You do enough," Lucie said, "more than enough. And do you want to know something, Professor? You and everyone like you; you're all my heroes."

16

Lake's advice to Lucie when he had first recruited her into the Overlappers, had been that the best spies were just ordinary people, and it had been advice she'd taken to heart. A person being themselves had no need of elaborate cover, and dressing up with cloaks and daggers had never been Lucie's scene. There were by necessity however, occasions when a greater degree of skulduggery than usual was required, and she found herself in such a situation this morning. Using the false name at the centre a couple of nights back had made her uncomfortable, but today at least she could fall back on the role of journalist which had previously helped her get close to the late Sir Geoffrey Hartnell, when uncovering his shrouded agenda.

Monika had proven every bit as professional as Tanja had claimed, responding immediately to the text, happy for Lucie to get in touch. A brief conversation followed, and Lucie found herself invited to her professional offices in Charing Cross for a chat. Upon arrival, Lucie had related the cover story of researching an article for *The New European* about life in the workplace for EU Nationals, and what such a prestigious contract as the *Red Mako*, given its importance to the Hard Right as a symbol of Brexit, meant to the day-to-day lives of EU Citizens within the industry. Monika, a Slovakian woman of similar age to Lucie, with short, cropped black hair, green eyes and high cheek bones, was immediately intrigued and the pair struck up an instant rapport.

Tanja had been correct in her guess that Monika was aiming to recruit for the project on behalf of her company, and the consultant was in fact preparing her pitch for the next round of recruitment shortly to commence. There was an unusual level of secrecy around the project, and suppliers were required to re-tender for each recruitment phase – a tedious endeavour but one unquestionably worth it given the size of the commissions on offer. With the women bonding so quickly, it became an easy task for Lucie to have herself invited along to the pitch meeting a couple of days later at *WaterWhyte Defence's* Rochester site, which housed the bulk of the project, software development and strategic work, while physical construction of the projects took place at the larger premises in Portsmouth. And so it was that Lucie found herself two days later in the passenger seat of Monika's BMW, heading down to Kent and silently praying that the car would not meet the same fate as Ismail's had only a few nights previously.

Ismail himself had remained in London, to examine the social media presence collated by Lake's team and await the additional electronic data that Lucie hoped to gain during her visit. The corporate fire walls around *WaterWhyte's* intranet were both sophisticated and formidable, and while Lake had been sure his specialists could break them, he had ordered a different approach and provided Lucie with a small piece of hardware, now held in her suit jacket pocket.

To the naked eye a simple flash-drive, when plugged into any computer, active or not, it would automatically access and store all information contained on the device, link to the local network and scan it for selected buzzwords. Lucie's light-hearted query as to whether her being kitted out with the 'Bond stuff' signalled her acceptance back into Lake's good graces had received only a customary frown from the spy master. Her initial sarcasm soon gave way to the realisation that she would need to engineer an opportunity to use it, and it was that that preoccupied her as they drove past the guard house and pulled into the vast and neatly arranged carpark of *WaterWhyte Defence* itself.

After having been welcomed into the gleaming reception area of the enormous, white-washed and thoroughly modern building, Lucie and Monika were directed to wait in the seating area until all the representatives of the various competing companies had arrived. Sitting down in a low armchair coated in blue fabric, Lucie looked up into the face of a skinny young man in his twenties, wearing an almost glimmering silver-grey suit, stiff collared white shirt and red tie, who grinned at her with a look on entitled smugness. His chin sported meticulously styled stubble which might have looked more effective had he been old enough to grow more of it, and what remained of his shaved and layered hair was gelled back with such rigidity he could have been mistaken for an action figure. The condescending wink he offered to the two women met only with a snort of disdain from Monika, and one of Lucie's more withering stares, before he laughed at his own display and turned to talk with his similarly attired colleague.

"I don't know how the hell you can do this job," Lucie whispered to Monika, who offered a knowing smile in return.

"It gets easier as you go along," the recruiter whispered back. "A lot of these guys are all mouth and no balls. They'll look down on you because they think you're an interloper in a man's world, even though most of them have no experience in either the business or life; they just stick on a flash suit, cover themselves in aftershave and hope that being an arrogant little shit will impress the people they need to do business with. It rarely does."

"Well good for you for not letting them get to you," Lucie replied.

"It can be difficult sometimes," Monika admitted. "When you start out and you're trying to get commissions and generate new business, you get stuck on the brew rounds and have all the usual comments about 'taking one for the team' to bring the jobs in. Then that's exactly what they accuse you of doing when you start out-billing them and earning big money. And if you stick to your guns and keep doing your job well, before too long you're heading a desk and they're all working under you and complaining about the evils of positive discrimination."

"While in reality you've had to work twice as hard as any of them to get the same level of recognition," Lucie finished, tired of having heard so many similar stories from female friends across so many different industries.

The reception area was beginning to fill with many more variants of the winking wonder and his friend and a number of perma-tanned young women with perfectly placed hair, pouting lips and unmoving features, juxtaposed with a smattering of more modestly presented professionals who looked to Lucie like they actually knew what they were talking about.

Monika gestured to the latter group, one in which she most definitely belonged.

"These are the people I'm really competing with," she said. "Too many in our industry think image is everything, but it's the ones who are low on flash talk and heavy on detail that really impress the clients and make the big bucks."

As she spoke, a figure emerged from behind the reception desk and walked over to the group.

"Excuse me," the young man began, before clearing his throat and trying again. "EXCUSE ME, LADIES AND GENTLEMEN."

This time he was met with silence and the stare of expectant faces.

"Thank you. If you'd like to follow me, Dr Rigson and the team are ready for you. Please step this way."

The group began to move en masse, Monika moving herself to the front with effortless and uncontested ease, Lucie falling into place alongside her. The spy shuffled and twitched uncomfortably in the stiff business skirt and jacket she wore, while walking on heels remained an activity unimproved since her attempt a few evenings earlier. It was a hindrance which Monika didn't share as she carried herself with professional confidence and led the way into the conference room. The pack of recruiters jostled and bustled themselves into the seats laid out around an enormous horse shoe table, some offering smiles to friendly competitors, while other faces twisted into resentful sneers as quicker rivals bagged seats closer to the end of the horse shoe and closer to the department heads who shifted uncomfortably under insincere gazes. Monika, at the head of the pack, led Lucie to two prime seats, closest to the execs and the large monitor clinging to the wall facing the tables, the remaining walls decorated with numerous framed photographs of previous projects and portraits of distinguished company engineers.

When the scrape of chairs, the rustle of papers and the tuts of discourteous opponents subsided, the room was silenced by a loud and authoritative welcome from the woman who had risen from her seat to stand in front of the screen, all eyes turning to her as she spoke.

Lucie took the opportunity to properly observe the room, feeling instantly alien in a chamber packed with sharp suits, glittering watches and a potent clash of expensive aftershaves and perfumes. And while there was an abundance of designer stubble, immaculate hairstyles and more than a few eyes glistening with the tell-tale signs of a well-fuelled coke habit, Monika's seemed one of the few genuine smiles in the room, Lucie admiring the strength it must take to forge a successful niche in an industry she did not appear suited to.

The speaker opening the event was a woman in her late thirties, dressed similarly impeccably, but possessed of a natural charm and authority of a type bereft from most others around the table. Her tone was professional but lively enough to hold her audience's interest as she explained the purpose and schedule for the day. They were all there, she recounted, to learn more about the *Red Mako*, and to pitch for a position on the new PSL.

"What's a PSL?" Lucie whispered to Monika.

"Preferred Supplier List," came the hushed answer. "The industry's taken a battering since the Brexit vote and everyone's desperate for a piece of the action. The company want to keep the number of agencies recruiting for them to a minimum, so they invite us all here and let us fight it out in front of them. It's like gladiator combat for young professionals."

The woman, who had introduced herself as Julie Woodlock, the HR Director, but whom Monika referred to somewhat cryptically as 'the Gatekeeper', went on to introduce a short video on the project. The lights were dimmed as a montage of CGI shots of the *Red Mako* itself played across the screen, accompanied by a sickeningly corporate musical backing track, over which a confident male voice extolled the project's virtues. All around the room, pens were furiously scribbling and brows furrowing in exaggerated intensity, though precious little of anything of any technical value was revealed in the short, which culminated in a shot of the lauded new boat speeding towards the camera.

The promo ended and the lights were raised, while some of the more sycophantic of the room's occupants attempted a round of applause that remained ignored by the rest of the attendees. Rather than Julie returning to her feet, a grey haired and bespectacled man rose from his chair at the end of the horseshoe and addressed the group, barely disguising the distaste in his voice.

"I'm Richard Wineheart, the Programme Director, alongside me is Dr Rigson, the Technical Manager. The video you've just seen should be enough for you to sell the project to your candidates," he said in gruff tones. "Technical specifics and requirements have all been written by Dr Rigson and will be provided in individual job adverts for those of you who make the list. I don't expect to meet or speak with any of you again, and be warned that anyone who tries to reach me directly will find their candidates disqualified and their company removed from the PSL. I shall leave the judging of your pitches to Julie and I would suggest a comfort break before you begin, I know only too well how people in your industry can talk. Thank you and good morning."

With that, he nodded to Julie, who seemed completely unfazed by his conduct, and exited the room. Julie immediately rose to her feet and passed a stack of glossy brochures to Monika, who took one and passed them down the table.

"I'm sending round the latest marketing information aimed at recruitment and HR," she said. "Inside you'll find details of the type of roles we'll be recruiting for to help you start looking at your candidate pools. Now, I think Richard's idea is the best one; let's have a comfort break before we start the pitches. For those who need them, toilets are down the corridor, Gents to the right, Ladies to the left. Back in ten minutes please everybody."

The room immediately filled with intense murmuring and movement as chairs were pushed back and people began heading for the door, their conversations growing louder as they pushed through and headed down the corridor. After the flurry of the first few seconds, only Monika and Lucie remained at the table, the recruiter studying the brochure with interest.

"Wineheart's an unfriendly bugger, isn't he?" Lucie opined, Monika laughing in response.

"You get used to it," she answered. "Really?"

"Oh, fuck yes, employers hate us, particularly huge companies like this. Recruitment's a dirty business; every other person in the industry will try and get one over on his competitors by kissing the hiring manager's arse and hoping that'll put their candidate at the top of the interview schedule. Wineheart's just letting people know he won't put up with any shit, it's all part of the game. In truth if I ring him directly on a Friday with the perfect candidate and he can't fault me on the brief, they'll be starting the job on the Monday. Believe me, they'd much rather do all their recruitment themselves and not have to deal with people like us at all, but that just isn't practical for an organisation this size, so they outsource it to us and let us do the leg work, while cursing us every time we get on the phone."

"I knew recruiters weren't exactly loved but I never knew they were so hated," Lucie laughed.

"That's putting it politely," Monika replied. "Everyone hates recruitment consultants. Now this is interesting..."

"What is?"

"The job roles in the brochure. They're looking for project managers, software specialists, engineers, systems designers, everything you'd expect in a massive project like this, except for..."

"Except for what?" Lucie pressed as her colleague's voice

tailed off and she flicked through the rest of the brochure, her frown increasing with each turn of the page.

"No weapons."

"What, none at all?"

"Nope. Not a single advertised role for weapons specialists, missile engineers, defensive systems quality technicians, nothing. That's bloody odd. And it's a shame too; we can charge big fees for good weapons people."

"Could the weapons be part of another contract?"

"They're not supposed to be. As far as we're aware the contract is wholly owned by the WaterWhyte umbrella. Bloody odd... anyway, excuse me a moment, I'm running to the ladies."

As Monika stood up and left the room, Lucie seized her chance, taking out her specialised flashdrive and clicking it into place in the laptop the HR Director, Julie, had left at her place before going to fend off unsolicited 'off the record' questions in the Ladies'. An L.E.D on the stick glowed a dull green as the virus inside it did its work and Lucie kept an ear and an eye out for signs of movement on the corridor outside. Footsteps began to draw closer and Lucie placed her hand on the device, ready to pull and pocket it, but wary of withdrawing it too soon before it had its chance to draw all the information it could contain.

The slap of hard soles against a tiled floor grew closer still, and Lucie slipped the stick from the port, dropping it into her suit pocket in one movement, just as Julie Woodlock returned, flashing a professionally plastic smile towards her. As she sat down and began shuffling papers, Lucie ignored the twinge in her own bladder and picked up the brochure in front of her, flicking through and feigning a professional interest.

"Excuse me, Julie?" She began, the HR Director raising an eyebrow in response, her weariness at 'off the record' conversations with recruiters evident upon her face.

"I've been going through the brochure and I noticed there's no weapons related jobs available."

"Well spotted," came Julie's response, her inflection ambiguous enough for Lucie to wonder if she were being sarcastic or sincere. "It just seems a little odd for a project of this nature," Lucie continued, mimicking Monika's curiosity. "I thought *WaterWhyte* was responsible for delivering the entire product."

"And so we are," Julie answered, this time with a touch of indignance. "At least, all aspects of the product that were open to tender."

"Some weren't?"

"As it happens, no." Julie's voice had now moved through indignancy and into defensiveness. "The Saudis removed weapons systems and munitions from the contract; they're content to handle that side of development themselves. Not that you should worry, there are other roles galore for you to fill your boots with. If you make the PSL that is."

Her last words were spoken sternly, and Lucie knew they were a warning not to probe further lest she abandon any notion of making the cut. Though her curiosity was unsatiated, Lucie opted to stay quiet and not damage her new contact's chances of making the fortune that could save her from the impending Brexit chaos, instead smiling in gratitude at the rigid Woodlock and returning her gaze to the brochure.

After what felt like several lifetimes, Lucie and Monika stepped out from the building and breathed in glorious lungfuls of cold, fresh air as they stretched their joints and headed back towards Monika's car, shaking their senses back to life after the dullest couple of hours either could remember. Pitch upon pitch from the well-dressed if nauseatingly cocky salespeople, all bragging about the size of their databases and the sincerity of their desire to listen to their customers, had nearly led to Lucie nodding off at the table, were it not for a well-timed kick from Monika.

As they breathed life back into themselves, Lucie replayed Julie's explanation about the weapons systems in her mind, before voicing them to Monika as they reached her car.

"I spoke with Julie while you were out of the room," she said as Monika searched in her bag for her key. "About the weapon systems."

"Oh, shit, you didn't piss her off, did you? I need the commission from these jobs..."

"Are you kidding? You gave the only decent pitch in the room, you'll be top of the list guaranteed. No, she said the weapons systems and munitions were never part of the contract; that the Saudis had explicitly taken that part out of the deal. Does that sound normal to you?"

Monika's features twisted in puzzlement, as she located the keys and de-activated the alarm.

"You know the more I think about that it just feels odd," she answered. "I've recruited for a lot of Naval defence projects – the Type 45 Destroyer, the Astute class Submarine – weapons tech was a crucial requirement for all of them. And the defence industry is a pretty incestuous creature, the same engineers can always be sure of finding work on the next project that comes along, whoever wins the tender, that's why so may of them do contract work; they know they'll always be in demand and they can charge big bucks for their time. And even if they want to build those parts in Saudi Arabia, we do international recruitment all the time; these kind of professionals go all over the world to work... there'll be a few people pretty pissed off at missing out on something as high profile as this, that's for sure."

The women opened the doors and climbed inside, Monika turning the key and setting the car moving.

"Missing out..." mused Lucie, almost under her breath. "What?"

"Oh, I was just thinking out loud."

"What about?"

"Nothing really, it's just..." She stopped herself finishing the sentence, which only succeeded in further peaking Monika's interest.

"Nothing's 'nothing'," the recruiter grinned. "What is it?"

"Just something you said just now; that there'll be lots of defence professionals pissed off at missing out on the contract."

"Yeah?"

"I was just wondering whether it was more than that."

"More than that? What do you mean?"

"Well," Lucie mused as the car pulled out onto the road and began the journey back into London, "if the industry is as incestuous as you say, and all the weapons and munitions engineers have worked on every other Naval defence project since the dawn of time, then maybe it's not as simple as them 'missing out' on the *Red Mako*."

"Go on."

"Maybe it's more like they're being *kept* out."

17

"I must admit," sighed a smiling Ismail the next morning in the coffee shop, "when you texted me about this 'big weapon theory' I had something more intimate than coffee in mind."

"Behave yourself," laughed Lucie, her cheeks flashing a momentary pink.

"If I must," he laughed back.

Arriving back in London the previous afternoon from her sojourn with Monika, Lucie's mind had been racing with possibilities, robbing her of any desire to be sociable, and so after Monika had dropped her off, she nervously contemplated whether to follow through with her plan to call Ismail and discuss findings over a drink. Standing outside the door to his flat, her knuckles poised to rap, she finally dropped her arm and instead posted the flashdrive through his letterbox, sending him a text explaining its presence and her latest theories, before cursing herself for the missed opportunity as she headed quickly back home. While her regret may have followed her into the morning, she at least had the work to focus her attention.

"So, what is this theory of yours?" Ismail quizzed.

Lucie recounted the events of the previous day with feverish intensity, detailing her 'business trip' with what could only be described as a pack of other recruiters, Monika's curiosity at the absence of weapons and munitions vacancies and Woodlock's defensiveness when pressed on the matter.

"Why should that be sinister?" Ismail queried as she paused to draw breath. "Why should it matter if the Saudis want to build certain parts themselves, or if they want to paint the bridge green and put a TV screen in the back of every chair? Contracts can be weird things to ordinary mortals like us."

"No, it's more than just the usual bollocks," Lucie insisted, "I can feel it. Monika said the defence industry is incestuous, everybody knows each other and that's especially true of the weapons bods."

"Not literally, I hope."

"Hey," Lucie chastised, forcing back the return of her strangely bashful smile, "I won't tell you again."

"Sorry," he answered with playful sheepishness.

"Think about it though," Lucie pushed, steering him back to the subject. "The *Red Mako* isn't just another paper promise from the Brexshitters, it's a massively high profile, state-of-the-art sea-based interception vehicle. The Saudis have almost as much riding on its success as our government do. Now, if you were in charge of building a new ship to help your country win a war, and there was a pool of massively experienced weapons specialists immediately available and itching for the chance to get on board, why the hell wouldn't you use them?"

Ismail's smile had gone, and his eyes had narrowed as he focussed on her words.

"Go on."

"Because whatever weapons you're planning to fire from your sparkly new boat, either rely on a technology entirely different to that used by all the major aerospace & defence companies for the past few decades..."

"Which is pretty unlikely."

"Or whatever it is you want to fire at your enemy isn't the kind of thing those engineers would have the stomach for."

Ismail absorbed the words like a blow to the head, and he sat back for a moment in a silence Lucie mirrored; the implications of her theory sounding all the worse when spoken out loud. After a moment, Ismail picked up his coffee and drew a deep sip before leaning across the table and lowering his voice, somewhat needlessly in the otherwise empty establishment.

"You realise what you're saying of course?" he asked.

"That our government is complicit in facilitating chemical weapons attacks on Yemen."

Ismail exhaled and pressed his palms to his face, murmuring behind them for a moment before dropping them back to the table and sighing once more.

"Lucie," he began, "that's quite a statement, not to mention quite a leap. I mean, I've no love for this shower of shit in government, but you're talking about war crimes..."

"Would it be the first time?"

"Dodgy dossiers are one thing, but this?"

"Maybe they don't know," Lucie conceded, "and maybe they do. But my gut is telling me I'm right on this. There's something not right about this project. Kasper was on to them and it landed him in hospital, put there by a bunch of fucking yellow vests employed as security for *WaterWhyte*!"

"Healey worked for *WaterWhyte*," Ismail cautioned. "There were a dozen or more people on that video attacking Algers, of all shapes and sizes, most pretty clearly physically unsuited to security work for a Blue Chip company; maybe a handful out of the crowd were Healey's colleagues."

"A handful is enough for it not to be coincidence in my book," Lucie replied, breathing slowly to calm herself.

"Maybe so, but it won't be enough for a court. Trust me, I know."

"I'm not interested in courts," Lucie answered, darkly, Ismail straightening up in response.

"Oh, really?" he said, their earlier roles of chastiser and chastised now reversed. "And what happened to the woman who prayed at the side of the guy she killed? What happened to the woman who fought back tears, insisting she wasn't a murderer? Because it sounds pretty clear to me that's what you're intending here."

He spoke the words sternly but calmly and without drama, and that was what made Lucie pay heed and catch herself before she allowed the clouds to regather. Ismail was right. She hadn't slept a wink after the events of the other night, instead spending the dark hours sat cross-legged on the floor in her living room, promising an atonement to God that she didn't know how to make and welcoming the stiffness and cold her position invited, reasoning that comfort was the very last thing she deserved. Though the instinctive desire to defend her remark flirted momentarily across her mind, it was quickly supressed, and Lucie instead offered a warm smile to the man who had very quickly become her friend. He was still so new to this world and she suspected he would always at heart be a police officer, honouring a system he found flawed and often corrupt, but which still represented to him the safety barrier that prevented justice falling into the hands of the mob.

"You're right," she said softly, allowing the smile to grow. "Sorry, I'm just... just pissed off."

"I understand," Ismail reassured her, reaching across the table and putting his hand nervously atop her own. Lucie hesitated for a moment and almost withdrew, but the warmth and softness of his touch felt so natural to her that she was content to sit in silence for a moment and simply enjoy it. The crash of a dropped mug from behind the counter pulled her from the moment and she quickly sat back upright, snapping her hand to her side as Ismail's expression dropped slightly in disappointment.

"Anyway," said Lucie, flustered, "what did you mange to learn from the flashdrive?"

"More than I thought I would, that's for sure," Ismail answered, finishing his coffee and sliding the cup away. "What you and Lake are lacking in gadget-laden spy cars you make up for with software, put it that way."

"Glad to be of service."

"First of all..." He paused as the chime of the door sounded and a young man with an unshaven face and a fearsome expression trudged in and made his way to the takeaway counter on the far side of the room. Turning back to Lucie, Ismail dropped his voice a notch lower as he continued. "First of all, you can tell your new mate that she's made it onto the PSL, seems she was already near the top of the list, even before yesterday's meeting."

"First on the list, eh? Good for her, she deserves it."

"From the sound of things, I agree with you, but she's not first on the list."

"What do you mean?" Lucie raised an inquisitive eyebrow. "The whole point of yesterday was to get the suppliers in place ahead of the mass recruitment."

"That's what the brochure said," he nodded, "but that's not what happened. There's a supplier in place already that no-one was told about yesterday; been there a few months now too."

"Actively?"

"Yep. And I could have missed it but I can't see that they ever had to go to tender or pitch in the way everyone did yesterday, it looks like they were just taken straight on. Of course, I might be reading too much into that, they could always have had a relationship with this lot..."

"So did half the recruiters at yesterday's meeting," Lucie mused. "The whole point of this was to refresh the list for the new project. Who are the company?"

"*Augustus Nairn Ltd.*"

"Fancy name. Anything dodgy about them?"

"For the most part they seem quite reputable, at least as reputable as recruitment companies can get. Augustus Nairn himself is a bit of a curiosity though."

"How so?"

"He doesn't exist. Never has."

Ismail pulled his phone from his pocket and quickly brought up the *Augustus Nairn* website, handing the device to Lucie.

"He's a made-up name, designed to give the company a grand, respectable image. It's not an uncommon business strategy. What's more interesting is who *really* controls things."

Lucie looked down the garish page, resplendent with stock photos of professionals in various poses, all appearing frighteningly stiff and smiling unnaturally, and pressed her finger against the menu. Locating the 'who are we' tab, she scrolled down until she came across the title of 'Director' above an image of a bespectacled older man with a high forehead and thin, greying remnants of what had once been flowing blonde hair.

"Jarvis Whyte," Lucie exclaimed, a cynical laugh in her voice. "Giving contracts out to himself, eh? Cheeky bastard."

"That's one way the rich stay rich," Ismail smiled, matching her cynicism. "But that's not the bit that concerns me."

"Then what is?" Lucie asked, handing back the phone.

"Since they've been on board with the project, *Augustus Nairn* have focussed exclusively on recruiting for administrative roles, personal assistants and the like."

"And?"

"And, I didn't see any record of any applications, no interview notes or anything, not even a record of any vacancies the successful candidates had applied for."

"Maybe you were looking in the wrong place?"

"Maybe, but I was pretty careful. And that's not all. I can't find any social media footprint for any of the candidates."

"Nothing at all?

"Nothing." Ismail leant closer still as the door opened again and the surly man exited clutching a large paper cup, while a slow trickle of people shuffled in to replace him, jingling with change and squinting at the menu board as they came.

"One person with no online presence I could maybe understand, at a pinch two, but that would be rare in this day and age. But there is nothing for any of these people, not even CVs on online job boards, or LinkedIn profiles or anything. There are just copies of offer letters on the *WaterWhyte* database, confirmation of appointment and immediate posting to the company's Portsmouth site."

Lucie drained then last of her coffee as she processed Ismail's words.

"If they had no online presence and there were no formal vacancies to apply for, how could they be recruited in the first place?"

"That's the million-dollar question," Ismail answered, his eyes focussed and unblinking.

"Something tells me you've got the answer."

"Maybe," Ismail nodded, "or maybe it's just coincidence."

"There's no such thing," Lucie answered.

"Let's have it."

"The jobs all went to women."

"Nothing too unusual about that," Lucie responded.

"Women still make up the bulk of administrative staff, whichever the industry."

"I agree," nodded Ismail. "But exclusively women with absolutely no electronic footprint, who all just happened to step out of the ether and accept jobs there's no record of them applying for, or that were even advertised? I'm not buying it. And then there's the number of them..."

"How many?" Lucie quizzed, her stomach beginning to churn and her mind already guessing the answer.

"Six."

Lucie's eyes dropped to the table and she shook her head, at once excited they now had a lead, and angry with herself for having taken so long to find it.

"Our women," she said softly. "You're sure?"

"The names don't tally but look at this."

Ismail reached again for his phone, holding it up for Lucie to see. On the screen was a photograph of an attractive, dark haired young woman, one of the missing six; the picture adorning her Facebook profile.

"You recognise her?"

"Hagne Pappas," Lucie answered immediately, the faces and names of each of the women etched across her mind. "Greek, twenty-four years old."

"Top of the class," Ismail grimaced, scrolling through his phone again for a new picture. "There were very few photographs in the files, at least that I saw, but let me introduce you to Khryseis Angelis."

He held up the mobile once more, and Lucie found herself staring at the exact same face. The pose was different, the hair more professionally styled and the features unsmiling and rigid, but it was without doubt the face of Hagne Pappas.

"Bastards," whispered Lucie as she took in the image. "They've robbed her of herself... what about the rest?"

"I couldn't find any more pictures, but the others have to be our women. This is a far bigger operation than we thought."

"You're telling me," Lucie frowned. "So, whoever is at the top of this tree is using yellow vest knuckle scrapers to kidnap European women they target on social media, pack them along to *WaterWhyte Defence* via *Augustus Nairn* under the guise of job applicants, where they get stripped of their identities and disappear to God knows where."

"Never to be seen again," Ismail finished.

"Well you and me are going to make bloody sure they are seen again, mark my words."

Lucie stood to leave as more people began filling the coffee house and the next table became occupied, Ismail following suit.

"I still don't understand why it's only been European women targeted so far," he mused, "or what the hell the motive could be for two multi-million-pound companies to be involved in people trafficking. And while we're on the subject, why would a long-standing MP be involved in it all? I mean, I know half the buggers are corrupt, but, trafficking?"

"And not just trafficking," Lucie added as they threw on their coats and headed to the door. "Don't forget about the mystery of the phantom weapons systems too. All in all, there's something decidedly bloody nasty going on and Jarvis Whyte is at the centre of it, which means there's only one place to start."

"Will Lake let us go for it?" Ismail queried, pulling open the door and holding it.

"Don't worry about him," she answered as she stepped through. "He's a bastard but he knows when a lead looks hot. If he's any sense he'll let us just get on with it."

"And what does 'getting on with it' look like?"

"Well that depends," Lucie mulled as they set off briskly down the street. "What else did you find in those files?"

"One or two things of interest," came the response, "but I also found something of interest in the social media of our missing women, specifically about that group they belonged to; or rather Lake's team did."

"Yeah?"

"Another member, also a professional European woman under forty."

"You think she's under threat?

"It's a reasonable assumption," Ismail confirmed, "but you should hear the name."

"Why?" Lucie asked, instinct telling her that the answer would not be good news and Ismail's face confirming it as he stopped walking and turned to face her.

"Monika," he said. "Monika Barenyi."

18

Lucie climbed the steps of Crewe House, London's Saudi embassy, with a professional determination fuelled by the uncooperative and belligerent obstruction of the man she was marching to face. Monika's membership of the Facebook group, combined with her name appearing on the *WaterWhyte* list, caused Lucie both further guilt and sufficient concern to place a guard outside the house Monika shared with friends in Shoreditch, while she took the information gathered a step further.

Ismail's reading of the files had led not only to revelations about the case, now inextricably linked with the *Red Mako* inquiries Algers had been wrestling with, but also reaped details of every press release relating to the project since its inception. While most of these didn't warrant a second glance, the latest entry had pricked Ismail's attention and presented them with a timely opportunity.

With the second phase recruitment team now in place and hundreds of roles about to open for application, a press conference had been arranged to herald the new era of independence for Brexit Britain ahead of a black-tie dinner at the Saudi embassy that evening.

A call to Lake and a hastily arranged press pass later, and Ismail was taking his place in the midst of a grand, parliamentary conference room full of scribblers and hacks, while Lucie sat in the ante-room, watching the spectacle unfold on the monitor alongside a handful of other aides and advisers.

Eventually, and to a fanfare of clicking cameras and flashes of light, three figures entered the conference room and sat behind the table set up beneath an ancient and impressive tapestry depicting Wellington's troops driving the Old Guard from the field at Waterloo.

The figure in the middle of the trio garnered most of the attention, and to any observer of current events it was obvious why. After the latest round of Ministerial resignations saw the government lose its Defence Secretary, the Prime Minister had opted – or some said had been advised by the Hardliners – to promote a junior Minister at the department rather than shuffle someone sideways into the role. In consequence, it was Adam Butcher MP who had sat facing the cameras, dressed in a suit sharper than any Mako's tooth and wearing the perpetual smirk which had made him infamous in political circles.

Although Butcher had never been blessed with an over-abundance of intelligence, at least none he had ever displayed, what he lacked in IQ he made up for in raw political cunning. To the extreme Brexiters he had long been the darling of the movement; handsome, despite the persistent sneer, and popular with the media. His charming voice and uncanny ability to twist whatever question he was asked into an opportunity to spout the latest Leaver soundbites, had proved unswervingly attractive to booking managers in TV studios up and down the country. It was a political charm that had taken him to the Cabinet. So too had he garnered support in the country, when the recent tragic suicide of his estranged mother had afforded him the opportunity to show a hitherto untapped emotional side to interviewers.

Having already piloted the trial 'Legalisation of Sexual Premises Act' through the Commons, and now having taken the Defence Portfolio, to many on the government benches he was ideally positioned to take the keys to Number Ten whenever Damocles' sword may fall on the PM, a prospect that looked increasingly likely.

To Butcher's right sat the apparently emotionless Bandeer Al-Khatani, a representative of the Saudi government whose immaculate white thobes and keffiyeh provided a neat and respectable contrast to the sartorial peacock display preferred by his two companions. Lucie had known nothing of Al-Khatani, other than his role as the Butcher's counterpart in the Saudi government, which the press release had spoken of. But it was the third figure at the table that held Lucie's focused attention.

It was Jarvis Whyte himself who sat to Butcher's left, sweat glistening on his high forehead as he reached for the jug of water before him and poured himself a generous measure. It had been obvious to Lucie that Whyte was not relishing this appearance. A career back-bencher, he was renowned in Westminster for preferring to stand just adjacent to the limelight rather than in its glare, focussing his energies on increasing his millions through business rather than political interests. In fact it was a known character trait of the politician that he quickly grew bored of the day-to-day handling of his many projects, preferring instead to get the ball rolling on the latest scheme before handing over the reins and taking a back seat to count his money. Never the most attentive of constituency MPs, politics had always been more of a hobby to him than a career, and his parliamentary longevity owed more to the inherent safety of his seat and the colour of his rosette than it did any tireless commitment to his constituents. Despite his natural reticence though, he had duly taken his place at the table, dressed in a suit that rivalled Butcher's own for bite. His black framed glasses were pushed up to his nose, his face pale and uncertain in front of the camera flashes and rows of journalists before him.

As predicted, it had been Butcher who had opened the conference, so passionately extolling the glorious future he predicted for Brexit Britain that even some of his more ardent press supporters had stifled embarrassed murmurs. The *Red Mako*, he said, would be the symbol of the new Britain, unconstrained by Europe and showing the world that Britannia once more ruled the waves. The flicker of embarrassment on Al-Khatani's face at Butcher's choice of words had been brief but obvious to Lucie, and it had been the Saudi Minister's quiet cough that informed the Defence Secretary his speech should come to a close. Al-Khatani himself had spoken only briefly, to praise the Saudi-British collaboration on the project and express his thanks to Butcher for his work, and to Whyte, whose company would facilitate it. In response, Whyte had merely given a shallow nod, a quiet 'thank you' pushing its way through his thin lips.

It was when the floor had been opened to questions that Ismail had come into his own, Lucie watching with a satisfied smile as he played his part to perfection. Sitting three rows from the front, far enough away from the cameras to not be picked up by them, Ismail had waited while the usual suspects made their comments and the planted queries were raised, everything being directed towards Butcher, who answered with his usual mix of pleasantry and soundbite. After several minutes of this Ismail's hand was picked out and he had stood to voice his question, only to address Whyte, who looked back in wide-eyed shock and reached at once for the water.

"Mr Whyte," Ismail had begun, "Mr Butcher has been keen to talk about the prestige of the project and what a boost it will be for the post-Brexit economy that all the *Red Mako's* component parts will be produced in Britain, coincidentally by companies which all exist under the *WaterWhyte Defence* umbrella..."

"The, er, the tender process was entirely above board and..." Whyte had stuttered, what little colour there was in his cheeks noticeably draining as he spoke.

"I'm sure," Ismail had interjected in apparent sincerity. "But perhaps you could explain why the weapons systems are being produced entirely in Saudi Arabia?"

Whyte had simply stared at his inquisitor, blinking and speechless, his mouth wordlessly opening and closing as though his vocal cords had stalled. Lucie had thought he might stay like that indefinitely before he was rescued by Butcher, who clarified that certain parts of the platform were being constructed by the Saudis directly, and the only contracts issued had gone to British companies so there was no reliance on European supply chains.

Undeterred, Ismail had followed up by quizzing how another of Whyte's companies, *Augustus Nairn*, had been able to source and employ administrative staff for vacancies which had apparently never been formally released to open application. Again, the perspiring MP had mumbled something about targeted headhunting for 'particular roles', before Butcher again interjected. "I think you've had your turn," he said in a professionally jocular tone, "let's give someone else a go," before pointing to a friendly face in the crowd and fielding a question about the significance of the new boat's colour scheme.

Whyte's reaction had been everything Lucie had expected, and she was not about to relieve the pressure now. The press conference was to be followed that evening by a reception and dinner at the Saudi embassy whose steps she now climbed, her jeans black, her overcoat buttoned tight and a modest black scarf respectfully cradling her head. Each Member of Parliament had receive an invitation to the Ambassador's reception, though it was expected that many, the indisposed Kasper Algers included, would politely – or not so politely – decline. A quiet word in diplomatic ears ensured that his invitation was re-issued in Lucie's name, and she wordlessly presented it to the embassy guards as she entered, refusing to allow her focus to be distracted by small talk or polite conversation as she scanned the splendour of the function room for her prey.

It did not take long for her to find him; Jarvis Whyte, immaculate in black tie, and with several members of Parliament's more extreme groups surrounding him in the centre of the spacious grandeur.

In the more social surroundings, Whyte was the antithesis of his earlier self before the cameras, charming an apparently inexhaustible string of guests with light conversation and laughing uproariously at whatever jokes were thrown in. The lack of alcohol in no way diminished his joi de vivre, and he behaved as though he were working the crowd at a constituency fund-raiser, holding his glass of water like it was an aged Scotch, with each sip to be savoured in the memory.

The first part of Lucie's plan was dangerous, not least because of the risk not just to her but that posed to Monika too; hence Ismail now busily preparing the second part of the plan. But she reasoned it was the only way. If the British press had paid so little attention to the disappearance of a number of European women including the murder of one of them, it would take something pretty special to wake them up now. Likewise, it stood to reason that the politician into whose businesses the women had vanished would have some idea how the political pressure on the police not to investigate the crimes had been leveraged. Lucie knew she had to create that unwanted attention herself.

She cut through the crowd silently, never taking her eyes from Whyte's face, until she hung at the back of the crowd around the MP as he regaled them with tales of his own back-breaking efforts in bringing the contract to Britain, and how the contract's success would send a message to the Remoaners with their 'project fear' that there was a prosperous future for the country.

"You didn't answer the question," Lucie coldly pointed out as the laughter and cheers died down.

The chatter stopped and Whyte looked pointedly at her, his brow creasing over his glasses and the slightest hint of pink appearing on his cheeks as he processed the unexpected question in a room which was supposed to have been wholly complimentary towards him.

"Excuse me?"

"I said, you didn't answer the question. Today, in the press conference. You were asked how it was that all of the sub-contracts for the *Red Mako* project are connected in some way to *WaterWhyte Defence*. Sounds almost like a monopoly to me..."

"Madam, I'm sorry but I've no idea what you're talking about..."

"Yes you do."

Whyte's brow, already furrowed in confusion at the unexpected and decidedly unwelcome approach, creased further still.

"I'm afraid I..."

"I suppose it must just be a coincidence," she cut him off, her voice still austere and controlled. "Just like it must be a coincidence that six women have disappeared without trace, at a time when six women seemingly appeared out of nowhere and were employed in admin positions within your company. Another was murdered, Mr Whyte. Perhaps she failed the interview."

The chattering had stopped, replaced with whispers and puzzled looks, Whyte's own features morphing from confusion to outright anger as he puffed and stumbled for some kind of answer, before a spark of distant recognition appeared behind his eyes.

"Wait a moment... yes, I thought so, you're Algers' girl, aren't you? I might have known that even unconsciousness isn't enough to stop him from being a pest."

It was enough for the laughter from the braying chorus behind him to start again, the sound reviving the confidence in Whyte's features.

"That's not very nice, Mr Whyte, Kasper is in in hospital right now, put there by a man on your payroll, no less."

"There's no evidence..."

"The same man who chased after me and a friend of mine in a car the other night, firing bullets at us."

"Look, if you have something the police ought to be aware of, then I can only recommend that..."

"And I'm nobody's 'girl' Mr Whyte," Lucie replied with fixed eyes above her cynical smile. "I'm the woman who will bring you down and reveal all your little secrets to the whole watching world. You Brexshitters have got most of the British press in your pockets, but there are still enough independent minds out there to take an interest in your handiwork, even if they have to go to other countries to be published."

Whyte's voice dropped to match Lucie's, and his face took on a stern and sinister quality totally at odds with his public persona.

"And they'd be bloody stupid to try," he almost whispered to her. "Let them publish what they like and they won't just be damned, I'll destroy them in every libel court in the land. I worked my fingers to the bone to bring this contract to *WaterWhyte Defence*, and I've made sure thousands of people can keep their jobs because of it. And for traitorous Remoaners like yourself to try and throw all of that into doubt, just because you don't like the result of a democratic vote is beyond the pale!"

"Democratic vote?" Lucie smirked, resisting her desire to relish the man's discomfort and keeping her mind focussed, knowing that every twitch of her features and inflection in her voice further infuriated him. "A vote that only certain people are allowed to take part in can't call itself democratic. You Brexshitters don't care about democracy, despite all your bleating; you just care about perverting it enough to suit your ends, and to hell with everyone who gets crushed in the process."

"Now, really, this is outrageous..." Whyte spluttered.

"Tough," Lucie interrupted, her voice calm and measured as she fought to control her rising anger.

"I know about the women, Mr Whyte," she continued. "And I know you know what happened to them."

The glamorously attired guests assembled behind the frothing MP were rising in number as voices hushed and eyes focussed on him, his cheeks rapidly turning from simple pink, moving with each syllable through dark ochre before settling on an indignant crimson. While ignoring her new audience, Lucie played to them masterfully, stepping closer to Whyte, her finger pointing inescapably at him.

"And I know who the next woman on the list is, too. It ends. Now."

The expression on Whyte's face twisted into one of pure hatred, and for a moment Lucie thought he might actually try to strike her, before he regained control of himself and spoke loudly to the guests still flocking around the scene.

"I'm glad you're all here to see this," he said loudly. "This woman works in the offices of the infamous Kasper Algers. And while all of us are sorry at the fate that has befallen him, we can at the same time condemn the attitude and opinions of those who claim him as a figurehead. They're so desperate to ignore the opportunities of Brexit that they'll even stoop to using the tragic murder of an innocent to smear those of us who champion those opportunities!"

The crowd was back onside, save for a small handful who looked curiously from Whyte to Lucie and hung back from the group. For the most part though, they laughed and crowed, some making boorish comments fuelled by the booze they had managed to sneak into the event, while others cried 'shame' and tutted, as though they were still sleeping off their lunches in Parliament.

Seizing his moment of victory, Whyte stepped closer, his voice once more dropping to a sinister level.

"I wonder if the press will pick up your story after all," he said, "or whether tomorrow's headlines will instead condemn the Remoaners who would use the memory of a murdered woman to attack Britain's future."

Before Lucie could respond, the elegant figure of Al-Khatani appeared beside her, his face as emotionless as it had appeared in the conference, his voice stern.

"My apologies, madam, but other guests have complained, and your behaviour is causing a disturbance."

"Well we can't have that, can we?"

"Though I would prefer if you stayed, I must ask you to address your behaviours, lest you be required to leave. Now, may I fetch you some water?"

"Don't bother," said Lucie, grinning, "this one'll do."

Snatching the glass from Whyte's hand, Lucie threw the contents at the MP, who gasped as the cold water coated him and a fanfare of condemnation blew up around her.

"Madam!" exclaimed Al-Khatani, at whose beckoning, two robed, muscular men began to move through the crowd towards them.

"Remember," Lucie hissed at the dripping Whyte, "it ends now, or I end you."

The look he fixed her with before she turned and headed from the building stayed burned into Lucie's mind as she walked, but she couldn't worry about that now. She had played her hand in the most public way possible, and she could only hope both that it was enough to provoke retaliation, and that she and Ismail could prevent another victim from being added to the list.

Brushing past the gate security, Lucie headed down Charles Street, before turning onto Queen's Street, where she had parked the car allocated to her after the untimely demise of Ismail's Peugeot. As she opened the door to the scratched and dented Fiesta, she wondered momentarily whether Lake had a side-line in crap used cars, before her thoughts returned to the danger she had placed Monika in.

It was a hunch, Lucie acknowledged, to believe that Monika was necessarily the next on Whyte's list, but she had learned to trust her instincts, and was grateful that Ismail had begun to do likewise. She also acknowledged, a little more shamefully, that she was gambling the woman's safety on Lucie's own ability to protect her; a wager she would feel significantly more comfortable about if she knew precisely what form the threat would take.

Monika's name appeared on their files for a reason, and she matched the profile of the others too completely for it to be a coincidence. Lucie's antics in the embassy would, she was sure, lead either to them making their move to have her disappear the same way as the others, or backing away before scrutiny became too great; she hoped it was the latter. Lucie switched on the engine and pulled into traffic, telling herself again that this was the only way to save her new friend. She could only pray silently that the second part of her plan would work.

19

The drive from Mayfair to Shoreditch took around forty minutes, and Lucie's nerves did not settle at any point in the journey. She had left Ismail earlier that evening, with Monika's safety his paramount concern, and she had sent a text as she left the embassy to let him know she was on the way, but the natural concern she had for the recruiter had soon given way to worry as no reply came. Twice on the way she had tried calling Ismail, but his phone remained stubbornly silent.

By the time she turned into the freshly gentrified Totter's Lane, her worry had turned to fear. There was still no answer from Ismail, while across the driveway of number 76, where Monika resided, sat a black Audi of the type that had chased them so relentlessly through Primrose Hill, nights before. Lucie cruised past the house, straining to see inside the curtained windows for any signs of life or activity but to no avail. Most likely, she mused, the road itself was being watched for either signs of trouble, or perhaps the arrival of Lucie herself; if she were the one inside the property, it was what she would do.

Pulling the car in at the far end of the lane, Lucie ducked into the driveway of the end house and scrambled over the gate which gave entry to the small back garden. Gentrified though the district had become, the houses themselves were still reliable old terraces, solid in construction and linked at the rear by a modest yard and garden space, punctuated by wooden fencing in various states of disrepair. Lucie negotiated those fences as silently as she could as she made her way towards number 76, pressing herself against cover whenever a kitchen light flicked on or a window opened.

By her count, the next garden would be behind 76, and Lucie could see that the untidily kept lawn was bathed in a shallow light, coming from the rear French windows, but still she could see no movement or discern any noise. The upper bedroom windows were closed shut and curtained, and while she could look straight into the kitchen, the light was off and there was no-one within, at least none that she could see. The French windows themselves were at too tight an angle for her to look fully inside.

The freezing damp in the night air had begun to provoke her bad knee into its usual belligerence, and she warned herself not to give in to its twinges as she slipped her gun into her hand and slid over the fence. Keeping to the edges, she skipped over unkempt flower beds and pressed her back against the cold bricks of the house, pausing to scan the area before ducking under the kitchen window and straightening up as she reached the edge of the tall glass panes through which the dim light shone out. A knot of anxiety tightened within her as she paused to fill her lungs in readiness for whatever lay within, and it grew tauter still as she cautiously inched her head around the brickwork, the sight filling her at once with horror and righteous fury.

Inside the otherwise unremarkable room sat Ismail, broken and bloodied, strapped to a wooden chair, his head lolling and his chest heaving erratically. Lucie's eyes flashed to all the alcoves in the room she could see, before calling her bad knee into action and kicking hard at the handle of the windows, slamming them open with tremendous force before rushing to her stricken friend and kneeling by him, lifting his head and willing his eyes to focus on her.

"Look at me, "he ordered, "Asif, look at me!"

The eyes, devoid of the mischievous charm she had come to depend on rolled up towards her and he began shaking his head, almost violently.

"Don't," he spluttered, "they're here for you, it's a trap."

"Of course it's a fucking trap," she answered, a sad smile on her face and her eyes dampening. "But that's not going to stop me helping you."

The thump of boots on stairs sounded above and Ismail leant forward to touch his forehead against Lucie's, both understanding what was coming next.

"My angel," he whispered.

"The foolish kind," she smiled softly back.

On cue, the living room door smashed open, splintering against the wall, and Lucie spun on her knees, the gun still clasped tightly in her hands, and fired off two shots into the shins of the of the first black-clad figure lurching towards her. Rolling away in time to dodge the shot from the second figure entering the room, Lucie re-aimed and fired a felling shot into his shoulder, the masked man crumpling alongside his fallen comrade.

"Look out!"

Ismail forced the warning from his battered body and Lucie turned just in time for the swinging knuckles of a third attacker, fresh from the adjoining kitchen, to connect against her temple. Dazed, she staggered backwards and felt the gun being knocked from her hand by the third thug, insults directed at both she and her mother as he did so. Her focus returning as a second punch came her way, Lucie caught the fist in the air with both hands and moved swiftly to twist the limb upwards behind her attacker's back. The man fell to his knees, reaching in vain over his shoulder, unable to break free from Lucie's grip.

"Where's Whyte keeping them?" she shouted into his ear.

"Fuck you, bitch!"

"Where?" she roared again, punctuating her request with a further twist to his arm.

"You'll find out soon enough!"

The new voice came from behind her, and Lucie cursed as another sickening thump struck across her skull, sending her sprawling. Her senses reeling, she could only listen in helplessness to the echoey voices of her assailants.

"Fuckin' whore," spat the one she had bested. "Take her upstairs, let's see how she likes it when she can't move her arms."

"That's not the deal," voiced the one who had struck her from behind. "Bring the van round, get her and the Paki inside."

"The van can fuckin' wait!" The oaf was becoming argumentative. "This is the bitch that did Jon in, now look what she's done to Nige and Jake!"

The screams of the two felled gunmen still filled the air, and Lucie tried to raise her head towards them.

"You might have thought the sun shone out of Healey's arse, but I couldn't give a fuck, now get them in the fuckin' van!"

"But Nige and Jake!"

A noise like the sound of a heavy book hitting a table filled the room twice, which even Lucie's addled brain recognised as the double shot of a silenced handgun, taking with it as it died away the screams of the injured men.

A moment of silence enveloped the room, save for Ismail's heavy breathing, before Lucie heard a quiet but angered voice cursing emphatically.

"See?" said the other, "I don't give a fuck about Nige and Jake, either, and if you think you're charming and intelligent enough to be the exception to the rule I'd advise to think again. Now fuckin' MOVE!"

Their arguing gave Lucie the respite she needed to stretch life back into her fingers, as her eyes settled on the gun that had been knocked from her hands. Stretching her arm forward a centimetre at a time, her middle finger brushed the grip of the weapon and a flame of excitement lit within her as she focused on the game-changer within her reach.

Instead of the sensation of the gun in her grasp, a boot stamped down onto her outstretched hand and a second met her ribs, sending a burning pain through her body which caused her to curl up in agony.

"Nighty night, bitch," she heard the calmer voice spit into her ear, before the hard rubber of a cosh smacked across the back of her head, and blackness overcame her.

20

———————

Lucie wasn't sure exactly how long she'd been out, and it took a few minutes for her mind to fully embrace lucidity after her eyelids first began to flicker back into life. She was in a vehicle of some sort, that much was obvious by the noise of traffic and the thuds that shook her body every few seconds as whatever she was in traversed the roads. Trying to move, she quickly found her hands tied behind her back. She was also hooded, something she had experienced once before when dragged through the Afghan desert by her captors.

Though her back was stiff, and her arms and legs ached and yearned for freedom, Lucie kept completely still. She remembered voices in the house saying something about a van, and it seemed pretty obvious that it was said vehicle now transporting her. She had no way of knowing who else if anyone might have been in there with her. Nor indeed would she risk any further harm to Ismail, who for all she knew was inside the van with her. As she half sat, half lay there, waiting to arrive at wherever her destination may be, she took comfort in her calmness. She might have been foolish to rush in to Ismail's rescue, but she was in control of her emotions now, and consequently had not completely lost control of her situation. She was a captive of her attackers, granted, at least until some suitable opportunity presented itself, but how she responded to that was her choice, and it was one undoubtedly better made with a clear brain.

The squeak of worn break pads and the slamming of cab doors told Lucie they had arrived at wherever they were meant to be, and she breathed in deeply to keep her nerves calm and stable. The engine was still running as the rear doors opened with a creak, followed by a stream of profanities from a voice she recognised as belonging to one of her attackers.

Still she offered no movement until she felt the grip of a rough hand on her collar, wrenching her head up. She allowed her body to follow with little resistance, until she reached the open doors and felt herself being pushed to the ground below. Though she had expected such an act and poised herself in readiness, the smack of her body against the hard gravel took the breath from her lungs.

It was the sound of a second 'thud' which confirmed Lucie's suspicion that she had not been alone in the van, and she tried to position herself closer to the second person as they were picked from the floor and pushed forwards, her feet crunching on the gravel as she went. There were three voices with them now, all men, two of whom she recognised from the house, while the third, a scouse lilt to his words, seemed to be in charge.

"You're late," the new voice berated them.

"Yeah, well, there were problems, weren't there," protested the less eloquent to the two. "She weren't there, none of them were. When we got to the house, the only one there was the Paki."

"So you don't even have the girl?"

"This other one's just as good, in't she? She's a fuckin' Euro too, so what's the problem?"

"The problem, dickhead, is that the boss handpicked the women he wanted, this silly bitch and her Muslim mate were supposed to be extras, and on top of that you put bullets through Jake and Nige!"

"That was him!"

"Ah, quit bitching."

Lucie allowed herself a smirk; their failure meant that Ismail himself had been successful in arranging safe haven for Monika and her housemates and keeping them from harm, not caring that it had cost him dearly to do so. Her affection for him had grown steadily since their first meeting, and now alongside it, Lucie felt the warm glow of pride.

The conversation, such as it was, ended, and Lucie found herself halted and the bag pulled roughly from her head. It was night, and there was little light from the grey, concrete wall in front of her to hurt her eyes, but her vision was still blurred and strained and she blinked hard to clear her sight. The night air rushed to her freshly unguarded cheeks, but with an added scent that Lucie would have recognised as the sea even without her days in the Merchant Navy.

Her vision clearing, Lucie took in her surroundings as quickly as she could. The grey wall was one part of what looked a huge building, but in the black of night and devoid of light, it was hard to properly gauge the size. A metal door was built into the wall which one of the figures, bulky and still clad in black, was straining to open. Lucie could feel a second figure standing behind her, breathing a sickly breath of stale booze and spent cigarettes onto her, while the third was stood closer to the door, a now likewise unhooded Ismail in his grip.

Ismail! It was all Lucie could do not to lunge forward and embrace her wounded friend, even with her hands tied, but she speedily repressed the urge, offering the battered policeman a surreptitious half-smile, obliquely reciprocated, before returning her stare to the man at the metal door.

He and his cohorts had removed their ski masks, the safety of home turf presumably affording them a confidence and invulnerability not felt back at the house. The man with the scouse accent, who now wrestled with the door, was skeletally thin, with shoulder length hair and a fading bruise on his cheek bone. Of his two comrades, one was squat and somewhat bulky looking, but wore an expression of cruelty on his face which assured her he was still capable of serious harm. His colleague, the one who had finished off his partners in crime at the house, was taller, with a shaved head. His eyes shone with an intelligence she didn't see in the other two, coupled with a resentment that he was taking instructions from a man he clearly considered beneath him.

"Mind the step," the first man sneered at the pair as they were led down a short flight of stairs into a brightly lit breeze-block corridor which stretched into the distance and was lined on either side with further metal doors.

Stopping outside one, the man at the front jangled with keys and heaved it open to reveal a barren storage room, lit by a single bulb. He gestured for Ismail and Lucie to enter, while she felt the flick of a knife release her from her bonds. Ismail's 'handler' helped him into the cold room, cut his hands free and deposited him unceremoniously onto the floor. Lucie dropped to one knee to check him before turning back to the three strangers who stood ready to close the door.

"You can have a rest in here for a bit," came the scouse tones. "Till we let the boss know we have you. Oh, and don't try to escape, eh?"

"Or what?" Lucie quizzed, coldly. "I end up like the French girl you raped and murdered?"

What sounded like a snort of contempt came from the shorter man, his cruel face twisting into a malicious sneer and his eyes fixing on Lucie with an all-too-readable intent.

"Well, you might have a bit of a problem there," the 'leader' of the trio laughed. "As long as you stay in here, you'll be alright, but if you try to get out, well…"

"Your guard dog tries his luck?"

"Something like that. You see, Gary here doesn't have many hobbies, he's not well-read or articulate like you and me. There is something he enjoys though."

"No prizes for guessing what that is."

'Gary' laughed out loud, a sinister, mocking sound which pierced the air between them.

"Never had much time for birds has Gary; thinks they're only good for one thing. We used to have a guy here who kept him in check as it happens, a bloke called Jon. Couldn't stand rapists, Jon couldn't."

"Honour amongst thieves, eh?"

"If you like. Jon was fine with knocking ten shades of shit out of MPs and activists; he was a bugger for that, but rape? Not his kettle of fish. But Jon and Gary got on, so well in fact that whenever Gary got his urges, Jon would have a quiet word and Bob's your uncle."

"I take it Jon was on a day off when this piece of shit killed Ines Aubel?"

"Ah, well," the man began, "those were special orders, you see, right from the top. But ordinarily Jon was on hand to make sure nothing like that went on. Trouble is, Jon's not here no more, someone put a bullet in his head a few nights back when he was out for a drive."

"Really? Shame Gary wasn't driving."

Lucie struggled to prevent the disgust she felt at the thin

man and his crew from showing on her face, though it seemed only to encourage him to continue his mockery.

"Funny how life turns out, eh?" he laughed. "You killed just about the only guy who could have looked after you."

"What makes you think I need a guy to look after me?"

"I'll remind you of that later, sweet cheeks, you might find yourself changing your mind."

"Yeah? Well, they say that life's a bitch," Lucie answered with murderous cynicism, "and then you piss off the wrong one and she kills you."

The thin man's eyes narrowed for a moment as he stared back at her, before taking hold of the heavy door and beginning to close it.

"Maybe," he laughed in contempt, "but I haven't met her yet."

She offered no further retort, but instead fixed him with a look of dangerous intent as the heavy door began to swing into place and she was left with nothing but the sound of 'Gary's' receding laughter, and the heavy breathing of her stricken friend.

21

Sat on the floor with his head back against the breeze block wall, Ismail was wheezing in low, regulated breaths; the tell-tale signs of an injured man trying to retain control of his battered body. Lucie had seen such sights before in the deserts of Afghanistan and remembered with dread how they so often preceded tearful requests for final prayers and absolution. Lucie had offered comfort to the dying so many times, but now it was her friend, *her love*, lying before her, the words dried up and refused to be spoken.

Was he dying, though? Lucie couldn't tell but it worried her that she wasn't moving close enough to find out, and she might well have stayed standing by the door for eternity had he not turned his face to her and grinned his infectious grin.

"Don't worry," he said through bruised lips. "It feels worse than it looks."

Though her emotions fought against it, Lucie chuckled, and she knelt down beside him, her instincts taking over as she checked his pulse and mentally timed his breaths.

"I've been waiting ages for you to check my vitals," the wounded man joked.

"Behave yourself or I'll give you a real injury to worry about," she replied in faux chastisement. "Your heart doesn't seem to be too bad, but we need to get you out of here and bloody quickly."

"Ah," he answered, "I think I've spotted the flaw in the plan."

"I'll get us out of here," Lucie said, as she stood and marched back to the door, pressing her hands against it in a futile search for a crack or gap she could exploit.

"Lucie..."

"There must be a way to prise this door..."

"Lucie!"

She stopped and turned to him; the injustice of her own impotence etched onto her face for him to see. She stared wordlessly for a moment before shaking her head in apology.

"I'm sorry," she said. "For what?"

"Everything. I'm sorry for turning up at your station, I'm sorry for telling you I was SIS, I'm sorry for dragging you into this whole, bloody mess."

For a second he was silent, and Lucie wondered if his mind was composing some particular condemnation for her, but then he fixed her with his kind eyes and opened his bloodied jaw.

"The only thing you should be sorry for," he began, "is being in here with me. You should have left me where I was."

"They'd have killed you."

"I saved Monika. I'd have died a hero."

"I'd rather you didn't die at all."

"Don't be so sure," he answered. "When we get out of here, I intend to put in for a medal."

"I'll pin it to your chest myself."

Ismail's warmth even as he lay injured helped soothe Lucie's own tumultuous emotions, and she leaned against the wall opposite him, sliding down until she sat on the floor, her feet touching his.

"Monika," she began, "how is she?"

"She was a bit confused, but she's safe and so are her housemates. Lake has them in a safe house on the other side of London. I thought I could take them when they came for her, but they got the drop on me."

"And here we are," Lucie finished. "Wherever here is…"

"Wherever we are it's by the coast; didn't you smell the sea air when we arrived?"

"My nose is having an off day," he said, gesturing to his freshly crooked proboscis, Lucie smiling at his warped humour.

"Point taken. But I'd bet all the money I have we're at the *WaterWhyte* plant in Portsmouth. That's what? About a two-hour drive from London?"

"An hour and a half in good traffic."

"And it makes sense that whatever is happening to us happened to the missing women: kidnapped from London, driven down to Portsmouth and stuffed into the sprawling labyrinth of a defence giant, to end up God knows where."

"It looks like we'll find out pretty soon," Ismail opined. "I think I'm going to ask Lake for a couple of days off after this."

"He's not a big one for paid leave," Lucie laughed. "When I tried to take a few days in France, I ended up with a dodgy assignment, a hit list and a bullet wound."

"You know what?" Ismail began, his eyes wide in pretend shock at Lucie's words. "All in all, I'm beginning to wish I'd never been invited onto this team."

Lucie raised her head from her knees and stared at him for a moment before her shoulders began to rock with laughter.

"I have those days myself," Lucie smiled in fatalistic amusement. "Wish I could promise tomorrow will be any different."

"It'd better be," Ismail responded through heavy breaths, "or else woe betide them when the staff survey comes around."

Ismail's voice was growing quieter and Lucie watched as his eyes began to flicker and close.

"Hey!" she snapped, shuffling across to sit beside him. "None of that, stay with me Asif, eyes open if you please."

"I don't think I can," he shrugged softly, all trace of the joviality from moments earlier vanished.

"Then try harder!"

The volume of her voice jolted the fading policeman, and he pulled himself upright and heaved as fresh a breath as his lungs could muster into his chest, wincing and clutching his ribs as he moved.

"Yes, Ma'am," he gasped as he settled his aching and battered frame into its new position. "If you ever fancy a change of career, you'd make a hell of a drill Sergeant at the Police training college."

"No thanks," she smiled. "My days in uniform are behind me, and believe me mate, this stuff is as bad. Worse than that, it's addictive."

"Ha! Not to me it isn't."

"That's what you say now," Lucie smiled. "I said the same. You think you'll just be in it for one job, then you find yourself doing another, then another, and even though you go to sleep hating it with every fibre in your body, you wake up the next day rushing to do it all over again, like a drunk running to the pub. Take my advice, if Lake promised to let you go after this job then take him up on it and get your arse back to your police station double time."

Ismail was wheezing, the pain on his face obvious though he tried to mask it with his smile.

"And what about you?"

"I still have unfinished business," Lucie said solemnly, quickly fighting back the lump in her throat that always arrived when memories of her murdered mother replayed across her mind, followed closely by Lake's promise to help her track down the man responsible, Trystan Dagonet. "But if it was up to me, I'd find myself a little restaurant that needs a chef and play harp in the pubs on my night off."

"You play harp?"

"Blues harp," Lucie laughed, "the harmonica."

"Oh, a blues woman, eh?"

"A female Charlie Musselwhite."

"I'll take your word for it," replied the stricken Ismail, as he pondered the unfamiliar name, his eyes flickering once more, widening only when Lucie's hand tapped hard against his cheeks.

"I said wake up, lover boy."

She reached out as his strength began to fail him, his broken body inching sideways down the wall. Cradling his head and shoulders against her breast she looked down at his face, surprised by quite how painful it was to see him in this state, but also strangely welcoming the sensation as proof that the growing affections she had felt towards him were genuine.

"Lover boy?" he parroted softly through smiling lips. "I like the sound of that."

"Yeah, well don't get too excited," she teased, "there's not much we can do about it in here."

"Actually, I think I'm feeling better..."

"I bet you are."

"In fact, I've a couple of ideas about how to aid my recovery."

"Get fucked," Lucie playfully warned.

"How did you guess?"

Laughter once again filled the freezing room, their grins wide but their eyes displaying only pain.

"Don't die on me, you bastard."

"Or what? Dying feels like a pretty good option right now."

"Because it's your turn to buy the coffee next."

Ismail clasped Lucie's hand and held it to his chest, bending forward to leave the softest kiss he could muster on her knuckle.

"You're something else, you know that? Okay then, I'll try not to die."

"You promise?"

"Only if you make me a promise in return," Ismail breathed. "We get out of here, I go back to the cops, you tell Lake to go shit in his hat and you find yourself that restaurant to cook in. And every spare night we have, we head out to the pub and you play that harp of yours."

"Yeah? And while I'm playing, what will you be getting up to?"

"Supporting you of course," he exhaled. "And, you know, drinking."

The laughs soon subsided and gave way to the sound of shivering bodies and wheezing lungs. It was just a dream and they both knew it; Ismail was losing the fight to retain consciousness with every minute that passed, and there was no way Lucie could get help to him. All she could do was feed the dream that kept them lucid, though the fear that she would soon be choking on the fantasy haunted her mind.

"Well," she said softly, "I suppose as long as you had a couple of beers waiting for when I finished my set, I could live with that."

"You could live with me too, if you like?"

"Live with you?"

"What's the point of us both struggling to pay the bills?"

"Careful lover boy, you agree a pub date and five seconds later we're moving in together?"

"Why not?" he smiled up at her. "I'm house broken, and a fabulous cook."

"I'm sure you do," Lucie conceded through her spreading grin, "but I have a job to do."

"A job you hate," corrected Ismail, "a job killing people…"

"Don't," she warned, "just don't."

Lucie had spent so many days since Lake had pulled her into this life doubting and even hating herself as she clawed around her soul for some kind of motivation to do the work she did. She had told herself that she wasn't a murderer, that she only killed as a last resort, but in her darker moments she knew that there had been lives she had enjoyed taking – perhaps even wanted to take. She had been born with a ferocious temper that her dad had always put down to the 'crazy arse Czech blood' she inherited from her mother. When depression took vicious hold of her mind her temper could grow to levels she couldn't control, and she would be lying if she claimed never to have killed while under its influence. Even her short tenure in this business had brought her into contact with true evil and true evil doers, and many were the nights she had asked herself if it was really a sin to send such evil from this world to the next? She knew of course that it was, and for every shot she had fired, she had spent hours wearing her knees to the bone in penitence. Her work was dirty, and she knew it. But hearing the man in her arms declare it so placed a knife upon her heart, and she had no desire for him to push it in.

Ismail looked wordlessly up at her. There was no judgement in his face and no condemnation, just an honest and loving concern for the soul behind the eyes he looked into. He squeezed her hand tighter, stroking her rapidly cooling flesh with his thumb.

"We've all done things we're not proud of," he said. "Sometimes we just need someone to tell us to stop."

"I don't know if I can," she answered. "I don't know if I want to."

"Well I'm not surviving unless you promise to."

Lucie returned his gaze and wondered if he could see the

tears she could feel building in her eyes. His broken body was growing colder and his voice weaker, and Lucie wondered whether his was a promise that could be kept, but if her acquiescence gave him even the slightest boost it was worth it. And in any case, it would have been another lie to say that the shared dream their words had built did have a hold on her heart at least as strong as did her employment.

She leant forward and pressed her lips against his, ignoring the turmoil in her mind and the blood, sweat and tears on their bodies.

"Ok," she softly said. "I promise."

"You promise?" he echoed, his voice already stronger. "You and me?"

"Why not? We could give it a go. Back to the cops for you…"

"And back to the…"

"If you even think about saying 'back to the kitchen' I'll finish you off myself."

"Point taken. Back to chef 's whites and blues for you. Mosque on Fridays and church on Sundays, unless you're working."

"I never miss church," answered Lucie, ignoring the tear that had fallen from her cheek onto his. He tightened his grip on her hand as tears of his own began to fill his eyes and trickle down the side of his head to mix with the blood.

"I think you might be missing it this week."

"We're not dead yet."

Goosebumps covered Ismail's skin, and Lucie slipped off her treasured overcoat and covered him with it, sitting back alongside him and letting him lean closer into her. She may not be able to save him but she would offer what comfort she could now, for as long as she was needed.

"Lucie?" His voice sounded from her lap. "Asif?" She replied.

"Now that we're about to embark on a whole new life

together, I feel I can finally tell you something that's been bothering me for a while."

"Yeah? What's that?"

"I really need a piss."

Their laughter warmed them as they huddled tightly together in a protective embrace, waiting for whatever would come next. Lucie knew that any window for escape would be brief and that she must be prepared for it, but right now this man needed her, and she was content in that moment to be needed. Her kind started to drift before being dragged back into the real world by the slam of a metal door and shouts of their captors.

Blinking away her blurred vision, Lucie jumped to her feet and threw a punch at the man coming for her as she tried to force her way through to Ismail, who was being dragged through the door by another figure. Her distraction was her downfall, as the felled attacker, the thin Liverpudlian she had earlier confronted, rose back up and thrust a rag hard into her face, while another pulled her arms behind her. The aroma was sweet and overpowering, like strong vodka mixed with sugar, and made Lucie sick to her stomach, her sinuses filling instantly and her senses failing. Still the man held the rag in place, not allowing any chance for her to recover her mind and fight back, but Lucie cared only about the stricken Ismail.

The last image she saw as her sight gave up and plunged her back into night, was of her partner and friend hauled down the corridor outside, a mocking thug on either side.

"Don't worry about him pet, worry about yourself," came the cruel voice, fading in her ears. "It's time for you to make a covenant."

22

———

The angered cry that shot through Lucie's ears as she awoke came from her own throat, and she threw herself upright, forcing her eyes open and air into her lungs as she waited the tortuous eternity for her senses to return. The movement exacerbated the dizziness she felt and the more her surroundings came into focus, the greater the pain in her head pounded and throbbed. Her forehead felt clammy and cold, and goosebumps had broken out all over her body.

Keeping still enough for the pain to subside, she examined her surroundings, expecting to have found herself almost anywhere except where she appeared to be. Around her were the walls of what looked like a sparsely decorated but otherwise average looking bedroom, containing a wardrobe, bedside table and a window with blandly coloured curtains drawn. Lucie was lying in a relatively comfortable double bed, made with white cotton sheets and a duvet devoid of pattern or colour, and as she risked the protestations of her aching head by inching herself upwards, she looked down to see she was dressed in only a plain, short nightdress.

Her anger at the violation rose in an instant, fuelling and re-energising her enough to overcome the debilitating pain in her skull and rise from the bed. Although ready and quite willing to rampage through wherever she was until she found those responsible, she knew that the reality of her situation demanded she retain her focus, and she had no intention whatsoever of giving her captors the satisfaction of witnessing an emotional response. Of her own clothes there was no sign, but fresh underwear and a business suit were hanging from the handle of the wardrobe. Ignoring them for the moment, the sound of traffic led Lucie to the window and pulling back the curtains she peered out onto the street, frowning in incredulity at what she saw.

She, and the building she stood in, were inside what seemed like an enormous warehouse structure, upon the walls of which the image of a dawn sky was projected, complete with a rising sun in the distance and accompanied by the chirp of early morning birdsong. The traffic she heard was in reality a single car, its hollowed out chassis attached to a pole, inside which sat a battered wax mannequin, 'driving' around a track on a makeshift street, encircling a row of 'shops' flimsily constructed from what looked like plywood, like some ghoulish merry-go-round.

"What the...?"

Ignoring the pain in her head and shaking free from dizziness, Lucie ran from the room, passed the immaculately laid out living room, kitchen and bathroom, down the stairs and outside onto the 'street', the noise of everyday life continuing to build, mimicking the sounds of any awakening city she had lived in. Everywhere she looked, worn out and clumsily painted mannequins, dressed in a multitude of attires, stared back at her through soulless plastic eyes, as though voicelessly willing her to join them in damnation. There had to be a way out of here, Lucie thought, resisting the stares of her morbid company and setting off barefoot around the bizarre town, her eyes analysing every nook and cranny as she ran towards its perimeter. As she passed the final building, the warehouse shutters beyond it in sight, an ear-splitting alarm screeched in hysterical objection, the spy crashing to her knees, her hands pressed so tightly to her still throbbing head that it thumped all the more angrily in protest.

The sound grew louder as she attempted to inch herself forward, until she could move no more, a stentorian voice booming the words 'NO EXIT' from somewhere high above. Lucie dragged herself back towards the plywood prison, crossing back over the perimeter and leaning against a fake wall as she breathed deeply and relished the sudden silence as the screech finally died and the agonising pulsing in her head began to subside.

Slowly recovering, she looked back at the exit she had run towards, which stood mirage-like, shrouded by the projection of rolling fields and a burgeoning sunlit day. Tempted for a moment to ponder why someone would go to the lengths of constructing such a set-up, or indeed populate it with what seemed like ancient wax figures, Lucie concentrated on finding a way out. Shifting her gaze upwards, she spotted the projector from which spewed the breaking day at three hundred and sixty degrees, fixed to a ceiling about thirty feet from floor level, too high for her to reach, even if she climbed atop one of the odd 'buildings'. Likewise, an array of cameras and speakers were peppered throughout the complex, seemingly to capture her movements and speak to her wherever she might go. She expected that her 'flat' such as it was would be filled with the same, and while she could at least try to take care of some of them, she reasoned that like the projector, it was unlikely she could reach them all. The pain in her head was lessening, and a rumbling in her previously nauseous stomach gradually replaced it. Rising to her feet, she re-traced her steps back towards her apartment, her bare feet slapping against the concrete ground as she properly examined each of the store fronts on this nightmarish street for the first time. A bar, a general store, and alongside that, a deli, through the window of which Lucie saw a motionless vendor alongside what looked like fresh ingredients.

Stepping through the door, Lucie examined further and found trays of freshly baked loaves and rolls stacked across from a counter resplendent with fresh meats, vegetables and condiments that set her mouth watering instantly, though no knives or utensils were anywhere to be seen. Reaching for a warm baguette, Lucie pulled it unevenly apart with her fingers and began filling it with items from the display, creating an overly large sandwich. A small warning had triggered in her mind, guarding against eating something which for all she knew may have been coated with poison or something equally harmful, but she quickly dispelled her concerns, reasoning that it would be illogical for anyone building such an elaborate prison to finish her off in such a way. Besides which, if she were to attempt escape, she would need her energy, and had no way to be sure when she would next be able to eat. Content in her decision, Lucie raised the sandwich to her mouth and took a bite.

"Only the first meal is free," a quiet but threatening voice suddenly sounded through a speaker grill on the counter. "After that, all items must be paid for."

"That's fine," Lucie voiced back, her eyes fixing on the speaker as she chewed her food, "I don't intend to stay."

"If you'd care to make your way to the edge of our little town, we can discuss things in person, though do please be careful not to cross it this time."

Placing her hastily prepared meal on the counter, Lucie stepped out of the shop and walked slowly back towards the fence, the chill of the cold, concrete warehouse breaking through her thin nightdress to frostily caress her skin. She remembered that clothes had been laid out for her, but there was no way she would appease her wardens by wearing them. Scanning the street, she spotted a mannequin stood alongside a row of traffic cones, dressed in dark blue overalls, hard hat and yellow hi-vis jacket, and she crossed over to him. Likewise determined not to allow the men behind the cameras watching her the satisfaction of seeing any embarrassment, she slipped off the nightdress and deprived the mannequin of its overalls, which though somewhat rough were at least a more dignified attire. The yellow vest she left discarded on the floor.

She reached the perimeter and stood waiting, her eyes searching for what she was sure must be motion detectors of some kind to capture any movement out of the zone. The shutters, over which the projection of green fields and blue skies now danced, were about fifteen to twenty metres away from where Lucie stood, no distance at all were it not for the instantly crippling noise...

The shutter began to creak open and Lucie parked her contemplations, strangely relishing the impending confrontation. "Good of you to show your face, Whyte...," she began, her voice tailing off as she realised her error, the shutters raising to reveal her captor's triumphant smirk.

"Butcher?" Lucie quizzed in surprise and contempt.

"That's 'Mr Butcher' if you please, Ms Musilova," the Cabinet Minister corrected. "The Right Honourable Mr Butcher, if we're being formal."

"I'd never thought there was anything particularly honourable about you, Butcher," Lucie retorted, "but I confess I didn't have you down as the kind of man who'd keep women locked up in some kind of pervert's playpen."

"Playpen," Butcher smiled almost nonchalantly, his face glowing with warped pride as he surveyed his creation, "yes, that's not bad. 'Pervert' is a matter of opinion but, 'playpen' isn't bad, although it's really more of a 'play street'. And there are no locks on any of the doors within it, you can walk in and out of any one of the buildings."

"Just not out there," she replied, gesturing to the door he stood in.

"No," Butcher laughed, his tone condescending and superior.

"That would present us with one or two problems."

"Well be sure that I have every intention of presenting you with more problems than you know what to do with".

"No doubt you do," he quietly intoned. "But unless you make the covenant within the next couple of days, the only problem I'll have is where to dispose of your body."

"Covenant?" Lucie snapped, "What covenant would I want to make with you?"

"What you want has very little to do with it," Butcher replied, his chest puffed out like some immaculately attired peacock. "Besides, I've grown utterly sick of it." The sneering mockery had disappeared from the politician's face, replaced instead by a cold and almost softly spoken malevolence. Lucie had heard such tones before in others, both in the Afghan desert and in the bars and tea rooms of Parliament, where the more extreme Members could voice their true opinions free from the glare of cameras and the scrutiny of the public.

"Sick of what, exactly?"

"Sick of what other people want," Butcher spat, "or more specifically you people."

Lucie balked at the expression and allowed her disgust to show on her face.

"You mean women? Or foreigners?"

"Both, actually," came the reply. "As if listening to women bleating on about 'equality' wasn't bad enough, we flung open the borders and before we knew where we were, we were up to our bollocks in nig-nogs and wops, all demanding the right to live next door to decent people and insisting on 'representation' – whatever the fuck they mean by that. In my grandparents' day women and foreigners knew their place."

"So that's what this is all about?" Lucie quizzed, "Nostalgia? You kidnap and murder women because you've got a boner for the days when a man could come home to his tea on the table and put his feet up in front of *The Black & White Minstrel Show*? Do me a favour..."

"Why?" he spat back, aggression in his voice. "No woman has ever done one for me."

"Oh, boo-hoo," she retorted. "No hairdresser has ever got my style just right, but I don't round them up and keep them in a B-Movie horror set."

"If you had power over them you might," he quietly countered. "I waited a long time to have power enough to punish one woman, but that wouldn't do when there's so many others out there who need bringing to heel."

"Ah..." Lucie voiced in perverse satisfaction. "We've got above ourselves, and so here comes Adam Butcher to put us back on the leash again."

"Someone has to," he coldly replied. "God knows the government won't, at least not with its current leader. But as soon as I'm sitting in Downing Street and the country is out of Europe, we can start to unpick all those restrictive 'employment rights' Remoaners get so worked up about. You'd be surprised what people will agree to when food and medicine are scarce and they've children to care for."

Lucie could feel the bile rise in her throat, as she took in the words of the preening monster before her.

"Bastard! Rather than fight poverty, you'd use the threat of dropping people into it to strip away rights they bled and died for?"

"The wrong people, Ms Musilova," Butcher replied, the smirk once more embellished with malevolent amusement. "You're the wrong person too. An MP's aide who solves crimes, an ex-priest with a gun? Well don't entertain any idea about your friends in MI5 coming to save you, I've got that little outfit sewn up..."

"I'm not with MI5," Lucie corrected, relishing the flicker of uncertainty across his features. "There's too much to do over at Cross Boundary Affairs."

Butcher squinted, the perpetual smirk twitching upon his permatanned face as the Overlappers official designation slowly registered with him.

"You?" he scoffed. "A fucking Overlapper? Bloody hell, I'd forgotten that shower still existed!"

Butcher's chuckle grew into a cacophony of unstable laughter "I knew SIS were struggling with the funding cuts, but I hadn't realised they'd stooped so low as to start hiring mongrels!"

"I'd be careful if I were you," Lucie spat back. "You haven't exactly caught me on my best day."

"But I have caught you," he countered. "And it's your own fault we did. When you first started poking your nose around the Camden whore house, I was content to just have you killed, like I tried with your friend Algers, but you proved so bloody persistent. You wanted so badly to know what happened to the

French girl, that it seemed only fair to show you, and besides we needed a replacement after you and your Muslim friend managed to spirit away the one we were after. Who'd have thought it eh? A Muslim working for a white woman; what would the *Daily Mail* say?"

"He doesn't work for me."

"Well he certainly doesn't anymore."

"What have you done with him?"

"He went for a swim."

Butcher played with the words, a smile spreading on his face as he spoke them, his enjoyment of Lucie's reaction plain for her to see.

Though she had expected the blow, the words thumped home harder than the punch of any hired thug, and she turned her head away from the murderous bastard before her and clenched her eyes against the onrush of tears. The pain in her throat and the rage in her lungs screamed at her to be released but she refused. There would be time to holler her outrage to the heavens for Ismail's death when she had got what she needed from his killer, and she fully intended to do both. Ismail would expect nothing less of her. "You'll...," Lucie began, before stopping to push the cry that was forming back down inside. "You'll regret many things when this is all over Butcher, but you'll regret that most of all."

"Alas," he answered, running his hand through his dark hair and straightening his tie, "in three days you will either no longer care about the late Mr Ismail, or if you do, you'll join him in deportation to the undiscovered country."

"Three days?" Lucie spat.

"That's the Biblically ascribed period for rebirths, isn't it? Today you died, at least to the world. You have three days to learn obedience; I usually give two weeks but having a priest occupy my little town brought out my sense of irony."

"Three days for what, exactly?"

"Three days for me to break you," he answered. "Believe me, I'd rather break your will than your body, but the choice is yours. In your new home I have provided instructions on how you will behave. They cover everything from what you will eat, how you will dress, what time you'll go to bed and wake up. A few buildings along from your flat, you will find an office. You will go there each morning, perform the tasks left for you, after which you will receive money from the Post Office over there to buy your meals. You will make no effort to cover or hide yourself from the cameras when dressing, showering or attending calls of nature, you will make yourself visible to the cameras at all times. At the end of each day you will be rewarded for good behaviour, and if after three days you have proven yourself, you will make a covenant of loyalty to me, and become my..., well, 'pet' I suppose, along with the others who passed the test."

Finishing, the MP stood, framed by the light from behind the door. Lucie was tempted even more than earlier to risk the ear-splitting screech of the alarm and charge into him, but the silhouettes of others behind him persuaded her now was not the time. His pointed tongue was flicking serpent-like across his lips as he watched her through eyes that seemed to Lucie to be glazing over, as though in anticipation of an evening's voyeuristic pleasure. Sadistic he may be, Lucie thought. Evil? Perhaps. But what was more obvious to her than either epithet was his state of mind. This man was not well.

"So much for the great Adam Butcher," she laughed, her own tone mimicking the mockery in his, breaking him from his perverted trance. "So much for the Hard Man of the Right. It's all just a con isn't it? Forget all the grand speeches, all those flag waving rallies; at the end of the day you're just a dirty bastard sat behind a screen watching women you could never hope to bed get their kit off. The only thing hard about you is what's going on in your pants when you're sat behind a monitor. You're pathetic."

The words came unnaturally to her, but Lucie knew they were necessary. She suspected an ego as big as Butcher's would be susceptible to popping, and so it proved, the grin disappearing from his face, which twisted into anger as he took a step towards her before stopping himself and breathing the cold air of the warehouse into his lungs.

"We'll see how pathetic I am in three days," he said, turning his back on her to walk away.

"Wait!" Lucie shouted after the politician, who turned around and stared back at her, all smugness removed from his face and replaced with something close to hate.

"What's all this got to do with *WaterWhyte*, with the *Red Mako*?"

Butcher sneered once more, latching onto her need for an answer and using it to further demonstrate his 'control'.

"Let's just say it's my 'bung'," he said. "Your three days have begun."

"I'll see you then," she said through a smile dripping with sarcasm. "Oh, and Adam? When you finish up in front of your laptop and start planning your new dog-eat-dog paradise, just remember who it is you've just put in a kennel."

Butcher wordlessly scoffed and spun on his heel, and the warehouse shutter creaked down behind him, Lucie watching it as it closed, her brain processing everything, from his ludicrous 'covenant' to the fragility of his ego.

Turning back and heading into what would at least for the moment be her home, she wanted nothing more than to drop to her knees and weep for Ismail. She would not give Butcher the satisfaction of giving in to her anguish, instead, the emotion she was prepared to let loose, if only for a short while, was her rage.

At the end of this plywood street of nightmares stood a

mannequin dressed in a business suit, a briefcase attached to its 'hand' and an archaic and dead mobile phone glued quite literally to its other. It was as unconvincing as the rest, its body chipped and worn, and its features crudely painted; but to Lucie, it was for that moment Butcher himself. She picked up pace, running towards it as the scream that had built inside her for days erupted from within, drowning out all else and echoing around her. Clenching her fist, she slammed her knuckles at speed into the model's face, breaking her skin and cracking the ancient dummy's neck, sending its head spinning off it and onto the road, where it rolled into the path of the perpetually looping car, the vehicle crushing it as it continued on its never-ending journey.

Lucie flexed her bruised and bleeding hand and heaved air into her burning lungs, watching with pleasure as the wax split and crunched under the weight of the moving metal. Butcher might think he had her trapped, but Lucie had been trapped before, and she reminded herself that her last captors had paid dearly for their abuses. As she walked away from the broken waxwork, she made a promise to Ismail and the others, that this time would be no different.

23

Lucie woke with a jolt. The pain in her head was finally gone, along with the rage that had consumed so much of her previous day, replaced though with the pain of cramped and sore muscles and a determination bordering on murderous.

After her confrontation with Butcher and her assault of the unfortunate dummy she had chosen as his proxy, Lucie had explored what remained of the 'Playpen'. Another model had graciously provided a well worn but oddly comfortable pair of trainers, which at last gave her feet some protection against the cold floor, and she had returned to the deli to hastily finish her sandwich and make another for the following day. In her flat she found Butcher's instructions for how she was to act during her period of 'testing'; lights out at 10:30pm, awake at 6:30am, when she would shower, dress in the clothes provided and proceed to the 'office' to perform the duties assigned to her. Having checked out her supposed new employment, Lucie found it to be another bland room, occupied by rows of desks, all empty and none with working computers, save for one, albeit with internet connection and next to which lay a hardback copy of Shakespeare's complete works and instructions to copy them out. Ignoring them, Lucie had continued her inspection.

Estimating that the warehouse was around fifty thousand square feet, the Playpen took up probably a quarter of its total size and had been built closer to the entrance than the rear of the structure. There was no fence around the perimeter, but having risked several tests, Lucie was sure that the alarm-triggering sensors existed all around it, and that she was in fact trapped. She could find no utensils of any kind that could be used for any attempted break out, and neither was there any obvious trap door she could locate, and she had cursed herself for imagining that there would be.

There had been nothing of use in the other buildings, though on the counter of the 'bar' stood a bottle of rum with enough still inside it for two glasses. Not standing on ceremony, Lucie had lifted the bottle to her lips and swallowed the contents in full, before fatigue had begun to overcome her, her tired eyes longing for sleep. Returning to the room she had woken in, she had jumped in surprise when a voice that didn't sound like Butcher's began speaking to her from the grill in the wall, telling her to dress in night clothes and settle down for the night. When she had responded with profanity and pulled the sheets and pillow from the bed, intending to sleep outside on the pavement as a small act of rebellion, the voice followed her to a grill on the wall of the deli she had earlier visited, warning her that she was 'breaking the covenant' and to expect punishment. Responding defiantly, she had pulled the blanket over her head, only to be woken from unsettled slumber by the sound of the warehouse shutter creaking open.

Throwing the sheet back and running to the edge of the Playpen perimeter, she had seen the silhouetted figures of two men approaching her, which meant the alarm was off! Not waiting a second, Lucie had charged towards the pair, aiming to fell them and take her chances with whatever lay beyond the shutter, but before she even drew level with the figures, her body was stricken with absolute and all-consuming pain.

The twin barbs of a taser had pierced the skin of her abdomen and sent twelve hundred volts of current into her body, leaving her crumpled in agony, her muscles screaming at her as they spasmed and pulled. Forcing her eyes open as the initial pain began to subside, she saw her attacker standing over her, his finger on the trigger of his device, ready to unleash another burst of pain into her system. His colleague soon appeared, carrying with him a bin liner filled with the vegetables and breads from the Playpen deli, her only source of food. Passing her, the man had reached into the bag and pulled out a handful of the salad leaves, tossing them to the floor in front of her.

"Feeding time," he spat.

Lucie, pushing herself with spent and sapped muscles to her knees, had scooped up the wet mixture and hurled it back at him, splattering it against his trousers, and earning herself a second jolt from the taser. The pair had reached the shutter before the pain let go its excruciating hold on her body, mocking her as they went, leaving her to stare after them in frustration. Mere seconds after the shutter locked down, the wail of the alarm had sounded again, cutting through her senses and causing her to force her bruised muscles to work and crawl back behind the perimeter, where she had struggled to her blanket and allowed exhaustion to drift her into a painful and tormented sleep.

There was no clock near her when she awoke, though she guessed it was still early, the projection of sunrise not quite yet reaching the warehouse walls, and there was none of the sound of simulated activity which she had grown used to so quickly. She stood and stretched her still aching but rested muscles and took a brief reconnoitre of the Playpen. All food was gone, the shelves in the makeshift shop and deli bare, as she had expected, save for a tap of cold water, from which she drank heartily. Discipline, she reasoned, was the focus here, or more accurately, 'training'; she was being trained as an owner might a dog, and her anger began to boil at the thought, before she supressed it with rational calm. This set up was designed to humiliate and terrify, through daily indignity and the threat of punishment. The only way to fight it, she reasoned, was to give in to neither and to do that, she must retain control of her emotions.

After spending her first minutes of the day in prayerful meditation, Lucie ate the second baguette she had prepared the day before, before returning to her 'apartment' across the street. Though the overalls she had taken from the mannequin already stank with sweat and grime, she again refused to wear the business suit laid out and went through instead to the bathroom. As expected, the cameras in the room were in plain sight and no curtain hung from the shower rail. She found nudity neither embarrassing nor shameful, and her first instinct was to simply defy their expectations of timidity and go ahead and shower but doing so would detract from her plan.

No amount of compliance over the next couple of days would free her Butcher's clutches, whether or not he deemed her to have successfully made a 'covenant' with him, and she had absolutely no intention of joining his own personal harem, or ending up dumped behind a brothel in the early hours. The only way to avoid those fates, she reasoned, was to break the rules of the game she was in as often and as flagrantly as she could. If the psychology of the torture was intended to instil a fear of punishment and therefore a lack of human contact for the period of captivity, then Lucie would do the opposite.

Collecting the blankets from the pavement, she knotted the

corners together to form a rectangular canopy, trapping one corner in the bathroom door and tying another around the shower rail, providing a makeshift but effective screen across the toilet and shower. Though she made use of both as quickly as possible, it still wasn't fast enough to avoid the water turning from hot to ice cold as she washed; the punishment for erecting her screen as expected as it was swift.

Dressing again in the rough and uncomfortable overalls and trainers, Lucie continued in her acts of rebellion while concentrating on the problem of how to get out once she had pissed them off enough to open the shutters. She had ignored the voice with all its fatuous talk of covenants and promises for so long that its warnings of dire consequences went almost unregistered, even when it raised several levels from its customary quiet and sinister level to almost scream demands for her to proceed to the 'office'. She did not do so, instead sitting cross legged by the perimeter in still concentration.

The shutter remained closed hours later, as though matching her own defiant intransigence in a waiting game to see who would blink first, and Lucie realised she was being starved into submission. She had gone hungry before, and the pain in her belly as her hunger pangs increased perversely gave her the focus to keep her mind calm and on the problem at hand. Lucie could not escape until the door was open, and shut it remained, as though her watching it for the slightest move was an extra torture for her captors to enjoy. It was when she broke from her vigil that she heard the creak of movement, and she rushed back in seconds, only to see it close again. She was being toyed with, and she would not make such a mistake again. If they wanted her, they would have to come for her, and Lucie knew that one way or another, she was wanted. Lacking any obvious weapon, Lucie retrieved the now empty bottle of rum from the plywood bar and placed it under her blanket with her as the projections rotated once more into twilight; she allowed herself to drift lightly away, her hand gripping the bottle neck and facing the shutter, ready to strike.

It was not the jolt of electricity that woke her but the scream of a siren and the glare of lights so bright they bore through her eyelids and into her fractured dream. The sensations did not lessen when she sought cover inside the buildings, the noise only amplified through the speakers that surrounded her prison. With no respite, Lucie returned to her bed and wrapped the blanket as tightly as she could bear around her head, clamping shut her eyes and shouting back in almost manic recalcitrance, before the siren ceased and the lights cut off in a glorious instant as quickly as they had arrived.

These tactics too she had experienced before, exhausted and broken in the Afghan cave; a sleep-deprived mind was a suggestible mind, and she knew this would not be the only time that night that those sirens would blaze. Returning her stare to the shutter and allowing her eyes to close once more, Lucie let her thoughts to drift to the heavens, preparing her senses for their next assault. Her prediction proved accurate as the sirens wailed repeatedly throughout the night, Lucie each time resisting despair and bellowing her passions in response.

When morning arrived, she was weary and fatigued, but took advantage of what seemed the cessation of the attacks to grab the few hours sleep she would need to refresh herself. Her hunger had tipped over into nausea and there was again no food to counter it, Lucie instead taking more water and contemplating her situation. She had neither the desire nor intention to go through such a day again, or more accurately such a night, and she knew that the motives of her captors were purely sadistic. Butcher had said it took two weeks of conditioning to 'train' his other victims, yet he had given her only three days; the purpose could only have been torture, unless there was something special about the date that had eluded her. Either way, it was obvious to her that simply refusing to engage was not an option which would leave her the strength to fight off any ultimate attack, and she had no intention of begging for for relief. Rather, she thought to herself, she would bring it to a head.

After freshening as best she could, Lucie resumed her position at the shutter, only this time not in quiet defiance.

"Hey!" she shouted over the soundtracked birdsong and revving of engines. "Hey, Butcher! Come and get me; you win!"

A crackle sounded from the speakers and the sinister voice returned, triumphalism masking the obvious puzzlement within it.

"You wish to concede...?"

"You bet your arse I do," Lucie shouted back. "I'm ready to make the covenant."

24

It was many hours later that the shutter clanked and creaked upwards and the vile smugness of Adam Butcher was revealed, Lucie waiting in what had become her regular position to greet him.

"You took your time," she spat.

"Well I do have a life outside of this, you know."

"Cabinet meeting? Or something more up your street, like an interview with a brown-nosed journo, or sharing a stage with the EDL?"

There was no warmth in the man's face, none of the political charm with which he had first made his name. His eyes were fixed unsettlingly on her and sweat was glistening on his brow, his tongue flicking against the back of his teeth as he relished the sight of his latest captive.

"Forgive me," he said as Lucie continued to scowl, "I'd been told you were ready to make the covenant, but your words suggest otherwise. Perhaps my people got the wrong impression."

"You know what they say about getting good staff after Brexit?"

Butcher gave a short, cruel laugh, never taking his eyes from hers.

"I must admit I was surprised to hear you'd broken so quickly, and you didn't seem the type to beg. I hadn't expected to have this conversation until the morning, but hey-ho. Which is it, Lucie Musilova of the Security and Intelligence Service for Cross-Boundary Affairs? Will you join my little harem, or join the French whore in the gutter?"

Lucie ground her teeth at his words, her eyes narrowing as she fought to maintain the control she had worked so hard to exert.

"You already know the answer to that."

"Hmm," he mulled, "pity. You might have been fun. Well, I'll leave you to enjoy the company of my subordinates here. You know they were really quite close to that fellow you killed a few days ago, in fact I don't think they've been quite themselves since. If I were you, I'd avoid mentioning it."

"Before all that," Lucie shouted, stopping the MP in mid-turn, "tell me what all this has to do with the Red Mako; what do you mean this is your 'bung'?"

Butcher's face creased into a mocking frown, as though he were being asked to demonstrate the tying of shoelaces by a stubborn child.

"Isn't it obvious?" he laughed. "It's how business has been done for centuries! The Saudi government wanted a product, the British government wanted the money, all the rest is just horses for courses; the public are informed of a tender process by papers which get a couple of days of nice headlines, and in the background the powerbrokers are busy thrashing out the real deal."

"You're saying this is a simple case of defence industry bribery?"

"Well, perhaps not 'simple'," Butcher conceded, "but the

principle's the same. Al-Khatani made it clear to me exactly what he wanted out of the contract, and I told him the same. As Defence Secretary I could bypass the tenders and choose exactly which company I thought would be able to accommodate us."

Lucie grimaced at his blithe delivery and breathed deeply to push down the rage that was building with renewed vigour within her.

"And I'm right, aren't I? The weapons systems aren't included in the contracts because Al-Khatani wants to fire something onto Yemen that the papers might not report so kindly?"

"It's not indiscriminate, if that's what you think," Butcher answered in continued nonchalance. "There are certain groups hiding out by the coastline, the *Red Mako* will help him pick them off, that's all."

"With chemical weapons."

"No-one cares what happens in Yemen," Butcher sneered. "Britain's falling apart, and if dropping a handful chemical grenades on a few Muslims puts enough sticky tape on the economy to delay collapse a couple of years then no-one who does find out will even care."

"Chemical warfare, and your own personal slaves," Lucie spat in contempt. "And you say this is based on 'principle'."

"Of course," Butcher objected. "The principle of the market."

"And it's as simple as that," decried Lucie. "You used social media to target the women you wanted, the women who you thought had got above themselves, then you trapped them in here and broke them with psychological torture until they were yours to control. And thanks to a tame press and the 'British services for British people' crap you've been sewing everywhere, no-one even stops to ask where they've gone. You might think you can get away with this, you bastard, but think again. My superiors are on to you, and when I disappear, someone will come after me."

Laughter echoed between them as Butcher almost doubled up with what looked like genuine hilarity

"You don't get it, do you?" he scoffed. "It doesn't matter how many scandals you uncover – and believe me there are far more than even you think you know about – it won't make any difference. Aside from a brief flare on Twitter and some colourful placards on the next march, nobody cares. That's the problem you have on your side; you think people still care about democracy when they don't. All anyone cares about is getting their own dirty and perverted version of it over the line then battening down the hatches. People have agendas these days and they're not just prepared, they're happy to disenfranchise any group necessary to pursue them. And nobody even cares."

What angered her most about his words was the fact that she knew there was truth in them. Since 2016 she had lost count of the number of people for whom she had laid out in detail all that was illegal and corrupt about the campaign and the wilful denial of voices to the five million and the young, but few had listened, instead shouting cries of 'betrayal' of a democracy they couldn't even define. This was not a battle she would ever stop fighting, but she feared daily that it was one that may never be won.

"The government knows about all this?"

"Well, 'knows' is a subjective word. Let's just say they're not inclined to listen to rumours and aren't too bothered about inspecting the minutiae. If anything ever came out about chemical attack, they have deniability, and with the economy on the brink, aside from anything else, it's good business. At the cost of some dead Yemenis nobody cares about and a handful of missing euro whores, the future of Brexit Britain is signed, sealed and delivered."

"Sealed with a death," spat Lucie.

"The people have chosen this, they handed us a blank

cheque; they can't complain now about how we choose to cash it."

Butcher was drunk on his own arrogance, and that was exactly what Lucie wanted him to be.

"And that's that, is it?" she pressed.

"You ride out to fortune and glory and leave me in the hands of the chuckle brothers back there?"

"You had your chance," he dismissively spat, waving her a casual and insincere farewell.

"I know, it's just…"

"Just what?"

"I just thought a man like you would take care of it yourself, not leave it to those idiots."

Butcher's smirk returned and Lucie saw him nod to someone out of her line of vision, butterflies playing in her stomach and adrenaline shooting through her as he took a long step towards her, the deafening siren remaining obstinately silent. The alarm was off…

"You?" he sneered as he stood barely feet away from her. "I wouldn't even bother."

Lucie merely smiled a wide, beaming grin and shook her head. "And you know what? You'd never get near me anyway."

In a second she was on him, flooring the MP with an uppercut to the chin and sprinting past him to the door, only to be rugby-tackled by two bulky figures who knocked her to the ground in a heap.

"Deal with her!" ordered a flustered Butcher as he strode through the shutter and disappeared up the corridor, a lacky in tow.

Lucie was struggling with her two assailants, and her sore muscles strained to resist her arms being spread out wide. The second man pulled away from her and she kicked out, narrowly missing him, while the man kneeling behind her began to laugh in a voice she recognised as belonging to the infamous 'Gary'.

"Go on mate, use it," Gary was urging, "then I'm having first go!"

The other man was pulling the taser that had caused her so much pain and her stomach turned at seeing it again. Gary's eagerness though was getting the better of him and as his friend levelled the taser, she wrenched herself free from his grip, wincing as the barbs penetrated Gary's groin and he writhed on the floor screaming.

"Try taking back control of those," she quipped, before ducking under the swinging arm of the second man and slamming the back of her hand against his head, knocking him cold.

Lucie ran at breakneck speed through the hated shutter and though the air in the corridor was stale and warm, it was the sweetest she had breathed in many a long year. A short distance down the hall stood an open door. She peered inside, finding its main wall resplendent with controls and monitors, upon which all the joys of the Playpen were displayed.

The room bore all the signs of well-worn untidiness, with unwashed plates, half-full mugs of tea and takeaway boxes galore strewn across the work surface and across the banks of monitors. Pulling the cables from the kettle and phone chargers plugged into sockets, Lucie bound the wrists of her felled opponents. Clutching a collar in each hand, she dragged them through the shutter door, her muscles bellowing in protest and demanding a rest she would not provide and deposited them in the middle of the Playpen.

"Enjoy yourselves, lads," she said as she leant them together against the headless mannequin which she had decapitated on her first morning there. "I think you know the rules."

Running back, she slammed down the shutter lever and

scanned the control desk for the alarm switch, briefly savouring the adrenaline rush it gave her as she flicked it, before turning back to the monitors to search for her remaining tormentors.

Butcher she found quickly, the external monitors displaying his flustered journey to his official car outside, the MP brushing himself down as he stepped inside his vehicle. Of the other man there was no sign, and Lucie allowed her thoughts to return to her predecessors in the Playpen. Control was Butcher's ultimate desire – of the project, likely too of the country – but certainly of those women caught in his perverted game. The purpose was conditioning through psychological torture; should any of his victims show signs of rebellion he would want them nearby where they could be easily dealt with, either through re-conditioning or the same fate which had befallen Ines. To have them too far away from the Playpen wouldn't make sense, Lucie reasoned, they *must* be here.

A map of the complex was on the wall beside the monitor bank, and Lucie grimaced at how considerably larger it was than she had expected, encompassing not only the storage and warehouse section she had been kept in, but an office block and a dock hall by the water's edge; where if the documents were to be believed, the *Red Mako* itself was being constructed. The playpen was in a building away from and apparently separate to the main complex, devoid of the security personnel who patrolled the rest of the site, suggesting to Lucie that Butcher's private staff were concentrated in this one place.

"First thing's first," Lucie muttered to herself, resolving to find the women then focus on the *Red Mako* afterwards. Cameras covered the whole complex and Lucie despaired at first of finding any clue to the location of the women, who she was sure were there. The controls were simple enough to decipher, one button switching the view to the Playpen, where her erstwhile captors were cursing and writhing against their bonds, and another switched to the dock hall, in which she caught her first teasing glance of the military boat that had been the centre of so much trouble.

Resisting the temptation to admire it for too long, Lucie pushed the third button, images of the office block appearing on the monitors before her. Each image corresponded to a room on the complex plan and she frowned in frustration as she realised that each was empty, aside from the occasional guard. She swore and pressed her clenched fist against her head, damning herself for believing the veracity of her theory. Having been so sure she was right it cut deep to realise she wasn't. Except... *except...*

Lucie went through each camera again, mentally checking them off against the chart on the wall. Each room was on the screen except for one. She felt a grin work its way onto her face as her hunch breathed new life within her. Noting the room number, Lucie spun around and ran out of the room, her mind composing plans for bypassing security and getting to the captive women, but in her haste she neglected to check the corridor and charged headlong into the trunk of a black clad figure heading the other way towards her.

Pushing herself away, Lucie clenched her fist, ready to slam it with what was left of her strength into the newcomer's chin, but stopped in shock as her eyes fixed properly for the first time on the face of the figure.

"I bet Lake that you wouldn't need my help getting out of there," said Kasper Algers through his wrinkled grin. "Looks like he owes me a Toblerone."

25

———

E motion engulfed her and she flung her arms around her friend. "Kasper!"

"Hey, hey, it's okay," Kasper replied as he untangled himself from her.

"It's not okay," she snapped back, her expression changing to one of intense concern. "What are you doing here? You can't be well enough to be back in the field!"

"I'm well enough to come and look for you," he answered, shooing away the question. "I came around a couple of days ago and I'm doing ok, really, just a bit weak."

His face was gaunter even than usual, and there was an uncharacteristic weakness in his voice the belied his claims.

"Don't lie to me," she said, softly.

He smiled down from his great height and nodded.

"Well," he said, "maybe I'm not quite firing on all cylinders yet but I'm 90% there. And when Lake told me you'd gone missing I couldn't exactly leave you to it, could I?"

"But how did you find me? I'm guessing we're in Portsmouth, right? At the *WaterWhyte* site?"

"Yeah, at the Shipyard; this building is away from the main

complex but they're building the *Red Mako* in the dock hall across the way," he confirmed. "I guessed your disappearance might have something to do with the same bastards that got me." He stared at one of the myriad screens behind her, projecting the struggle of the captors she had bested. "Looks like I was right."

Algers looked as though there was something else on his mind, but there was still work to be done and people to save.

"It's fantastic to see you," she grinned, "but we have to get into the office blocks. I think the missing women are held up there, I'm sure of it. What's the security like around here?"

"In this part not too bad but the main dock hall is well looked after and there's no way of knowing who's in on this and who isn't." She started down the corridor, the adrenaline overcoming her exhaustion as she broke into a jog. After a few seconds she realised Algers wasn't alongside her and she stopped to look back over her shoulder.

"Come on," she said, "we need to get in there quickly before we find the *Mako*."

Algers simply smiled back and walked up alongside her.

"I might be able to help there," he said. "You see, I didn't come here alone."

When they had reached the edge of the warehouse, Algers stopped running and ordered Lucie to do the same, reaching into his pocket and handing her a plastic visitor pass on a lanyard.

"Put that round your neck," he said as he unbuttoned the black jacket he had fastened up to the neck, revealing a shirt and tie beneath it. "And try and look presentable."

She fixed him with a 'look' as they walked towards the blocks, which he acknowledged.

"What's going on?"

"You'll see."

Reaching the office block, Algers took his card and swiped it through a reader beside the main thick glass doors, which swung open before them. Pressing for the lift, they stepped in and Algers pushed for the top floor, cursing the flow of muzak as they rose.

"Do you mind telling me what's going on?" Algers turned and looked at her for a moment. "You could do with a wash," he said.

"I know."

"I mean, would you like me to find you some deodorant or something...?"

"No, I'm fine."

"It's just that we've got a bit of a Pygmalion thing going on here right now..."

"I'm fine."

"Ok, I'll shut up about it then."

"That'd be great."

The lift stopped and Algers led the way down the corridor, Lucie frowning at his lack of explanation.

"Kasper!" she hissed at him. "Where are we going?"

"To see someone who's feeling pretty bloody sheepish at the moment."

They reached a grand set of doors and Algers barged through them without knocking, shepherding her in to a large, and well-furnished office in which stood a sharply suited and uncomfortable looking man, a clutch of papers in his hands.

"Ah, Algers," he began, before looking up and seeing Lucie, blood draining from his face as his eyes settled on her.

"Jarvis Whyte," Lucie spat.

"The very same," Algers confirmed. "He's not what you think, Lucie. He's not in on all this, he's been duped by Butcher. The only thing Jarvis here is guilty of is taking his eye far, far off the ball and letting himself be led a merry dance."

"It's true, Ms. Musilova," a flustered Whyte insisted, keeping a diplomatic distance from her. "I've not had any hands-on involvement in my companies for some time now; I had no idea there was any substance in what I thought were your ravings. If I'd known..."

"And how do we know he's telling the truth?"

"Because someone came to Lake with the details, and Lake went for a cosy chat with Jarvis here and ensured his cooperation in harvesting evidence, didn't he Jarvis?"

Whyte nodded slowly.

"Hang on, who told Lake about this?"

"That would be Ismail, Lucie."

Whether it was the news itself or how quickly she swivelled to face him, she wasn't sure, but Lucie felt her legs weaken and her knees almost give way. Steadying herself she stared back hard, almost daring her friend to repeat his words, so fearful was she that it would turn out to be untrue.

"Ismail?" she whispered.

"They dumped him in the sea but he managed to get back to shore and was picked up by a local dog-walker."

"How is he? Is he alright?"

She asked as earnestly as she had ever asked anything, and the conflict of emotions on her face must have been obvious to Algers, who moved quickly to reassure her, at least as best he could.

"He's alive, that's the main thing, and he's making sense. Now he just needs time to heal."

"Thank God, *thank* God..." she breathed, looking upwards

with her tears unhidden, before looking pointedly back at Algers. "And you couldn't tell me this outside?"

"I couldn't find the words. He was very insistent that someone came to find you."

She reciprocated his smile and re-ordered her mind as quickly as she was able, parking both her elation at Ismail's survival and the sudden and unexpected unease she felt at the prospect of making good on the promise she had made him.

"Well now you have it's time we found the others, too. Mr Whyte?"

"Oh, Jarvis, please."

"Jarvis," she said, acknowledging the curiosity of good manners in such circumstances. "Over in the storage block I saw blueprints of the whole complex; there's a room on this level somewhere that isn't covered by the security cameras, not even the corridor outside."

"Can you remember where?" Jarvis quizzed, his forehead crinkling, as he began tapping at the computer on his desk.

The trio gathered around the twin screens as Whyte brought up floorplans and diagrams, Lucie frowning as she tried to remember the layout she had seen.

"There!" she shouted, triumphantly. "That's the one!"

"And you think the missing women are there?" pressed Algers. "I'd bet my favourite harp on it. Jarvis, can you show us where it is?"

"Of course," he replied, the eagerness to be of help obvious in his inflection. "Should I bring these papers too?"

"I'll look after those," said Algers, reaching over and plucking them from his hand. "Now where's that room?"

The two spies followed the perspiring Whyte out of his office and past several others before turning down a corridor that could well have been untouched since the building was erected, the paint on the walls chipped and faded, and the atmosphere muggy and dusty with lack of use. At the very end of the corridor stood padlocked double doors and Lucie banged upon it, receiving no answer for her trouble.

"Where's the key kept?" she asked Whyte, who stuttered in response.

"Never mind," Algers cut in, slipping a thin and well-worn skeleton from his pocket and jimmying the lock open. "I never leave home without it."

The door was rigid and stiff, and Lucie pushed hard until it opened, and she half-fell, half-ran into the room, her eyes wide with elation that she had found them.

Her face dropped as elation turned instantly to disappointment and landed with a hollow thud in her gut. The room was bare, the only sound within it the hum of the industrial lights called reluctantly into action as Whyte flicked the switch. Of the women there was no sign.

Lucie shrugged off Algers' outstretched arm, determined to at least do the victims of Butcher's actions the honour of indulging her rage at their loss. There were four windows in the room, all blocked by blinds, and Lucie pulled at the nearest one so violently it came loose from its hinges and clattered to the floor. Lucie directed her furious stare to the floodlit gravel below.

"I'm sorry, Lucie," said Algers, softly.

"Not as sorry as Butcher will be," she answered, half-turning back to her friend. "Except..."

Her eyes caught by something on the back wall. Moving over to the spot that had captured her attention, Lucie reached up and pressed her fingers against a row of nails, following them until they met with the ceiling in the corner.

"What's underneath this room, Jarvis?"

"Nothing of any importance," he answered her, confused. "Tell me!"

"It's the motor-pool," he blustered, "the garage."

"Thought so, the wall stops here but the windows keep going."

Algers had joined her at the far end of the room, running his own fingers over the opposite edge.

"Hardboard... It's a false wall! Can you hear anything?"

"Not sure," answered Lucie, her ear pressed against it. "Need to take a look."

"On three?"

"Three."

Taking a few steps back, the pair charged their shoulders against the hardboard, a gargantuan 'crack' sounding as their weight clattered against it, leaving the façade dented and splintered. A second second charge saw them break through, leaving them crumpled on the floor, a cloud of wood dust in their eyes and lungs.

Coughing heartily, Lucie blinked her sore eyes free of the rough particles, straining to see what they had uncovered, but it was the voice of Whyte that told her what she wanted to hear.

"Oh, my..." said Whyte as he stepped over the sprawled pair. "Oh... oh, my."

Scrambling to her feet, Lucie stared open mouthed at the sight before her. The space was larger than she'd expected, as though a conference room had been cut in two by the now destroyed false wall. The windows had been boarded up, the only light coming from a single light screwed into the roof and the wall they had broken had collapsed upon a neat row of sleeping bags, now covered in splinters and dust. Across from them were three couches arranged in a group, and it was to them that Lucie's eyes were instantly dragged.

Two women sat on each couch, unwashed, dishevelled and pale. None had moved despite the manner of the trio's entrance, though their eyes were wide and staring. The faces of each of them were imprinted on Lucie's soul. She wanted at once to embrace them with joy yet weep for the tortures they had endured, turning them into living shadows of themselves. Algers moved to go to them but she put her hand gently on his arm and stepped ahead of him. "Hagne?" Lucie asked, moving slowly towards the woman closest to her on the first couch. "Hagne Pappas?"

Hagne's blank eyes almost flickered for a moment before drifting off focus and staring at the wall behind Lucie's head.

"Bastards," she whispered, shaking her head. "Bastards."

"The fruits of Butcher's labour," spat Algers, grimly. "Do you think they can be treated?"

"Anyone can be treated, Lucie. I just hope it doesn't take too long to work."

"Hagne," Lucie urged again, returning to the woman and kneeling by her side, I need you and your friends to come with us, is that ok?"

"You can't ask her like that."

Lucie spun around to the new voice, accented with a Polish inflection and coming from a woman with dirty blonde hair on the next couch.

"You have to order her," the woman said weakly. "You have to order all of us."

Lucie crossed to her and looked into her face. Like Hagne, her eyes would not focus, as though she were talking to a dream.

"You're Aga, aren't you?" she softly asked.

"Used to be," came the answer, her voice so weak Lucie could barely hear it. "He calls me something else now."

"Butcher?"

Aga stared, the strain of trying to remember showing on her face, but no more words came. Lucie took her hand and softly held it, turning back to Algers who was swallowing emotion of his own. "That wall wasn't something they took down and put up every day," she said. "How was food brought to them, how did he get here when he wanted to..." She tailed off, the words she intended to speak making her angry and sick.

"How about through here?" Algers said as he scanned the room and spotted a square hatch beneath a large table.

Pushing the table out of the way he dropped to the floor and examined the hatchway.

"Locked," he said, "from the underside."

Rising to his feet he stamped hard but fruitlessly at the hatch, which stayed resolutely rigid in the face of his assault.

"It won't budge?"

"Not an inch. Damn it! I'd much rather try and get them out through there than try walking them all through the site in full view of security. If we can get them into the garage, we can grab some vehicles and drive them straight out."

"With no way of knowing who's on Butcher's payroll and who isn't we can't risk walking them anywhere. What about from the other side, up through the garage?"

As she spoke, the hatch began to move, Algers gripping the edge and yanking it upwards, dropping it on the floor beside him as the head of Jarvis Whyte popped up through the hole.

"Sorry if I shocked you," he said in his irritatingly polite tones, "but I suddenly remembered where the old fire escape used to be before we refurbished."

"Jarvis, I could kiss you," Lucie shouted with a grin. "If, you know, you hadn't voted away my rights and freedoms..."

Jarvis nodded in understanding and Lucie helped Aga to her feet.

"Aga, we're to here to take you home, all of you. This is Jarvis, he's going to lead you down some stairs."

Aga nodded and walked painfully to the hatch, Lucie turning back for the remaining five who stayed sitting on their couches.

Lucie went to each of them in turn, urging and coaxing them to stand without success, before Aga turned back as she stepped through the hatch and spoke again.

"I told you," she said, "you have to order them. They'll only respond to commands now."

"But you don't," replied Lucie in admiration.

"No," Aga acknowledged, "but I do what I have to, to survive."

She stepped through the hatch and Lucie turned to Algers who cleared his throat and winced in distaste of what he was about to do.

"You will stand!" he commanded in his most booming voice, the prisoners responding weakly but without complaint.

"I can't do this," he whispered to Lucie who looked at him with sympathetic understanding.

"You have to," she told him. "Walk to the hatch!"

The captives shuffled slowly to the hatchway and began to follow Aga down the cold concrete steps. Lucie held Kasper's hand as he became the unwitting director of a macabre puppet show they both hoped would soon be at an end.

26

The stairway was cold and poorly lit but led at the bottom through double doors to the large garage, filled with fleet vehicles of all shapes and sizes. Immediately catching Lucie's eye were three minibuses emblazoned with the *WaterWhyte* logo, Whyte explaining that corporate transport was often more cost effective when transferring engineers between sites or to other locations for sub-contracted work. The explanation didn't interest Lucie as much as the vehicle's usefulness, and the erstwhile captives were quickly aboard the lead bus, Algers assuring her that this would not be the first vehicle he had hotwired.

Aga's voice was becoming stronger with each step she took away from the hated room and Lucie felt comfortable leaving her with the others while she and Algers took care of the unresolved issue of the *Red Mako*, an uncertain Whyte tagging behind them. Leaving the motor pool, the trio walked the couple of hundred yards to the site's pièce de résistance, at least according to Whyte.

The dock hall was an enormous structure of iron and steel,

and Lucie could not help but be impressed by the engineering skill which went into building it, let alone what it contained. Though Lucie's less than business-like attire raised the eyebrows of the guards they passed en route, the three proceeded unhindered to swipe themselves in.

Inside, the structure was even more impressive, housing three drydocks, upon two of which small vessels sat in early states of assembly. But it was the slipway built into the central drydock that captured their attention. The *Red Mako*, or at least its skeletal frame, patiently awaited the attentions of its builders. Sleekly lined and resplendent in gleaming scarlet paint where complete, with the outline of a bridge that would not have looked out of place on a yacht, the boat sat in mute expectation of the praise most observers would afford it. Not so Lucie, whose face twisted contemptuously at the thought of the plans Butcher and Al-Khatani had for the project.

Algers skipped ahead, climbing over the port bow with unexpected alacrity and ducking out of site. Lucie and her unexpected new ally stepped to the edge, Whyte reaching out and touching his product as though it were a treasured but aloof lover. "There she is," he said, a hint of awe in his voice. "The *Red Mako*. Forty-five feet long, diesel and water jet engines giving it a speed of up to fifty knots, carrying a crew of eighteen. Similar to the American Long-Range Interceptor, only far, far superior."

"Would you like a moment alone with it?" asked Lucie, her eyebrow raised.

"It was to be my company's crowning achievement," Whyte responded with whimsy. "Our statement to the world that Brexit Britain was open for business and would thrive."

"By ramping up arms sales to dictators?"

"Someone was always going to," Whyte justified, unrepentantly. "It's just a matter of markets."

"It's a matter of genocide now Jarvis."

Their eyes turned to Algers as he appeared back on deck, his creased features even grimmer than usual as he clambered over the guard rail and made his way back down towards them, clutching something in his hand.

"At least an intended genocide."

Whyte's face grew as pale as his name and he shook his head in defiance of reality.

"No, no. no," he insisted. "That's nonsense. Butcher might well be a pervert and I'm sorrier than you can imagine for the horrors those young women have seen, but the only weapons intended for the *Red Mako* are three machine gun turrets a couple of grenade launchers, plus a short range missile launcher for retaliatory strikes on coastal invaders."

"Yes, Jarvis," Algers calmly concurred. "But the problem is what those launchers are firing."

"You mean?" Lucie interjected.

Algers produced the object he had carried from the boat, holding what looked like a large metal egg, dull grey and with white words painted around it.

"Hydrogen Cyanide grenades, at least that's my guess; but we can get Lake to confirm it. There are no missiles present yet but they'll probably spread volatile liquids while the grenades are useful for close range gas attacks."

"What...?" Whyte's voice was as weak as his flesh was pale and he reached out to take the object from Algers, rolling it around in front of his eyes in disbelief. "We don't use chemicals..."

"You do now. That's what your project was being used for, Jarvis," Algers rammed home. "Imagine a small fleet of these bad boys firing nerve agents onto Yemen from the sea; imagine the carnage that would cause..."

"But I don't understand," Lucie interjected, "the weapons systems weren't included in the contract, why is the prototype...?"

She broke off as her mind began to answer her own question. "Of course; good old plausible deniability at work again."

"Exactly," Algers confirmed. "If any trace of the chemicals was found, the government can legitimately claim that Britain did nothing but provide the shell; the weapons systems were none of our business."

"And by not throwing weapons open to general recruitment, the industry is none the wiser and there's no risk of a leak. Butcher and Al-Khatani use their own people and if anyone asks too many questions, the only paper trail leads back to *WaterWhyte*... and you."

She plucked the grenade from his hand and held it up in front of Whyte's eyes.

"Al-Khatani gets his massacre, Butcher gets his harem, and you? You get stiffed as the patsy."

No words fell from Whyte's open mouth and Lucie ignored him, turning back to Algers.

"You need to get the women out of here and to safety."

"What about you?"

"I've got unfinished business with our friend the *Mako*."

"Are you sure? We can leak what we have to the press and..."

"That won't be enough Kasper, you know that. Butcher's allies in the press will tip him the wink and before any authorities get here this place will be clean as a whistle and the women out there slandered and pilloried, if they're even reported on. No, I've got an idea..."

~

Lucie and Algers argued back and forth, cursing each other's stubbornness and raising and dismissing alternatives while a bewildered Whyte looked on. Eventually it was settled, and Lucie walked with them both to the dock hall entrance, embracing Algers and offering Whyte her hand.

"Ms Musilova," Whyte began, his voice nervous and embarrassed. "It seems I was wrong; about a great many things. I must apologise for my part in this, and I unreservedly do. You can be assured at least that there will be no cover up from me. I'll do everything in my power to expose what's gone on here, and to help those women get back to some kind of... normality?"

The man was struggling to articulate what his face told Lucie he felt, and she nodded in curt understanding.

"They're going to need a lot of care," she replied. "And the government are going to do their best to wash their hands of all this."

Whyte nodded vigorously.

"I'll certainly do my part to ensure they can't."

Lucie began to break away but the Brexiteer interjected once more.

"Look, I realise that ignorance is no defence, and I realise I've been somewhat lax in my affairs of late, but nonetheless I want you to know that this wasn't what I intended, either of the project, or..."

His words failed him, the collapse of his world hanging heavily on his shoulders. This man had blinded himself to the worst excesses of the people and movements he had promoted, naively trusting in the soundbites they spun, so sure was he in the righteousness of a cause he couldn't define. Though he may not have called himself an enemy of people like Lucie, he had stood with those who emphatically were, his presence lending credence to the poison others gleefully spread, never objecting to their words, never challenging the injustices; content instead to ride the waves of chaotic populism to a comfortable retirement, until his own interests were threatened. He was a money man, an investor, and it had been his lackadaisical and cavalier attitude towards the running of his own companies that had made *WaterWhyte* such easy pickings for Butcher and Al-Khatani. Many had suffered because of the indifference of people such as he, yet Lucie felt no malice toward him as he stood broken before her in wordless apology.

Instinctively she reached out and placed her hand on his shoulder.

"Hey," she began as he looked back at her. "Hand-wringing is no good to anyone; it's what you do to make it better that counts. Now get these women somewhere safe."

Whyte nodded and sat back, his eyes displaying the racings of his mind. Algers pushed past him, his face etched in profound concern.

"Are you sure about this?"

"As sure as I can be," she replied. "Just put your foot down and hope I get this right."

"And if you don't?" quizzed Whyte, his eyes wide. "Then name your next business after me."

She reached into the pocket of her overalls and pulled from it the grenade recovered by Algers and handed it back to him.

"Here, you'll need this."

She turned away from the pair, heading deeper into the hall, Alger's voice stopping her in her tracks.

"Hey!" her friend called. "I'll say a prayer for you tonight."

They were simple words, but powerful to Lucie, and coming from the irreligious Algers, all the more moving.

"Thanks," she smiled back. "Let's just hope it's not the prayer for the dead."

She watched them as they headed back to the garage, Algers half-supporting, half-carrying his fellow MP as they went, and Whyte doing his best to offer nonchalant 'good evenings' to the security patrol they passed. Lucie ducked out of sight of the same patrol and waited until the minibus's headlights beamed out into the night, followed by the grind of an engine and the crunch of tyres on gravel. Lucie watched the vehicle pull away and strained to see inside the windows at the faces of the women she had come so far and through so much to save, to see if that first glimmer of recovery had bloomed into something more; but to no avail. The minibus gathered speed as it reached the main barrier and despite the shouted commands to stop, drove faster still, splintering the barrier and earning cries of admonishment and an immediate siren call.

The bus grew smaller on its way back to London, and the air filled with the crunch of boots on gravel as security personnel raced from across the complex to the gate, leaving Lucie to heave the deepest of breathes into her lungs, readying her body for its next test.

Slipping back inside the dock hall, Lucie ran to the wall behind the command desk and smashed her clenched fist against the plastic sheet covering the bright red bomb alert button, an intermittent siren echoing immediately around her. She poked her head slightly out of the door and could hear the sound of scurrying footsteps as the security staff rushed to the rendezvous point, cursing what was turning into a night of confusion.

Whyte had told her that M.O.D sweepers would soon arrive to scour the area for bombs, and she had little time to complete her task. Reaching for the lever Jarvis had pointed out, she pulled it down, the colossal double doors sliding open, allowing the sea waters to wash further up the greased rails of the dry docks. The *Red Mako* was but bare bones and if released to the sea would crumble at once and be lost to the waves, which was precisely what she intended to do. The boat was constructed upon a cradle, designed to ease its passage to the water, and Lucie searched for the switch to send it on its way, but dropped to the floor when the whoosh of a bullet screamed past her head, clanging off the metal behind her.

Two more bullets missed her as she rolled behind an iron strut and peered round to pinpoint her attacker, her gut twisting as she realised who it was. The scrawny man with the Liverpool accent who had taken such delight in her torment days earlier was firing down at her in a furious rage. She broke cover, before twisting mid-run and hurling herself backwards as her crazed attacker fired again. Lucie slipped from the dry dock's edge and onto the rails by the Mako's cradle. Stunned, she strained her neck upwards, her assailant grinning down at her, levelling his gun.

As he did so, the doors were wrenched open and a handful of soldiers rushed into the dock hall, bellowing orders to freeze and throw down weapons; voices which earned the contemptuous glare of the wiry man, who scowled deeper as they fired warning shots into the air. Lucie pulled herself to her feet and watched in horror as the man pulled an object from his belt and raised his arm towards the newcomers.

"Grenade!" bellowed Lucie who looked frantically around for some way of stopping him. Closest to her was a large metal wrench, and she threw herself towards it, plucking it from its holder and hurling it towards the gunman, striking him on the temple.

The grenade dropped from his hand, leaving him scrambling on the deck. His scream was consumed by the explosion which engulfed the *Red Mako*, and sent its cradle creaking into a fiery roll towards Lucie, who turned and ran ahead of it. The burning carcass picked up speed behind her as it collapsed in upon itself, and Lucie launched herself headlong into the icy waters, kicking as hard as she was able, hoping against hope that it would be hard enough. And as she kicked, Butcher's heralded new symbol of Brexit Britain, now a flaming mass of indignant impotence, rolled inexorably towards her.

27

The explosion stopped presses and dominated bulletins from almost the moment the flames were first seen licking the Portsmouth skyline, relegating all other stories to the status of also-rans. Within minutes the internet had been awash with rumours of who to blame, with concocted stories galore pointing the finger at everyone from Muslim extremists to Remoaners looking to sabotage the glories of Brexit; the absence of any official detail only fuelling the flames of falsehoods.

As far as the authorised story went, the explosion was merely a regrettable accident brought about by 'human error', with the actual costs minimised due to the early stage of the project's development and the damage to the dock hall easily repairable. Rather than catastrophe, the government machine went into overdrive to present the fire as an 'opportunity' to refocus and show strength and resilience in the face of adversity. The press were told to expect a personal statement from Adam Butcher himself, who would be flying in to the Portsmouth site on WaterWhyte's own private Learjet, direct from a conference in Edinburgh.

The cameras followed his arrival and subsequent statement made against the backdrop of firecrews working the scene, and he played to the gallery as he had done a thousand times before; a patriotic comment here, a dog whistle there, and an abundance of soundbites designed to portray him as the iron man Britain so desperately needed. All was going swimmingly for Butcher, and he soon opened up to questions, assured that his regular plants among the assembled journos would stroke his ego as they had so many times before. They proceeded to do just that, until one question shouted from the back made the Minister stutter and blink.

"Excuse me?" Butcher said, uncertainly.

"I asked," the voice shouted again, "if we could see the damage to the storage depot, too?"

Butcher coughed slightly and grinned insincerely.

"The, erm, the damage I'm assured was limited to the dock hall and the *Red Mako*, there are no reports of any other areas of the site being affected," Butcher said, looking around to take a question from a friendlier face, but still the voice shouted back at him.

"Well the damage from the explosion was limited to the dock hall, yes, but I hear there was quite a kerfuffle at the storage depot too."

The other journalists began to mutter, and Butcher squinted to see who was putting him under pressure.

"I'm afraid you must be mistaken," he said, the first beads of sweat beginning to form on his brow. "The storage depot is off limits to press and there was absolutely no 'kerfuffle' as you describe it."

The gathered journos began to part, and from the back stepped Kasper Algers, his weathered face strong and bearing no ill from the previous night's exploits.

"No?" he replied, the cameras now upon him. "Well I know someone who begs to differ."

"Really?" sneered Butcher. "What 'someone' is that?"

Algers reached backwards and a young woman took his hand and stepped forward beside him, her hair and face bright and clean and her clothes fresh and new. The colour drained from Butcher's face as the woman stared piercingly back at him, unfazed by the flash of cameras around her.

"You remember Aga, of course Adam," said Algers, loudly. "She's keen on asking you why you saw fit to keep her and her friends locked up in the storage block."

More chattering followed as Butcher began to shake on his podium.

"But," he stuttered, "but, Whyte said..."

"Yes, Jarvis told you on the phone that the fire was contained to the dock hall and that the rest of the site was uncompromised, but let's face it, that was a pretty white lie compared to what your lot put on the side of that bus, don't you think?"

"But..." For the first time in his career, Butcher had no words. Nothing had prepared him for this moment and even the friendliest faces in the crowd were now staring at him in a mixture of confusion and disgust.

"And while we're chatting about that," Algers continued, "maybe you could shed some light on this."

He pulled out the chemical grenade retrieved from the *Mako* the previous night and held it up for the cameras to see.

"I'm sure everyone here would be fascinated to know why you intended for the *Red Mako* to fire chemical weapons into Yemen." The murmers of the assembled press turned instantly into chaos, with microphones thrust into the panicking Butcher's face and demands for answers pounding at him from all sides. Shooting a look of pure hatred towards Algers, he pushed his way through the crowd and ran as fast as he had in his life back towards the small airstrip and the Learjet on which he had arrived. As he drew level, an armed military officer blocked his path.

"Excuse me sir," said the young lieutenant, "I think there's call to discuss the matters just raised in more detail..."

The sentence went unfinished, Butcher striking the young man hard in the midriff, and clattering his fist against his temple as he dropped. The youngster fought back but Butcher kicked at him viciously, freeing himself of his grip and fumbling to grab the sidearm the officer carried, firing it into the air above the pursuing army of press. With nowhere else to run, Butcher climbed the airstair to the jet and kicked it away. As he wrenched closed the heavy main door, the pilot stepped from the flight deck and started towards the politician, an expression of pure confusion on his face.

"What's going on?" he quizzed, "did I just hear a gunshot?"

"You'll hear another if you don't get back there and get us off the ground." Butcher swung the weapon towards the pilot, who froze for a second, staring at the gun in incredulity.

"But..."

"I said fucking move!"

Butcher roughly grabbed the man's arm, turning him around and pushing him back towards the cockpit.

"We don't have clearance!" the pilot objected as Butcher pushed him down into his chair.

"Do I look like I'm waiting for clearance? Take off!"

Butcher pressed the barrel of his gun against the pilot's cheek, who stared back at him in fear before flicking the switches and pulling the levers that heaved the plane into life.

The rising roar of the engine drowned out the shouts and protest from outside and the cries to block the runway. The plane was already moving, and Butcher watched through the windscreen as people scurried quickly from its path as it built momentum and hurtled down the runway, followed by the wail of pursuing police sirens.

Reaching reluctantly for the thrust lever, the pilot eased the plane high into the air, wiping sweat from his frowning brow as they rose. Butcher, the gun still pointed at the man's head, clung on with white knuckles to the back of the pilot's chair as the increased g-force threatened to knock him off balance.

"What's our heading?" shouted the pilot as he began to level out the flying metal beast.

"Just head out to sea."

"To sea? We don't have the fuel for a long-haul flight!"

"Just shut up and fly! If you turn us around, you're a dead man!" Butcher stepped from the flight deck into the main fuselage, the sweat of his palms making the gun slippery in his grip. Pulling with his other hand at his suddenly tight collar with such force that he pulled the top button from the shirt and dragged the shining red tie scruffily low around his chest. This couldn't be happening, not to him. Everything until now had been so easy, he held one of the safest seats in the country, he was the darling of the Brexiteering Right. The PM was on the brink and he had been the man standing behind her with the crowd bellowing for him to push. And now?

His face was full of blind panic, his mind feverishly racing and his eyes flashing back and forth.

"Looking for a way out, Adam?"

Butcher's arm swung up at once, pointing the gun in the direction of the voice, and he laughed in disbelief as his eyes settled upon the woman who emerged from the galley, her tied back hair dirty and her flesh and clothes stained and bloodied.

"There's only one way out that I can see," said Lucie

Musilova. "Whiskey and pistol time, eh?" Butcher answered in soft disdain, the panic that had etched onto his face giving way to a pure and unsullied contempt.

"We can skip the whiskey if you like, no point hanging around. You're screwed, Butcher, there's no coming back for you. Papers and TV all over the world are reporting on you, Al-Khatani and your little 'harem'; even the British press can't ignore it now. You've nowhere to run."

The smirk twitched as she spoke, even now his voice imbued with a potent vibe of arrogant mockery.

"You're so sure of that aren't you," he laughed, his eyes displaying to Lucie the tell-tale signs of a man whose grip on his own senses was growing looser by the second. "You're so sure you've got me beaten."

"It's looking like it to me."

"I'm not surprised," he snapped, "you're so two dimensional."

"And what are you, a fucking Time Lord?"

"In a manner of speaking. Or more accurately we're all children of our own time. This isn't the nineties, people don't give a shit anymore about the morality of politicians, as long as they tell it like it is."

"You mean as long as they pander to the prejudices, as long as they give simple soundbite answers to complex problems."

"It's the same thing! You've done me a favour in a way," he said, his pupils widening as he spoke. "What have I done apart from win a money-making contract for Britain and get rid of a few uppity foreign bitches along the way. Whether you and your filthy Remainer friends like it or not, there's a big audience for someone prepared to fight for Britain's prosperity, and who doesn't balk at stepping on a few insects on the way. And they'll do anything to see that person reach the top. The Party might wash their hands of me but there'll be others queuing up to knock on my cell door, just waiting for the day I get out of prison. You take me in, and you make me a hero."

"Who said I'm taking you in?" replied Lucie.

"Oh, so you're here to kill me, are you? Another mark on the bedpost for the Overlappers. Well tough shit, my dear, I'm the one with the gun."

"Who needs guns?" Lucie answered, "When you've got brains instead?"

"Brains?" he sneered. "In just a few short years we've turned Britain from the gateway to Europe into a land where the front pages of newspapers decry anyone who questions the legitimacy of the referendum we blatantly corrupted as an enemy of the people. You don't do that without brains, Lucie."

"No," Lucie answered, still facing down the gun with measured calm. "It wasn't clever, what you did. Cunning, yes, Machiavellian even, but not clever. It may take them a while, but people will open their eyes one day soon and see what you've done, and when they do, they'll demand an end to the perverted mess you've made of their democracy. And you, your *Red Mako* and your pervert's Playpen will be a distant memory that nobody gives the slightest shit about."

Butcher twitched, and for a moment Lucie thought he would pull the trigger. Instead, the MP took a step closer, shaking his head at her in apparent frustration.

"You just don't understand, do you?" He spat, contemptuously. "You don't get representation with your tax receipt these days, not anymore. Since 1832 people have tried to expand the franchise, but now it's about restricting it. Little by little, both at the ballot box and online."

"What?" Lucie quizzed in confusion.

"It's easy," Butcher answered, relishing his control of the

exchange. "We restrict the electorate and we push those left in the way we want them to go. People put their lives online and wherever they are, we are, inside their minds, inside their souls; we know how you think, and that knowledge is power. A little twist here, a little advert there, and before you even know it, you're dancing to our tune and would vote against your own mother if we told you to. We're already half way to convincing the country that you don't buy your vote with tax anymore you buy it with your blood; British blood. And yours is decidedly watered down..."

With each word Butcher spoke, Lucie realised all the more clearly that he meant what he was saying, as though he were narrating a delusional fantasy playing out before his own eyes. Had she not seen the fruits of his efforts first hand, she might even have pitied him, but the indignities she and the others had suffered because of him had taken her way beyond that. Instead, she fought through her fatigue and looked him directly in the eye. "Maybe it is," she answered. "But then, some men never could handle their drink."

Butcher's face twisted into hatred and as he levelled his gun at her, Lucie braced herself for the shot.

It never came. As he poised to fire, arms reached around the MP, knocking the gun from his hand and wrestling him to the floor.

Butcher heaved and strained, trying to topple the pilot and throw him off balance, Lucie joining the fray to force the politician back down to the floor. At her feet lay the gun, and the desire to break her pledge ignited immediately within her, but instead she kicked it back towards the pilot.

"Grab it!" she ordered the pilot, who scooped it from the floor and scrambled to his feet, levelling it at Butcher, who raised himself up to his knees, his face twisted with rage.

"Thanks," breathed Lucie to the perspiring man. "Autopilot?"

"Yes, but we're low on fuel, I'll need to get back there."

"Let me get him restrained," she answered.

Lucie ducked into the galley, returning with scissors she used to cut through lengths of seatbelt, intending to fashion restraints for the sneering Butcher.

"Where are we, over the Channel?"

"Yes, Miss. When you've finished up with this one, I'll turn us around."

"Do you think they'll thank you?" Butcher sneered. "What?"

"You heard me. You've won the day, you've saved your little litter of foreign bitches, you've got me bang-to-rights and no-one's going to be firing any chemicals into Yemen, at least not from our platforms now. Oh, there'll be some lovely headlines tomorrow for somebody, but not for you. You're a spy, an operative; there won't be any headlines for you, no recognition, even though you're the one responsible. You know, I don't think I could do anything without having somebody praise me for it..."

"Like a roomful of women abused and tortured into fawning over you? I don't need that kind of recognition."

"Well that's good. Because while tomorrow might bring good headlines, the day after is when they'll start looking at the cost."

"What cost?"

"You know what cost," Butcher chuckled. "Women rescued, yeah great! But why all the effort to save foreigners, when so many crimes against British people are unsolved. Humanitarian crisis averted, wonderful! But at the cost of one of the most valuable contracts this country has seen in years. Your little victory hasn't solved anything, and in a few days the papers will be blaming everything on foreigners again and screaming for the heads of federalist traitors like you. We'll be closer than ever to purging ourselves of your kind for good. And that's really all we wanted."

"Who, Butcher?" Lucie snapped, ignoring his diatribe despite the uncomfortable ring of truth it contained. "Who's 'we'?"

Butcher's eyes narrowed and his smirk twitched in condescension.

"Sorry," he said, "I can't remember."

Lucie stared back at the unrepentant man, both his smugness and his pride in what he had done twisting a knot in her stomach. Her straps were ready, and she pulled them tight in her hands and she stepped closer.

"Don't worry," she said. "I know someone in London who's particularly good at helping people like you remember. Ordinarily I'd find any reason I could not to make such an introduction, but I admit, in your case it'll be a pleasure."

Crossing towards him, Lucie felt the shudder of turbulence rock the cabin, and she braced herself to keep upright. The pilot's concentration though was broken, and he turned his head for a second back towards the cockpit, Butcher seizing his chance and twisting to knock the gun from the pilot's hand. Lucie charged for him, but the politician was already swinging towards her, his fist connecting hard with her temple and sending her sprawling across the cabin, the sound of gunshots ringing in her ears.

The blow knocked her senses from her. The wail and cry of charging wind filled her ears, bringing her back from the brink of oblivion and she shook the stars from her eyes and scanned the cabin, her eyes falling on the body of the pilot, a fresh bullet wound in his head. Sparks flew from the cockpit, where other bullets had been fired, the jet stuttering in indignant response.

Butcher stood by the cabin door his features twisted into unbreakable mania. The politician had thrown open the door of the falling craft, letting the sky rush furiously inside to claim it as its own, scattering papers and folders throughout the cabin. Scrambling to her feet and struggling for balance in the unstable jet, Lucie found Butcher's gun training steadily on her. Adjusting his balance, the MP reached above himself and opened the storage locker, fishing out the five parachutes it contained, and throwing the first four towards the open door, where they began their descent into the Channel below. The last chute, he retained, his perpetual sneer twitching as he hooked the strap over his gun arm and slid it over his shoulder.

"The Twitter mob used to laugh at me when I told them I was in the TA," he smugly recounted. "But it wasn't only picnics in the woods we got up to; we did parachute training too."

"Ooh," Lucie mocked, "I hope you got a badge for it."

"Funny, funny bitch. I'm sorry I won't get to see how funny you find it when you land."

"Where do you think you can go, Butcher?" Lucie shouted over the rushing wind.

"It's a big world out there," he sneered. "Time for me to global! Whereas for you, it's just time to go."

Panic began to rise in Lucie's gut as she looked around for an exit, some way out of this which refused to reveal itself to her. Her passions once more threatened to cloud her judgement, and she could feel her heart beat rapidly in fear.

"There's no getting out of this one for you," smirked Butcher as he pulled the harness tight around him. "You'd better say those prayers you're so fond of."

The clouds of emotion pushed back, Lucie had waited patiently for her moment, for the mistake her mind had told her would come, and now it did. The harness sat unclipped on Butcher's back, waiting to be fastened into place.

"I've prayed enough for the both of us already today," she

grimly replied. "You might want to try one of your own; it's best to go with a clear conscience."

"Go?" he snorted with derision. "Oh, I plan on hanging around for a good while yet, so forgive me if I don't take up your offer quite now."

"No rush," she answered, her eyes narrowing in determination as Butcher lowered his gun to clip the harness together. "It's a long way down."

The weapon no longer on her, Lucie pushed away from the desk and with every last ounce of energy she could muster, charged herself headlong into the shocked Butcher, knocking the gun from his hand and him through the beckoning cabin door. His protestations were drowned at once by the rush of wind assaulting them as they tumbled from the rapidly falling jet that began to dip into its death spiral. She locked her arms and legs intransigently around the shocked and struggling politician.

A screaming Butcher tried to shake her loose, and she gripped all the more tightly as they tumbled, her knuckles whitening and her muscles straining as she held them together into a mutually assured fate.

Lucie had jumped before, in her RAF days, and the barked lessons of her instructors sounded once more in her mind, berating her for not controlling the descent ahead of deployment. They were falling too quickly for her to comply with the orders of memory, there was no way she could release her grip to settle them into a glide and free-fall, and Butcher himself was clawing and biting too feverishly to do it himself, his writhing and squirming bestial in its ferocity.

Wrenching her head back from his chest Lucie looked into cruel, wild eyes, devoid of any trace of reason or sanity, the howling wind lending him a monstrous quality as though he were some undead wraith, scratching and tearing at his prey.

Thrusting forward, her forehead smashed against Butcher's nose, bespattering them both with his blood and sending it spritzing into the air pockets they tumbled through. The blow's effects were exactly as Lucie had hoped, Butcher's hands releasing her and clutching his face, giving her the precious seconds she needed to act. Squeezing her legs tighter still around him and digging her fingers into the flesh of his shoulder, she let her other hand slip free just long enough to pull down on the ripcord, the canopy unfurling in a tumultuous second, pushing them back up with such force that Lucie was shaken from her precarious clutch and she scrambled and snatched to reclaim it. Jarred by the canopy's release, Butcher clung onto the risers in panic, kicking out at the displaced Lucie, who clenched her arms unyieldingly around him while her legs were blown and buffeted in the air.

She had deployed in time, but Lucie knew it was insufficient to totally soften the rough landing ahead. The choppy sea was still settling from the jet's entry a distance away, and as their glide took them closer to the foam, Lucie could have sworn the waters were reaching out to claim them. With seconds to go, she swung her legs upwards and closed them around Butcher's calves, leaving his ankles to strike the hard water and break their fall. The politician had barely opened his mouth to scream before they plunged into the depths, salt water filling their mouths and stinging their eyes. Lucie pulled herself away from the struggling man and surfaced, heaving air into her lungs and trying to shake the disorientation from her brain. Neither the fall nor the water had diluted her anger and she watched the struggling man as he fought to free himself of the canopy and tread water with battered ankles, bellowing at the wind as he flailed. They were both dead now, she knew it. The waters were freezing and demanded their submission, and she knew she would relent soon enough. She may not be able to bring Ines back, but she could at least ensure her killer went out knowing who had sent him on his way and why.

Butcher surfaced and heaved air desperately into his lungs, but as he struggled with the spent chute, he was unprepared for the tug of cords against his throat. Lucie pulled on the lines, twisting them around the soft flesh, Butcher grasping fruitlessly to free himself.

"I hope you've made your peace with The Lord," Lucie spat into his ear as she tugged harder, "because we've been invited round to see Him, and I wouldn't want us to be late."

She pulled Butcher under the waves with her, pulling with all her strength until his struggles faded, and his thrashing limbs grew limp. At once she despised herself and she whispered unheard apologies to her victim as she surfaced, surrendering him to the water. She should have found a better way, but once more she had given in to the emotions that raged within her, and now there was so little time to repent.

The sea was pushing its way into her lungs, her mouth filled with the overpowering taste of salt and her voice powerless against the water. There was no point in shouting; there was nobody even to shout to, only the damning voice inside her head that she, a supposed woman of God, had made murder the final act of her life. Her arms and legs began to fall limp, ceasing their unwinnable struggle against the might of the waves, and allowing themselves to instead be rocked to their rest in their watery embrace. She was struggling to think any more and had almost forgotten why she was there. Her memory of why she had murdered was fading, but so was her guilt for it. Yes, she had killed, but that wasn't her final act. She had saved people too, people who would now have pains and sorrows and loves and joys they would have been robbed of without her. Where they had death, they now had life, and if the price of their freedom was the loss of her life then fair enough, she could think of worse ways to go. The damning voice had gone, replaced by a sense of peace and reassurance that things would be okay. She was sorry that she had killed, sorry that she hadn't found some other way to save the killer from himself, but violence would not be her final thought. Instead, as she gave in to the flirtations of the sea, her final thoughts would be of love.

28

The vaulted, octagonal grandeur of Parliament's central lobby was filled as much with ego as with people; esteemed Members of all Parties quick to catch a brief exchange with the influential and the powerful, while scurrying twice as fast from those constituents who prowled the hall with spleens to vent and axes to grind. Lucie's eyes were drawn through the puffing and preening figures and past the huddled groups of whispering plotters, towards the tall, grey haired figure of Kasper Algers, who stood apart from the horde.

The fall from the plane and the battering of the sea had left her in a stupor, her senses addled before finally giving in to the engulfing waves and her own unconsciousness, fully expecting her next breath to be drawn in eternity. Instead, it had been on a fishing trawler, wondering why she had responded by vomiting sea water onto herself and him. It had taken several days of hospital observation before she had been deemed recovered, during which time she had received a parcel from Algers, containing a brand-new black overcoat, and a stack of newspapers. Following an accident at *WaterWhyte Defence*, the papers informed her, and allegations of chemical misuse appearing in the foreign press, the *Red Mako* project had been suspended pending review, while the Saudi government refused to comment. Adam Butcher himself had died in tragic circumstances when his private jet had crashed into the English Channel leaving no survivors. Butcher's estate denied in full all 'spurious allegations' of involvement on his part of the abduction of six women, now receiving professional care and expected to make full recoveries.

Her strength returning, Lucie had checked herself out and headed back to London in time for the 'Urgent Question' about the fiasco, tabled by the Opposition, the word being that Jarvis Whyte, devastated both by his company's involvement and his own blindness, was to intercede to ensure the matter was not swept under the carpet. Having spotted her friend and mentor, Lucie pushed past some of the Commons' more lethargic Members and raced up to meet him, unaware at first that her own smile was every bit as wide as the one that appeared on his wrinkled face as he spotted her.

Their embrace was swift but sincere, earning the tuts of some of the more priggish passers-by, whom Lucie imagined were not so superior on their visits to the trial 'Establishments' now also under review.

"You're looking well," Algers smiled.

"I could say the same," she answered. "Thanks for the coat, by the way."

"No problem, can't have you catching cold when we're hunkered down looking for bad guys."

She looked away, the memory of her promise to Ismail to give up this work tugging at her gut.

"I suppose not," she said. "What happened?"

"After your impromptu sky dive, you mean?" he asked, winking at her. "I wish I could say I rode in to save the day, but quite honestly the answer is luck. The trawler that picked you up was in the area and witnessed the crash, but by the time they made it over, Butcher was already dead."

"Wish I could say I was sorry," Lucie muttered.

"The pilot's body was recovered with a bullet hole in his head."

"That was Butcher."

"I didn't doubt it," Algers answered, his voice low and grave, "but don't expect to see that in the papers."

"And Butcher?"

"At the moment people think he died in the crash, whether that changes will be up to Lake, I suppose. He's had the autopsy done in secret; the poor bugger got tangled up in his parachute cables apparently. Is that what really happened?"

"If that's what the autopsy says," Lucie answered, her face making clear she had no wish to discuss the matter any further. "He wasn't the only one, though. Al-Khatani was up to his neck in it too, it's not fair he gets away with it."

"I wouldn't worry about that," Algers smiled. "Our friend Mr Whyte is so racked with guilt by all this that he had a quiet word with his good friend, the Saudi Ambassador, who it seems is very keen on deflecting attention from his country's human rights record. He swears that his government had no knowledge of or involvement with any chemical weapons programme, and that any such allegations should be laid solely at the door of Al-Khatani himself."

"And?"

"And, I understand that he will shortly be taking a trip to explain his actions face to face with the people of Yemen; I'm told that several people there are very anxious to meet him."

"Ah," Lucie acknowledged in perverse satisfaction. "Bon voyage." As she spoke, a brief but profound hush came over the hall, marking the arrival of Jarvis Whyte, himself. Ignoring the clamber of the journalists who badgered him for comment,

Whyte strode with purpose across the lobby towards the Commons, pausing as he reached Lucie and Algers. Turning his head briefly towards her, he offered an understated and silent nod of the head; a gesture which seemed curiously anachronistic now but which in the past would have been considered the act of a gentleman. Without waiting for a response, he continued his journey into the Commons, politicians of all hues following in his wake as he drank deeply from the bottle of water he always carried before speaking in the House.

"Funny," Algers mused as they watched him go. "Reading out his political suicide note might just be the most effective and honourable thing he's ever done as an MP."

"At least he'll be remembered for trying to set the record straight."

"Maybe..."

He grinned widely at her, then began to pull away to join the trail of Parliamentarians heading into the chamber. "Catch you after the statement, yeah?"

"Kasper!" Lucie shouted after him as turned away.

Algers spun around and stepped back to her, his eyebrows raised in query; but nothing came, she just stared at her older mentor, her lips wordlessly moving. Algers' face relaxed into melancholy, as though he knew by instinct what it was she was trying to say.

"Hey," he whispered, "it's okay."

"I'm sorry," she said shaking her head gently as his hands rested on her shoulders. "I made a promise..."

"I know."

"You know?"

"We all make that promise, Lucie, sooner or later we all say, 'just one more job and I'll put it all behind me'. It's just it's not a promise that many of us keep."

"I have to keep it," she answered, her eyes beginning to mist. "I've never been the right fit for this job; I let my emotions influence me, I spend half my time killing people and the other half on my knees to God, trying to say sorry for doing it. I swear Kasper, when I get into bed every night, I go through a list of all the reasons to hate myself and I can't think of any reasons not to. All I wanted to do with my life was help people, that's why I signed up and became a Minister. I was a bloody good one too, but now? Now I walk around with a gun, killing people someone tells me are the bad guys... You have no idea how badly I never want to see a gun again in my life."

"Lucie," Algers interrupted. "You've just saved the lives of six women. You've ended the career of a man who would have caused fuck knows how much harm if he'd ever got behind the PM's desk, and while you may not have singlehandedly stopped the war in Yemen, you've made damn sure things aren't going to get any worse for them, at least for a while. You're not just good at this job, Lucie, you've *done* good by doing it."

"By waving a fucking gun around and killing people..." Algers sighed in patient understanding.

"Lucie, only you can decide whether or not you feel suited to this job, but don't let anyone ever tell you you're not good at it. So what if you spend your days off praying? I usually spend mine getting pissed and watching re-runs of *Randall & Hopkirk*. I can't give you any theological answers, Lucie, I'm not a religious man, but if I were, I'd say that this job, well... I think it might be your calling."

Lucie's eyes widened at his words and she looked silently back at him, nodding her understanding. Algers hands slipped from her shoulders, though his eyes remained on hers a moment longer before he gave a final smile and turned back to join the procession of the vainglorious into the chamber.

Making her way up to the gallery, Lucie politely reciprocated the few nods and half smiles in her direction as she took a seat among the dispirited journalists and sketch writers occupying it, high above the shining, green leather benches of the Commons. Below them at the despatch box, stood the latest automaton from the governmental conveyor belt, droning passionlessly on about a topic so unclear, even the half-hearted and half-cut cries of 'hear, hear' from honourable and not-so honourable colleagues were less sincere than usual.

She spotted the waving order paper of Algers from his position on the opposing benches, as he rose to make his first comments in the House since his injury, to the generally agreeable mutterings of those around him.

"I'm sorry, Mr Speaker, but while I'm grateful to the Right Honourable gentleman for giving way, I feel it is my duty to point out to the House, that he is talking absolute horse shit."

The immediate flurry of order papers and cries of righteous indignation were every bit as vociferous as Algers had expected, and more so; the Speaker's impassioned cries for 'Order' unheeded for some moments before volume returned to a manageable level. The Speaker, a short, grey haired man who never allowed his stature to in any way diminish his authority, allowed a wry smile to play across his face as he stood to enforce the laws of the House.

"The, ah, Honourable Member," he began, in not entirely unamused tones, "is an accomplished and intelligent man, and is well aware of the rules of this place, and what language is considered acceptable. I invite him to take this opportunity to withdraw his comments and... modify his language."

Algers made his perfunctory apology and re-phrased his statement to a blander one, objecting to the government's considering work of one hour a week to be reason to claim that the employment figures had risen; a statement the Minister pooh-poohed before continuing.

As the government minister reached his overdue conclusion, the benches began to fill and the leading figures of all Parties hurriedly took their seats ahead of the expected drama; notepads around Lucie opening at the ready, their owners already scrawling imagined headlines about what was to follow.

"Urgent question to the Defence Minister," boomed the Speaker, the House erupting in cries of adversarial posturing as the Leader of the Opposition rose to his feet, and demanded an immediate response to the situation at *WaterWhyte Defence* and the status of the *Red Mako* project, as well as the allegations appearing in the foreign press of Adam Butcher's involvement in the kidnapping of foreign nationals.

Responding for the government was a young and terrified looking junior Minister, thrust into the unwelcome limelight in the absence of his department's Secretary of State. He had not spoken long before a shout came from his own benches.

"Point of order, Mr Speaker!"

Lungs exhaled and heads turned towards the third row on the government benches, to see Jarvis Whyte, his order paper clutched between his fingers and raised in the air. A tortuous tension hung over the assembled Members, as they waited for the Speaker to allow him to speak or direct him to remain silent in his seat.

"Point of order," roared the Speaker from his position of grandeur, to a cacophony of cheers and a volley of condemnation. "Mr Jarvis Whyte."

The barrage of braying and jeers which typically peppered the chamber, gave way to murmurs and whispered rumblings as Whyte rose to his feet. Across the House, they stared in wide-eyed expectation, like children watching the chimney for Santa, while the features on his own front bench were rigid and grey, as though awaiting pronouncement of sentence. Whyte himself looked to Lucie more confident than when she last saw him, facing down the rows of parliamentarians as he might the boards of his companies, his high forehead free from perspiration and his eyes piercing and sharp.

"Mr Speaker," Whyte began, the chamber falling into ominous silence. "The Minister states that the government had no awareness of the activities of the late Mr Butcher, nor their connections to the *Red Mako* project, or indeed the company I long ago founded, *WaterWhyte Defence*. I'm afraid to inform the House that this is simply and demonstrably untrue…"

The sentence remained unfinished, as Whyte coughed and tried to speak, only to cough again. His brow furrowing in confusion which quickly turned to panic as he struggled to heave air into his lungs. Clutching his chest, the man's legs gave way and he tumbled forward over the benches, landing crumpled on the floor, by the feet of the politically and physically intransigent. Shouts for help and screams of horror ignited chaos in the chamber, punctuated by cries for order and paramedics to attend.

Lucie ran from the gallery, towards the Commons, out of which poured the powerful and the terrified. Cries from one quarter of 'terrorist' had thrown fuel onto the furnace of panic, while cooler heads appealed fruitlessly for calm. Lucie pushed her way past the fleeing Members and the bemused ushers, who struggled to apply sanity to the mayhem. When she reached the fallen Whyte, Algers was already kneeling beside him, his fingers to the man's neck.

"Dead," he confirmed as he looked up to Lucie.

"How?" she asked. "He looked fine!"

They stood back as two paramedics arrived and set about what would be futile efforts to revive him, Algers taking Lucie aside and whispering to her.

"I've seen sudden death syndrome before but not in someone Whyte's age."

"And just as he's about to expose government complicity in the *Red Mako*? That's too much of a coincidence."

"Absolutely, I just wish we had an explanation for it."

Lucie frowned in frustration as she scanned the chamber, looking for anyone or anything which might give some clue, before her eyes settled on a single MP, who had remained seated while the others ran, staring in pure maliciousness at the fallen body, before standing slowly and heading for the exit.

"Don't worry," Lucie told Algers, who followed her stare. "I think I know someone who might."

29

"Come in!" Lucie shouted as a knock rapped loudly on the door of Kasper Alger's Parliamentary office early the next morning, followed by the creak of wood as the visitor entered.

"I was expecting to see Kasper," said Amber Robyn as the door closed behind her and she surveyed the cramped and dusty office, puzzlement on her face.

"Yes, sorry about that," Lucie answered, "he's running a few minutes late and he asked me to look after you. Drink?"

"I'm not sure I have the time," the MP answered, displeasure at the altered arrangement, not to mention who she was expected to deal with in the meantime, etched onto her face.

"Oh, please, Amber," Lucie insisted, pulling a bottle of aged malt Scotch from Algers' drawer. "Kasper got this in especially; have a glass while we wait, he won't be long."

Not waiting for an answer, Lucie poured two measures into glasses ready on the table and handed one to Robyn.

"What shall we drink to?" Robyn asked. "How about to Jarvis Whyte?"

"Forgive me," she replied, "but I wouldn't have thought you'd mourn the passing of a man who campaigned so vehemently against people like you?"

"I'm not a monster, Amber," Lucie answered, winning the battle to keep her emotions contained. "Nobody deserves to go like that."

Robyn's eyes flickered for the briefest of moments as she held the glass to her lips.

"I don't know," said Robyn, her voice almost sinister in tone. "I understand it's not uncommon for a comedian to die on stage."

The words didn't stun Lucie, instead they told her that the woman sat across from her understood she may not be there to discuss casework with Algers.

"To Jasper," said Amber Robyn, her eyes betraying suspicion. "To Jasper," said Lucie Musilova, her own giving no reason to doubt it.

The women drank, their eyes remaining on each other, and neither at first offering a word or gesture to break the rapidly ossifying tension, until Robyn broke her stare for a second to glance at the clock on the wall behind Lucie's head.

"How long did you say Kasper would be?"

"There's been word from the coroner," Lucie stated, ignoring her counterpart's question. "Unofficially of course."

"The cause of death's already been released, it was a stroke, everybody knows that."

"Well yes, everybody knows that, or at least thinks they know that, and it would certainly fit the story of a man under enormous pressure, whose world was collapsing around him. But that doesn't necessarily mean it's what the coroner found."

"Really?" Robyn answered, her eyebrow raised. "And just why would the coroner tell you something not included in her report?"

"Oh, friend of a friend, you know how these things work."

"Indeed?"

"Anyway, at first glance, you're absolutely right; acute respiratory failure, wholly consistent with stroke victims, but when you take the coniine found in his water into account, it puts things in a completely different light."

"Coniine?" Robyn snapped, "I've never heard of it."

"It's nasty," Lucie replied. "You might know it better as hemlock poisoning. It induces flaccid paralysis and hypoxia, eventually killing you through lack of oxygen to the heart and brain. Horrible way to die..."

"So, it was suicide?"

At first Lucie answered her only with her eyes, staring unflinchingly into the MP's own.

"Was it?" she eventually responded. "Now, surely you're not suggesting..."

The anger that had begun to spread onto Lucie's face softened, replaced by something approaching sorrow, a sadness overcoming the fire in her now watery eyes.

"Amber," she began, her voice soft, almost whimsical in tone, "Kasper told me once that he and Jarvis were never close, either socially or politically. He was an unashamed Tory, he looked at Parliament as a club and it's fair to say neither would make the other's Christmas card list, but do you know what? When Kasper was first elected, an Independent MP, alone in the Palace of Westminster, without the first fucking idea of where to go and what to do, Jasper Whyte was the first one to go to him and offer his hand. He showed Kasper around the place, bought him a drink in the bar and they chatted, only for an hour or so, about the things they believed in, what made them want to get involved; they even found a little bit of common ground here and there. And that was it, other than a nod and a smile in the Chamber, or on their way to vote, but do you know what that tells me about Jarvis? That he was a decent person. He didn't care about High Office, or careering. Maybe he wasn't the best constituency MP, and maybe he should have been booted out of here years ago, but I can point to hundreds of people downstairs who that could apply to. No, he might not have used his position for good, but neither did he try to cause harm to people like that. It's a shame you can't say the same."

Robyn's eyes widened at the insult, and for a moment Lucie wondered if she might actually strike her, but a modicum of restraint appeared to take hold and control returned to her still ferociously beautiful features.

"If you think, young lady, that you can sit there and make insinuations..."

"I'm insinuating nothing, Amber," Lucie interrupted, "I'm saying that you killed Jarvis Whyte."

"I..?" Robyn laughed in outraged indignance. "What makes you think I was either able or inclined to kill a man I've known for twenty years?"

"That's just it, Amber," Lucie continued, "You'd known him for twenty years. You knew him as well as anyone, some would say perhaps too well, not that that's any of my business. But whatever the nuances of your relationship over the years, you were still close, at least he thought so. You'd campaigned together in the Referendum and you were both still involved in Leave pressure groups pushing for a No Deal Brexit; you'd been in and out of his office a hundred times in the last few weeks, including the day of his speech."

"So?"

"Coniine poisoning can take about three to four hours to kill a person. You'd met with him at six, he died just after two. I think you poisoned his water during your meeting in the hope he'd die before he could expose government complicity in the House, the extra sip just helped him on his way."

The anger was burning behind Robyn's eyes as she listened

to Lucie's words, objections forming at her lips only to be swallowed away and replaced with more as her rage continued to bubble.

"If you were to repeat your words outside of this office, madam, my solicitor would come down on you like a tonne of bricks. How, exactly would I have access to this 'coniine', and more importantly, why would I want to kill Jarvis, if we were as close as you suggest?"

Lucie finished her drink and picked up a folder of papers on Algers' desk, flicking through it as she spoke.

"Well, that's the interesting thing, Amber," she began, "you see at first it was just a hunch, but then someone got in touch with me about some interesting paperwork that's turned up."

"Another friend of a friend?"

"Something like that. It turns out that one of the major shareholders in *WaterWhyte Defence* is an investment group called *The October 17th Group* made up of several investors. I did some digging and wasn't too surprised to find Whyte and Butcher's names among them, along with one or two prominent if slightly distasteful business world figures. There was only one other politician in the group; any guesses who?"

"My private investments," Robyn hissed through her rigid jaw, "are my own affair, and nobody else's."

"Maybe so, but I don't recall seeing them mentioned in the Register of Member's Interests, Amber?"

Robyn's scowl deepened further still.

"An oversight," she curtly replied, with obvious insincerity. "I'm sure. I know you won't mind that I've taken the liberty of reporting the, erm 'oversight' to the Parliamentary standards authority, and of course, being a shareholder and a personal friend of the man who set it up, you'd have access to the company's premises, including their chemical facilities. But that isn't your only connection with Butcher, is it?"

Lucie leafed to another page in her folder and held it up for Robyn to see.

"Just before the referendum you co-authored a pamphlet about the 'dangers of immigration', in which you repeated several discredited theories and laid the blame for austerity on what you called the 'uncontrollable tsunami' of immigrants from Europe. After that you campaigned together under several controversial banners, and at least before Butcher's elevation to Cabinet, you revelled in your reputations as mavericks, didn't you?"

"Hardly a motive for murder."

"Not on its own, no," Lucie replied, her calmness countering the burning anger of her counterpart. "But when you consider that *The October 17th Group* are also significant investors in 'Adult Entertainment Centres' up and down the country, it does raise a few questions about the speeches you've made condemning them, wouldn't you say?"

Robyn straightened herself in her chair, winning at least for a moment the struggle to compose herself.

"I had no idea such investments were being made on my behalf," she retorted. "And I will ensure that they discontinue immediately."

"That's it, is it?" Lucie responded. "You think you can just pocket the cash and rattle off a quick apology and everything will be alright?"

"Why not?" Robyn sneered. "This country's more polarised now than it's been since the civil war. You'd be surprised what people are prepared to excuse if you cover yourself in the flag and talk of the 'great Brexit betrayal'."

"I'm not sure they're quite ready to excuse murder."

Lucie slammed her folder to the desk and fixed her eyes intently on Robyn's.

"You knew Whyte was a man with money who'd set up

businesses, lose interest and hand them over to others to run while he has content to sit back and get richer. You and Butcher knew he was just a figurehead for the company, leaving the way clear for Butcher to negotiate whatever 'perks' he wanted in return for providing him a platform to launch chemical weapons at Yemen. I don't know what your relationship with Butcher was, but I'll find out; and whatever it was it was close enough for you to be fully aware of his 'tastes'. Al-Khatani gave him the funds he needed to build his little pervert's paradise and the people he needed to staff it – thugs hand picked from the yellow vests and who'd buy into his mantra that European women deserved what was coming to them, for having the brass neck to be here in the first place. That just left someone to source the women, someone who'd have access to not only the details of the people working in the brothels, but the people campaigning against them. Damn it Amber, you probably even campaigned alongside some of these women, no-one argued more passionately against the centres than you did; how the hell could you give these women up to a man like Butcher?"

The flesh of Robyn's face had drained of colour, melding with her tamed hair and ivory blouse to present a figure of chilling and ghostly white, no longer the firebrand of her youth but instead the very image of the death she had visited upon others. The pretence was gone, as was the angered resentment, replaced instead with a condescending snarl and the visage of a woman who no longer cared about keeping up appearances.

"You misunderstood, Lucie," she answered, coldly. "It wasn't all women I wanted out of those brothels, only the British ones."

The words chilled Lucie, though she had almost expected them, more frightening was the passionless nonchalance of their delivery, as though what she said should have been obvious, or even conventional, to all, and it turned Lucie's stomach to hear them.

"I see," the spy answered.

"Do you? You accuse me of hating foreigners, but I don't, some of them have their uses."

"Like the ones prepared to sell themselves in sex dens while you pocket the cash?"

"Better they do it than a British girl," came the casual response. "Fruit will always need picking and backsides wiping in care homes. It's only when they get above themselves, wanting to compete at the top, to tell proper people what to do, that the hate begins to burn."

Lucie grimaced as Robyn spoke, the echo of Butcher's words only too clear.

"So, knowing that Butcher shared your hatred, you pointed him towards people you thought fit the bill and he used social media to tighten the grip. The *Red Mako* would be delivered, Butcher would get his 'perks' and you could further cultivate the hostile environment; your own pockets full while the country fell off the Brexit cliff edge. And if anyone asked too many questions, there was Whyte as the perfect patsy."

"Poor Jarvis," Robyn mused, her eyes beginning to wander. "Lovely guy, just not much vision. If only..."

Her voice tailed off and she shook her head in an apparent lament which Lucie was disinclined to endure.

"You're finished, Amber," Lucie declared, her voice devoid of sympathy. "You're having the Whip withdrawn as we speak and even if you manage to weasel your way out of charges, your Party will never take you back, not after this."

Robyn's face, through eerily ashen, began to twist into the arrogant sneer that had hissed soundbites and crafted insults in the House for years.

"There are other Parties," she smirked, "and no-one is ever completely finished in politics anymore, not these days. Remember what Trump said? That he could stand in the middle of Time Square and shoot someone without damaging his rating? Well he was right. People will forgive you anything as long as you speak to their fears and give them someone to blame for them. All you need to do is find your constituency and you're politically untouchable."

She stood to leave, her beauty twisted by the hate within her soul.

"I'll be the leader of a whole new movement, now," she predicted with confidence. "Even if you get your way and they send me down, I'll be a political prisoner to many who'll flood the government with more protests and petitions than they'll know what to do with."

She headed to the door and pulled it open, turning back to Lucie who stared at her with undisguised pity.

"You think you've won, Lucie, but you haven't. You've just made me a martyr."

The door closed and Amber Robyn's footsteps receded down the corridor, Lucie closing her eyes and settling her emotions for a moment before turning back to the desk, upon which the empty glasses still lay.

"No-one can be a martyr, Amber," Lucie sadly intoned as she reached for a handkerchief and carefully lifted Robyn's glass, placing it inside a large, plastic sandwich bag and fastening it shut, "if they don't live long enough for anyone to know what they were really dying for."

30

———————

The day, which had begun brightly enough, retreated into a dark and miserable bleakness as Lucie approached *Coffee Posse,* her regular haunt in which she had shared many a word with the man she now dreaded to meet.

He had been out of the hospital for a week before she called him, and even as she approached the door now, she couldn't explain why. For that moment, locked together in the storeroom, the promise they had made to each other, whether driven by fear or a desire simply to raise two fingers to cruel fate, had seemed the most perfect vision of a future she could have wished for. But it was a vision she had said goodbye to when she thought him dead, and even though her elation at his survival had reached every sinew of her body, and as much as she wanted to reach out and claim it back, the dream remained in the distance, like some cherished childhood memory; her love for it real but no longer present.

He deserved an explanation, Lucie knew, she owed him that much at least; a reason why she would break the promise that had meant so much, and she had come here to the scene of early flirtations and garnered trust to ensure he got it, however painful it might be.

She pushed open the heavy door and stepped inside to a room recovering from the early morning rush and enjoying the temporary relief of its own near emptiness.

Ismail was there at their usual table, staring out into the street, though his stare was more absent than she had grown used to, as though not all of him had made the trip back from the brink of death; his face was hollow and bruised and his mug was gripped in a gently trembling hand. On the table before him lay a damp and crumpled broadsheet, emblazoned with Amber Robyn's photograph, beneath the headline: 'DEFENCE SCANDAL CLAIMS 3RD MP AS NET TIGHTENS'. Lucie felt no temptation to celebrate Robyn's death, announced to the world as a suicide, despite the pain she had caused. Instead she silently lamented the further loss of life and the perversions of justice that the 'national interest' too often demanded.

"Hi," she said.

He shifted his gaze to her, his mouth twitching as though trying to form a smile that refused to wholly arrive.

"Lucie," he answered, his voice softer than she remembered. "I got you a coffee."

He gestured to a still steaming cup opposite him, Lucie taking it as an invitation to sit and sliding into her seat and placing her phone on the table.

"You didn't have to get me anything."

"It was my turn."

It was Lucie's smile that now struggled to form, and the pair sat across from each other in a silence as uncomfortable as any she had known. It was Ismail though who eventually broke the quiet. "Great news," he began in a voice which suggested it was anything but. "My suspension's been lifted, the disciplinary dropped and guess what? I've been short-listed for Detective Chief Inspector."

"That's wonderful!"

"Don't pretend you didn't know already."

He spoke the words coldly, his eyes falling away from hers and towards the contents of his mug. A spasm of guilt gripped Lucie's stomach at the words. She had known. It was not only she who had asked Lake to follow through with his arrangements, she had also suggested the promotion, she had thought as a reward for his exploits; but now began to wonder if it was instead to salve her conscience. Though she searched desperately for the right words to say to him, she found her mind empty of them, as though her brain had been plundered, leaving her with only banalities with which to answer.

"I thought you'd be pleased," she whispered.

Ismail shifted himself up in his seat, wincing as he did so, the effects of his not yet healed injuries all too apparent.

"Do you want to know something?" he began, his voice fragile but stronger than before. "When they dragged us out of that damn shithole we were in and pointed a gun at me, I was all for just giving up, walking into the light and getting myself a luxury suite in heaven, but two things wouldn't let me. One of them was the thought of going back to the cops and forgetting this shit ever happened. I fought so, so hard to get my position; the cops didn't want me and my family sure as hell didn't want me to join up. I have a brother who hasn't spoken to me in twenty-two years... I mean, I've tried, I've done my best, but he just slams the door in my face, he won't even pick up the phone. He says I'm a traitor."

"You're not a traitor." The words stumbled almost silently through Lucie's lips and were met by a harsh laugh from the police officer.

"It sure felt like I was. It felt like that for years and I couldn't handle it. It cost me my marriage. But then when I got into CID, when I made sergeant, then inspector, it actually felt like I was doing some good, that I was helping people, and more than that, I'd got there by myself, through my own work. And now I don't even have that, because the promotion I've worked for is down to a man I hate and a woman I love, who thinks she can make up for breaking a promise by pulling a few strings."

Lucie looked down at the table, unwilling to react to chastisement she felt she deserved.

"What was the second thing?" she finally asked, only to be met with Ismail's hurting eyes.

"You know," he said.

She looked down again to her untouched coffee.

"When we were in that room together," he continued, "you and me, we made a deal."

"Asif, we were just trying to stay alive, it didn't mean anything..."

"It meant something to me!"

Lucie swallowed the words she wanted to say and looked back up at him.

"It's not that I don't want to do those things with you, I do," she insisted in earnest. "It's just one more job..."

"Don't," Ismail sighed, putting up his hands and turning his head away. "Just don't. If I wanted to hear an addict's excuses, I'd go down the cells and talk to the crack heads."

"No, I mean it. I still don't know the connection between Robyn and Butcher and Lake's picked up a new lead on a child abuse ring we've been hunting. I screwed up on the last lead we had, I just need to finish this up..."

"I said don't!"

His chest refused to support the rise in his voice, and Ismail sat back, trying fruitlessly to stifle the cough his recovering body forced upon him. Lucie reached her hand out to his only for him to withdraw it before their skin could touch.

"You don't see it, do you? For God's sake, Lucie, you're not stupid! Wake up and see that Lake's got you by the short and curlies; there'll *always* be another job for you, another reason why you shouldn't walk away. That's why you have to walk away now, before you become like them."

She toyed with the handle of her mug, understanding only too well the veracity of his words but unable to yield to their logic.

"I can't," she finally said, Ismail turning his face away hiding from her the tear on his cheek and fighting to keep control of his breathing. He pushed his mug away and made to stand up, Lucie reaching out again, desperate to feel some warmth or sensitivity from him again, though unable to offer the words that would make it happen.

"I'm an idiot," Ismail spat, "you're already like them."

"I'm not!"

"No? Look how easily you took the gun from me that night in the car, how steady your aim was."

"I'm not going to use a gun again," she protested.

"No," Ismail conceded, with sadness in his face. "You'll just find some other way to make the kill."

Lucie was taken aback by the bluntness of his words, and she knew that her objections lacked any substance. In the silence, her phone began to ring, rattling against the table, the pair looking accusingly at it until it vibrated to a stop.

"I'm not like them," she quietly repeated. "Then prove it!"

Ismail checked himself as the server behind the counter looked pointedly at them, his voice having raised with each syllable.

"Prove it," he said again, softly but with undiminished intensity.

"Walk out of here with me now. Forget your phone, let it ring. Forget Algers, forget Lake, forget all the bastards waiting in dark corners and walk away with me."

"Kasper's a good man, he..."

"And Lake isn't," he interrupted. "You, Lucie, you are a good person. But if you stay with this lot any longer then I don't know how long you'll be able to say that."

"Do you have any idea what he'll do to you if I came away with you?" Lucie sorrowfully quizzed. "He nearly took away your career once, he'll do it again, and worse..."

"Then I'll stack shelves at ASDA!"

Lucie's eyes were everywhere except Ismail's, at once desiring and afraid of accepting his own outstretched palm. He was someone with whom at last she could be herself, with whom her so often raging mind was calm... The fingers of her right hand began to move across the table, inching towards Ismail's as though he were dragging her painfully from the quicksand of her life.

The renewed buzz and rattle of the phone against the counter was enough to pause Lucie's hand before her fingertips brushed his. Their eyes locked in mute resignation, Lucie could feel the tears he no longer hid matched in her own eyes as her hand drifted downwards and closed tightly around the device.

"Yes?" she replied to the sound of Lake's greeting, praying that her voice would not break until she could stumble through whatever instructions he had.

Ismail withdrew his hand, and slid from the chair, blinking away the water in his eyes as he walked to the door and headed onto the rain-soaked road. Lucie turned and watched him through the window as he walked, her hand pressed to the glass and her heart aching for him to turn and offer her even a regretful glance. None came.

"Of course," Lucie Musilova, the Overlapper, heard herself answer. "I'm all yours."

ACKNOWLEDGEMENTS

Any notions I entertained that writing books would become easier with experience were, I now realise, as foolish as they were naïve. I am indebted to many for their love, help and support as I scribed furiously (and often feverishly) away on Lucie's latest mission. In particular I would like to thank the administrators of Crime Fiction Addicts, for allowing me to post a question in their Christmas competition, and Karen Small, who won it with her splendid suggestion of 'Jarvis Whyte' as a character name. The British Czech and Slovak Association, Ed Peacock in particular, must also be thanked for their greatly appreciated support.

My thanks as well to Professor Tanja Bueltmann, for agreeing to cameo within these pages. Her work, and that of others such as the splendid Axel Antoni, and all at @3Million, is a true inspiration in these dark and worrying times, and while my thanking them is hardly adequate recompense, it is at least sincerely meant.

I thank Miroslava for her love and support, and my family and friends who continue to mystifyingly put up with me. Thanks also to the Good Lord for seeing me through it. Tim and

Georgia, I thank for simply being themselves (though if you could just let me have a little peace and quiet now and then, that would great).

I am grateful as ever to Bloodhound Books for their continuing faith in my stories, and to my fellow writers out there who know who they are, and whose support means so much. Thank you.

And finally, thanks to you for picking this book up and reading it; I hope it doesn't disappoint.

A NOTE FROM THE PUBLISHER

Thank you for reading this book. If you enjoyed it please do consider leaving a review on Amazon to help others find it too.

We hate typos. All of our books have been rigorously edited and proofread, but sometimes mistakes do slip through. If you have spotted a typo, please do let us know and we can get it amended within hours.

info@bloodhoundbooks.com

ABOUT THE AUTHOR

James Silvester's debut novel and sequel, *Escape to Perdition* and *The Prague Ultimatum*, embraced his love both of central Europe and the espionage genre and was met with widespread acclaim. This was followed by the first book in the Lucie Musilova thriller series, *Blood, White and Blue*, reflecting topical events in the UK and Europe.

James has also written for *The Prague Times* and his work has been featured by *Doctor Who Worldwide* and travel site *An Englishman in Slovakia*.

James lives in Manchester.